When Will the Dead Lady Sing?

WHEN WILL THE DEAD LADY SING?

• A THOROUGHLY SOUTHERN MYSTERY •

Patricia Sprinkle

WHEELER
CHIVERS

This Large Print edition is published by Wheeler Publishing, Waterville, Maine USA and by BBC Audiobooks, Ltd, Bath, England.

Published in 2004 in the U.S. by arrangement with NAL Signet, a division of Penguin Group (USA) Inc.

Published in 2004 in the U.K. by arrangement with the author.

U.S. Softcover 1-58724-753-4 (Cozy Mystery)
U.K. Hardcover 1-4056-3103-1 (Chivers Large Print)
U.K. Softcover 1-4056-3104-X (Camden Large Print)

The text of this Large Print edition is unabridged.
Other aspects of the book may vary from the original edition.

Set in 16 pt. Plantin.

Printed in the United States on permanent paper.

British Library Cataloguing-in-Publication Data available

Library of Congress Cataloging-in-Publication Data

Sprinkle, Patricia Houck.
        When will the dead lady sing? : a thoroughly southern
        mystery / Patricia Sprinkle.
        p. cm.
        ISBN 1-58724-753-4 (lg. print : sc : alk. paper)
        1. Women judges — Fiction.   2. Georgia — Fiction.
3. Large type books.   I. Title.
PS3569.P687W488 2004
    813'.54—dc22   2004053564

THANKS TO . . .

sister mystery writer Toni Kelner for the diamond story. Steve Kelner also did not propose until he'd earned enough to pay for her diamond, which puzzled and bewildered her. Toni, however, was a more faithful soul than MacLaren. In MacLaren's defense, she was a little younger at the time, and hadn't ever had a boyfriend except Joe Riddley. And Burlin was so very attractive.

Cast of Characters

MacLaren Yarbrough: Georgia magistrate, co-owner of Yarbrough Feed, Seed and Nursery

Joe Riddley Yarbrough: MacLaren's husband, co-owner of Yarbrough Feed, Seed and Nursery

Ridd Yarbrough: MacLaren's older son, high-school math teacher and part-time farmer

Martha Yarbrough: Ridd's wife, emergency-room supervisor

    Cricket (4) and **Bethany** (17): their children

Hollis Stanton (17): Bethany's best friend, lives with Ridd and his family

Tad Yarbrough (10): son of MacLaren's younger son, Walker, visiting Ridd

Hubert Spence: Yarbroughs' former neighbor, owner of Spence's Appliances

Maynard Spence: Hubert's son, antiques dealer

Augusta Wainwright and Winifred "Pooh" DuBose: Hopemore's elderly aristocrats

Hector Blaine: ne'er-do-well resident of Hopemore

Bailey "Buster" Gibbons: Hope County sheriff

Charlie Muggins: Hopemore police chief

Isaac James: assistant police chief

Burlin Bullock: Georgia politician, former congressman

Lance Bullock: Burlin's son, running for governor

Renée Bullock: Lance's wife

Georgia Tate: Burlin's sister

Edward Tate: Georgia's husband, Burlin's partner, Lance's campaign manager

Abigail "Binky" Bullock: Burlin's younger sister

|

The Hopemore water tank murder was news all over the world. It happened right after my own face got plastered on the front page of every major paper in the country, so for a time Middle Georgia had two national celebrities: Judge MacLaren Yarbrough and the Hopemore water tank. I am the shorter of the two.

With the town swarming with reporters and cameras, was I going to have to confess what I'd done?

However, I'm getting ahead of my story. For me, it began one September Friday when it was finally cool enough to shove our windows up. I looked out my front living room screen and gasped.

"Joe Riddley, there's a buffalo in our front yard!"

From the dining room table, where he was trying to summon the energy to lift his first mug of morning coffee, my husband gave a little snort I suppose he meant for a laugh. "Is a coyote slinking through the bushes?"

I have known that man since we were four and six. It's a miracle I have let him live this long. "No, but there is a buffalo. Shaggy shoulders, big hump on the back, great clumps of manure falling on the grass —"

He sighed, but didn't bother to turn around. "Then he's fifteen hundred miles and a hundred and fifty years off course. I've been telling you to get your eyes checked. It's probably a big dog." I heard the thump as his coffee mug hit the table. "What's it doing?"

"Cropping grass. And there's nothing the matter with my eyes. It's a buffalo, dang it!"

I spoke so loud that Bo, Joe Riddley's scarlet macaw — prancing around his own placemat — flapped his wings and demanded, "Back off! Give me space!"

At that, the huge creature on the front lawn raised its head and looked straight at me.

There was no mistaking the gleam of interest in those tiny eyes, which were almost lost in its huge fuzzy face. Weighed against its horns and massive head and shoulders, our new brick house seemed real flimsy. Why hadn't we looked for a place with two-foot granite walls?

The buffalo stood in the grass and stared at me. I stood in the living room and stared at it. My brain was sending frantic signals to my feet and legs, but my lower body had shut off the phone.

Until then, it had been such a *normal* morning.

I'd gotten up around six, like I usually do, and padded into our new kitchen, thinking how much I liked its yellow walls even if Joe Riddley did ask if the paint came with sunglasses.

I found coffee and filters on my third try. We'd been in the new house nearly four weeks, but our cook, Clarinda, was still shifting things around, trying to find "where they feel themselves to home." Apparently, only the toaster and coffeemaker had settled in so far, although Clarinda assured me the rest of our stuff was "beginning to get the feel of the place." A friend who stays abreast of modern trends suggested Clarinda was practicing fêng shui. I figured she was just being Clarinda.

Around six fifteen, Joe Riddley padded in, scratching, unhappy at being up. He invariably is, that early. I took a mug of hot coffee to the dining room table, since our new kitchen was too little to eat in. He slumped into his preferred chair, facing the backyard, and sat there glaring at the coffee like he expected it to rise and meet him.

"You bring in the paper?" he muttered without looking up.

"Not yet, but I will." I regarded him fondly from the kitchen door while I finished my own coffee. We'd been married over forty years, and I still thought him the handsomest husband in Hopemore. I even liked the touch of gray that was beginning to appear in his thick dark hair. He was generally real sweet, too, so long as you didn't expect him to be charming before eight.

"Are you going for the paper," he demanded, "or do I have to go get it?"

"You can't go outside in white boxers and that tacky robe. I wish you'd let me rip it up for rags."

"It's got a little life left in it, just like me." He shoved back his chair. "I guess I'd better feed Bo." He left his coffee untasted and pushed past me.

While he opened and shut cabinet doors, I tried to insert a little culture into our morning. "You know that odd red-and-green bird I've been seeing over in the woods between us and the next house? I looked it up in Audubon, and it may be a male scarlet tanager, changing from summer to winter plumage."

Joe Riddley peered into the pantry. "Where's Clarinda hiding Bo's food this week?"

"Your guess is as good as mine." He hadn't heard a word I said. Still, I try to educate him whenever I can. You never can tell how much a husband will absorb unconsciously.

He found Bo's cereal next to our own, carried it to Bo's green plastic place mat on the dining room table, and dumped out a bit. Then he headed to retrieve Bo from what the real-estate agent enthusiastically described as "your screened back porch." It was scarcely big enough for a large birdcage. We'd put Bo's perch as far from the screen as it could get and still, on nights when rain blew in, we'd hear him shrieking something he'd picked up from our four-year-old grandson, Cricket: "I need help here. Did you hear what I said? I need help." Still, he had to stay there. I wouldn't let him in the new house except for the living and dining rooms, which had floors we could mop. Unless you have had a bird, you have no idea how filthy they can be.

I scowled at the doo-streaked green cement porch floor while Joe Riddley stroked Bo's bright red breast to wake him up. Bo is even grumpier than Joe Riddley in the morning. He finally hopped onto Joe Riddley's shoulder and perched there, muttering inaudible words I probably didn't want to hear. We'd inherited Bo when his former owner, Hiram Blaine, had been killed down at our house,* and Hiram had a colorful vocabulary.

As Joe Riddley set the macaw down on his green place mat and gently stroked its breast, I reminded myself for the umpteenth time that he loved that bird and it had been real good for him in recent months. I would not suggest that we give it away — yet.

*Who Invited the Dead Man?

Joe Riddley watched until Bo had started pecking away, then turned to me and announced, "Tanagers don't generally get this far south. Must be migrating. We're in a migration pattern."

How did he know that? I was the one who read bird books. "I suppose you heard that from Audubon personally?"

"Just common knowledge." He pulled out his chair, fell into it again, and lifted his mug. "Did you get the paper yet?"

"I'm *going*." Grumpiness is a contagious disease. "Just let me get some windows open first. This place gets stale, all closed up at night."

I shoved up the windows in the kitchen and dining room and the side ones in the living room, thinking again how fortunate we'd been to find a house with windows on all four sides. So many builders put up houses with no more circulation than apartments. It was when I shoved up the front window that I noticed the buffalo.

Which was still staring at me.

I gave a little wave.

It nodded its big head and took a step in my direction.

I took a step back.

It took another step.

I froze again.

We stood there for a hundred years.

I wished my beagle, Lulu, wasn't down in

14

the barn at our old house, recovering from having a litter of pups. She wouldn't hesitate to take on a buffalo she thought was threatening me. On the other hand, I hadn't met all our new neighbors yet. I'd hate for them to label me "that woman who ran after the three-legged beagle chasing a buffalo down the block."

Finally the buffalo got bored or hungry and lowered its head to graze. I stepped out of its line of vision and headed for the kitchen. Let Joe Riddley be the first to face the "dog" if it decided to pay a house call. He's a foot taller than I am, with longer legs.

At the kitchen door, I muttered, "I'll call Tad to say we've found an ecologically sounder lawn mower. He won't complain." Tad was the son of our younger son, Walker, and had begun, reluctantly, to cut our grass each week.

I could have saved my wit. Joe Riddley was feeding Bo from one forefinger, not paying me a speck of attention.

With a disgusted sigh, I dialed the number for Ridd, our older son. Ridd and his wife, Martha, were keeping Tad that week while Walker and Cindy were up in New York City attending an insurance convention and seeing plays. Part of the deal was that Tad was to feed, groom, and exercise his mother's new hunter, Starfire, which Cindy was boarding in Ridd's barn.

15

With a buffalo on my lawn and my husband in denial, however, it wasn't really Tad I wanted to talk to — it was Martha. An emergency-room supervisor, she is Queen of Unflappable. She deals daily with situations that would sizzle my gizzard, and that fall she was not only raising her own two children but had agreed to let her daughter Bethany's best friend, Hollis, live with them for her senior year of high school.* If anybody would know what to do with a buffalo in the yard, Martha would.

When she answered, though, she didn't even wait to find out what I wanted before she started right in. "I'm glad you called, Mac. We've got a problem, and I need some advice."

Martha asking *me* for advice? I was so astounded, I sat down and forgot my own problem for a second. "What's the matter?"

"Tad. He's smoking."

The ice maker rumbled and dumped its load while I thought that over. "He's ten years old," I reminded her.

"I know. But Bethany and Hollis caught him smoking down in the woods after school yesterday."

"Where could Tad get cigarettes?" I was thinking aloud, but Martha answered anyway.

"He said a friend swiped them from his

Who Let That Killer in the House?

16

parents' stash while they were at work. Tad swears this is the first time he's tried it, but Bethany says he looked pretty experienced. I don't know whether to tell Walker and Cindy, or hope his little chat with Ridd will do the trick. Why do these things always happen when a kid's parents are away?"

"It's a law of the universe, honey, just like the law that says toilets will overflow and furnaces break when your husband leaves town. It was part of Eve's curse in the Garden of Eden. Somebody just omitted it from the text."

As I had hoped, a gurgle of laughter rolled over the line. I love Martha's laugh. It reminds me of a stream running over rocks. "Oh, well, I guess we'll get through this. It's just one more of life's little stretching experiences. Are you still planning on walking with me tonight?"

Martha and I both tend to be a little rounder than we'd like to be, so we'd decided to begin walking around the high-school track each evening.

"Yeah, I'll be there. But I called to ask you a question. What would you do if you had a buffalo in your yard?"

"Call a cowboy?" From the tentative way she said it, I knew she was waiting for a punch line. After all, she did live with a four-year-old who loved silly riddles. Before I could say anything else, she returned to her own problem.

"I guess I'll have to tell Cindy and Walker, but do you think I ought to call them in New York, or just wait until they get home?"

I peered around the door as I thought that over. *My* problem had abandoned the grass and was now moseying across the yard toward Joe Riddley's new silver Town Car. "Wait until they get home. I gotta go. Call you later."

I announced loudly from the safety of the kitchen door, "That two-ton horned dog is about to test-drive your new car."

That got Joe Riddley's attention. He'd bought the car in August to celebrate the anniversary of the day he'd gotten shot and survived to tell the story.[*] He would scarcely let me ride in it, he was so scared I'd leave a scratch on the finish.

Joe Riddley heaved the sigh men reserve for times when they think a woman who expects equality in other areas ought to be able to cope with the present situation — a dead rat in the pantry, a flat tire in the rain, a buffalo on the front lawn. He shoved back his chair, strode to the front door, threw it wide open, and stopped dead. "By golly, it *is* a buffalo. *Hi-ya!* Get away from that car!" Waving his arms, he dashed into the yard.

The animal had been ambling peacefully across the grass, but he stopped, turned, and

[*]*But Why Shoot the Magistrate?*

18

lowered his head. I could see the headline in next week's *Hopemore Statesman*: "Former Judge Trampled to Death."

I might get mad at the old coot from time to time, but I didn't want him flattened by a buffalo. I ran after him in my red-striped coffee coat and red slippers. "Get back in here!" I grabbed his arm and tugged.

The buffalo headed toward the excitement.

Do you know how fast a buffalo can run?

I never found out. Joe Riddley grabbed me around the waist, lifted me from the ground, and hightailed it to the porch. "That red must be making him mad," he gasped as he slammed the front door behind us.

Trust him to blame me. I'd have pointed out that he was the fool who went outside in the first place, but I was too busy trying to breathe. Besides, some of the best advice Mama ever gave me was, "Honey, you'll stay married a lot longer if you don't make a war out of every arrow aimed in your direction."

We leaned against the door panting for breath, our two hearts thundering as one. I didn't hear a thundering buffalo on the front stoop, though, so I dared to look out the front window. The buffalo had stopped about ten feet from our front step and was looking at the door with an expression that said "If *that* was the morning's entertainment, I want my money back."

Joe Riddley was still pressed against the

door. How long did he think he could hold it against a determined buffalo?

"Call animal control," he ordered. "I'll keep an eye on him." He locked the dead bolt — did he expect the animal to try the knob? — and moved to the front window. "Hurry. He's looking at my car again."

Animal control wasn't open, so I called the police. After all, as a county magistrate, I regularly get up and drive down to the sheriff's detention center in the middle of the night to save deputies the trouble of coming to me. I figured it was time somebody paid back the favor.

Royce Wharton, a deputy who regularly had the night shift and had roused me four times in the past month, answered. "Hey, Royce. This is Judge Yarbrough. Can you send somebody over here to remove a buffalo from our front lawn?"

I had to hold the receiver six inches from my ear to keep from being deafened by his laugh. "Our cowhands haven't arrived yet, Judge, but as soon as one gallops in, I'll send him over."

"This isn't a joke," I informed him. "We have a buffalo in our yard, and if you don't help me deal with it, you'd better call somebody else next time you need a judge to sign a warrant."

"What's it doing?"

"What does it matter what it's doing? It's

there. What do you suggest we do? And I don't want to hear a smart aleck answer, either."

"No, ma'am, but I don't know what to suggest. We don't do buffalo."

I was about to suggest that he didn't do much of anything when I saw, out of the corner of my eye, that the blasted animal was wandering happily across the yard in a new direction.

"My roses!" I slammed down the receiver and grabbed the broom. The way Joe Riddley tells it, I mounted the broom, flew out the front door, and zoomed over the yard. I didn't, of course, but I was determined to save those roses. I'd transplanted them from our old yard, and had grown them originally from Mama's cuttings. I wasn't going to lose them to any varmint, even if he had strayed fifteen hundred miles and a hundred and fifty years off course.

"Get out of here! Out! You hear me?"

I yelled at the top of my lungs and waved my broom. I was just about to bring it down on the creature's hump when I heard a shout.

"Wait, Mackie! Don't hit him. It's okay. Sarge will get him."

A man in gray slacks and a yellow polo shirt stepped from behind the big Emily Brunner holly tree up by the street. Another man, short and stubby, hurried around him

21

with a chain in his hand.

The short man wore jeans and a green T-shirt and walked with a limp. "Hey, boy. Hey, boy." He sidled toward the buffalo holding out something on one palm. That brute nuzzled his palm as nice as anything and let the man snap the chain through a loop hanging from its neck. "I'll get him back in the truck," he called to the taller man. He and the buffalo strolled amiably across the lawn and down the street.

I wished I could go with them. I'd rather walk a buffalo than remain where I was.

Every woman worth her salt has at least one guilty secret in her past. Mine was staring me in the face.

2

"Hey, Mackie, surprised to see me?" Burlin Bullock squinted against the morning sun. I wished a sinkhole would open in our lawn and swallow one of us. I wasn't particular about which one.

Mama always said that women who don't fix their faces before they come out of their rooms in the morning are asking Fate to fix their wagons. I stood in the early-morning sunlight wearing no makeup whatsoever, my hair at its day-before-beauty-parlor worst, dressed in fuzzy slippers and one of those snap-front coffee coats that are so easy to throw on. Why hadn't I developed a taste for flaming-orange satin pajamas with matching high-heel mules?

Burlin was handsomer at sixty-four than he'd been at twenty. His smile had always been wide and attractive, but over the years it had chiseled deep lines into his face that passed for character. His once-blond hair was now silver, but still thick and straight, parted on the left. His gray slacks had a crease you could use to slit boxes, his yellow polo shirt was soft as butter, and his black loafers were polished so the shine hurt my eyes. Or maybe that was the sun's reflection off his gold Rolex watch. He smelled like he'd just come out of the shower, and although he'd put on weight since I'd seen him last, it suited him. Mama would have said he'd finally grown into his potential.

Burlin always had considerable potential. When we were both at the University of Georgia, he'd been president of the drama club and a steadily rising star in student government. He'd gone on to Yale Law School, with an eye to following his daddy's footsteps in Georgia politics, but he'd done his daddy one better: He had served a couple of terms in Congress.

Now his gray eyes twinkled down at me from his tanned face. "Cat got your tongue?"

Burlin was always tanned. These days, he docked a sailboat at Lake Lanier, owned a condo at St. Simons Island, and went out several times each winter to ski in Colorado. How did I know? Because he was a regular guest on one of Joe Riddley's favorite talk shows, was often asked to sit in on newscasts to comment on national situations, and was a familiar face in the *Atlanta Journal-Constitution*. We seldom went a month in Georgia without seeing Burlin in the paper for something. He was the kind of politician men admire and women adore.

For one moment of treachery to all the life

experiences that have made me who I am, I wished I could strip off my face and look twenty again, and I gathered my wits to say something intelligent. "What the dickens are you doing here?"

He shifted so the sun wasn't right in his eyes. "My boy is running for governor, you know." Of course I knew. The election wasn't for another year, but the campaign had been in the paper for months. Lance Bullock was one of two strong candidates in our party, and with none in the other, whoever won next year's primary was likely to get elected.

However, having Lance run for governor was one thing. Having Burlin in my front yard was another — particularly when he said, "We're running his campaign out of Hopemore for the next week or so and staying down at the Annie Dale Inn. I guess you know it?"

I guess I did. Annie Dale Wilson was a year younger than me, and we'd bicycled all over town together, growing up. We'd drifted apart during junior and senior high — Annie Dale got a little wild back then — and lost touch after I went to college and she stayed home to work, but we still enjoyed an occasional chat or a wave when she passed me on her bike. Annie Dale was still a serious biker and spent two weeks each year bicycling in a different country.

"We're proud of Annie Dale," I told Burlin.

"Some people scoffed when she turned the old house her granddaddy built after he retired from the railroad into an inn. They said she'd never make a go of it because it's too close to the tracks. But trains don't come through town anymore, and she's had folks from thirty-nine states, so far, and a lot of weekend wedding parties. Having a gubernatorial candidate will really float her boat."

"It's handy for us. She's turned the whole second floor over to us, including a sitting room we can use for an office."

"Still, Hopemore is a funny place for a campaign center," I pointed out.

"Oh, I don't know. It's the county seat of Hope County, has several thousand voters, is centrally located between I-20 and I-16, and you're here." He smiled down into my eyes. When I didn't rise to that lure, he added, "Besides, it's smack in the middle of everything, including the gnat line." He ruefully scratched one arm.

I'd already noticed the pesky creatures nibbling my ankles in the tall grass. We'd had a lot of rain that week, and our grandson Tad hadn't mowed yet. I surreptitiously rubbed one ankle with the top of my other foot and wondered why Burlin's son's campaign couldn't be run out of some other deserving town to save me from my current predicament.

Burlin reached out one hand toward me, but I stepped away. His voice was low and husky. "You've still got those big brown eyes, and your hair is just like I remember it. The very same shade of honey brown."

I didn't bother to tell him about the part my hairdresser, Phyllis, plays in the color of my hair. Instead, I took another step back and demanded, "Did you put that buffalo in my yard?"

He threw back his head and laughed. "Same old Mackie."

Nobody but Burlin ever called me Mackie. For the first time in minutes I remembered Joe Riddley sitting in the dining room with nothing but a window screen to keep him from hearing every word we said.

Burlin was easy and relaxed, not the least bit worried about whether my husband was listening. "I wondered how long it would take you to get your dander up again. The buffalo is Lance's mascot. See?" He fished in his pocket and handed me a red button with the white silhouette of a buffalo and navy blue words: BULLOCK GIVES YOU NO BULL.

He chuckled. "I asked Sarge to let him graze your yard a little this morning, figuring maybe it would get your attention and lure you out of the house." He waved away my attempt to hand him back the button. "Keep it. We've got thousands."

"I won't wear it," I warned. "I'm a magistrate, and I never display a political endorsement on my property or my person."

It's just as well I hadn't expected him to be impressed. He shrugged and said, "Then put it in your jewelry box."

I would drop it in my kitchen wastebasket, but I didn't need to say so. Besides, he wasn't giving me time to say anything. "I tried to see you last evening. We got to town before dinnertime, and I wanted to look you up before it got dark, but when I found the address listed in the phone book — a big blue house out in the country — there was a crew of kids playing softball in the front yard. I asked where you lived, and one of them said you moved here last month."

"We did. That house was built by my husband's great-granddaddy, and it's a family tradition to deed it to the oldest child. We finally got around to doing that in August."

"It's gorgeous." He looked at the front of our small brick home. "You must really miss it. It was real private, too." He glanced back over his shoulder.

That reminded me how close our new neighbors were. They probably were hovering behind curtains, watching me entertain a man while wearing my pajamas. "I do miss the privacy," I admitted. "After living for thirty-five years at the end of a gravel road, with the nearest neighbor a quarter of a mile away, having folks across the street feels a bit like living onstage."

The truth was, I missed a lot of things

28

about the big old house. I missed turning down our road after work and leaving the whole world behind. I missed eating on our big screened porch, or reading out there while fireflies punctuated the dusk. I missed sleeping where the only sounds were owls, nighthawks, crickets, frogs by our pool, and an occasional truck grinding gears up on the highway. I missed high ceilings and big dim rooms, the smells of new-mown hay, honeysuckle, and the gardenias I'd planted near the house. I even missed Joe Riddley's noisy hunting dogs, who had stayed behind in their outside pen. I greatly missed my swimming pool.

But I wasn't admitting more to Burlin than I admitted to anybody else, so I told him what I told them: "Some folks get real teary about leaving their homeplace, but Joe Riddley and I aren't two of them. We like walking to work and church, and appreciate this little yard after taking care of five acres. We're glad not to have stairs to climb, and our housekeeper finds it a lot easier to clean six rooms than eleven. Of course, she grumbles about our 'little bitty kitchen,' but she used to grumble about having to walk so far between the stove and the sink. Grumbling is Clarinda's preferred mode of conversation."

"You cry only in your own bathroom, right?" Burlin always did see right through my scalp to my private thoughts. It discon-

29

certed me back then, and it annoyed me now.

"Not very often. I like this house. We brought most of the things we liked best with us — including some of Mama's roses, which your dratted buffalo nearly trampled. If it had —"

He held up both hands and backed away, laughing. "Hey, it didn't. I came to the rescue, remember? And I grow roses, too. What kinds do you have?" He headed in their direction with his usual purposeful stride. Burlin always gave his full attention to anything that interested him.

I sighed. Why hadn't I paid attention when Mama was trying to teach me the graceful way to get rid of unwanted guests? Next thing I knew, we were standing side by side discussing varieties of roses, and Burlin was prosing on about his attempt to develop a new variety. Suddenly he interrupted himself to demand, "Have you stayed married all these years to the same fellow?"

"He's changed a bit over the years, but he's basically the same fellow. How about you?"

That was a low blow and I instantly regretted it. Thirty years ago, Burlin's wife had been notorious for drunk and disorderly behavior. I'd felt a secret sympathy for the woman — any woman married to a Bullock would need some solace. In years since then,

I'd seen pictures of Burlin with several other attractive women — most often his sister Georgia — but I hadn't seen a picture of his wife in ages.

He rubbed one hand along his long jaw. "I didn't do so good. I married a folk singer — she gave it up, of course, when we married — and she developed a drinking problem. Maybe you read about her accident —"

Everybody in America had read about her accident. During Burlin's second term in Congress, Sperra Bullock ran over and killed a five-year-old boy in Virginia, then sped away. A bystander got the tag number, though, and she'd been arrested that same night. In court, she had tried to get off by claiming she was in an alcoholic blackout. That infuriated people. Then she got into several shouting matches and one hair-pulling fight with the mother of the dead child, who wanted the court to take Sperra's five-year-old son away to atone for the loss of her own. It had been the kind of nasty, brawling case the media loves. Sperra went to prison and Burlin finished out his term. He never ran for another elected office.

"Was that why you decided not to run for re-election?" I asked now.

"Partly," he admitted, "but I also decided I prefer to work behind the scenes. I had a history teacher back in junior high who said something I've never forgotten: 'The history of Georgia is men who loved this state and cared enough about her to give their lives to making her great.' That's what I've always wanted to do."

He might have been on a stage, but I didn't intend to stand there as an audience of one. "What finally happened to your wife?"

He shrugged. "What happens to every drunk who doesn't quit. She went in and out of rehab for ten years, but she couldn't lick the stuff. She died twenty years ago." He moved so close I could feel his warmth through my thin robe. "I wouldn't be this frank with everybody, but it was actually a blessing as far as we were concerned. She was neither a wife to me nor a mother to Lance after the accident. She couldn't stand to be near him, in fact. The other mother claimed that Sperra didn't deserve to have a child because she'd been so careless about somebody else's, and that nearly destroyed her. She and Lance had been as close as any mama can get to a kid when she needs to suck a bottle half the day, but after that she couldn't bear to hold him or touch him. Even having him in the same room could make her hysterical. She said she kept seeing that other little boy's face over his." He turned away to fondle a yellow rose, and his voice dropped to a whisper. "When she lost Lance, she lost everything."

Tears clogged my throat. "She still had you."

He shook his head and said softly, "She never had me." He stroked the rose.

It wasn't until he turned back toward me that I remembered again that Burlin Bullock was not only a politician, he was a darned good actor, and we'd just played a scene. I hoped Joe Riddley and my neighbors didn't know they were supposed to be our audience.

"Don't you have somewhere else you have to be?" I demanded.

He reached into his pocket and pulled out a little Swiss Army Knife. "Actually, I do. But before I leave, may I?" He pointed to the yellow rose. When I nodded, he cut it off and held it to his nose for a moment, then grinned and stuck it behind his ear. "Dashing, right?" He took it down and cupped it in one palm. "I've been experimenting with a new rose that I think is going to bloom this next year. Shall I send you a cutting? It's a real spicy red. I'm thinking of calling it the MacLaren. Would you like that?"

Before I could answer, Joe Riddley spoke from the front door. "Little Bit? Your toast is stone cold, and I've drunk all the coffee. You fixing to go to work in your nightgown? And where's the paper?"

Burlin gave Joe Riddley a genial wave. "I'm just going," he called. "Was admiring your wife's roses." He held the yellow rose aloft, then added in a low voice, "I didn't mean to get you in trouble." He turned and strode across the lawn without looking back.

"Who the Sam Hill was that?" Joe Riddley demanded as I headed for the door. "He's the spitting image of Burlin Bullock, but you didn't need to stand out there entertaining him in your bathrobe for God and all the neighbors to see."

I hardly heard what he was saying. I was hearing Burlin whistling what he always used to whistle when he left me at my front door: "I'll be seeing you."

3

Joe Riddley made me cinnamon toast and fresh coffee while I dressed, and he read the sports section of the *Augusta Chronicle* at the table while I ate. "Georgia ought to have a great game tomorrow, even with all those players they had to bench."

I couldn't believe my luck. "You want to drive up for it? Maybe stay overnight? We could even go on to the mountains for a week. We haven't been anywhere in so long, I'm growing moss." When he didn't agree right away, I offered, "I'll call and see if Ridd can manage the store." Our son is a high-school math teacher by profession and a farmer at heart, but he is willing to stop by in the afternoon after school a few days at a stretch to compensate for all the plants we give him for his yard and garden.

"Ridd's gonna keep the store tomorrow, but we can't go to the game." Joe Riddley's voice was sour as last week's milk. "I told Gusta we'd come to a Do she's having over at her old house." No wonder he looked like he'd asked for sweet milk and gotten buttermilk. For eighty years Augusta Wainwright had been the self-appointed queen of

Hopemore. Joe Riddley hated Gusta's Do's. "Bite-sized sandwiches and watered wine," he muttered, going back to his paper.

I wasn't real fond of Gusta's Do's myself. "You said yes without even asking me?"

"It's for an old friend of hers, some sort of political shindig. You ought to be there."

Joe Riddley had been a county magistrate for thirty years and kept up with the whole political ball of wax. When I'd been appointed to replace him after he retired a year ago, I'd figured if I signed warrants that were set before me, held probable-cause hearings and bond hearings, and presided over such courts as were required of me, I could skip politics. After all, I didn't seek the appointment. If they took it away from me, it wouldn't block my sunshine. But Joe Riddley was bound and determined I'd at least show my face at political events from time to time. It was one of the ongoing dissonant chords in the harmony of our marriage.

My stomach went down a long sliding board. It was highly unlikely that two politicians would be in Hopemore this one weekend. "It will serve you right if she serves nothing but tuna-fish sandwiches and watery punch."

The coward hid behind his paper to avoid my glare. "You still need to go. Besides, you've been wanting to see what Maynard has done to the place."

I did want to see the place. Gusta's former house was one of three antebellum houses in Hopemore that Sherman didn't burn. Her best friend and rival for Hopemore's throne was Winifred "Pooh" DuBose, who lived two doors down, in a fine Victorian. The previous winter, Pooh had begun to show increasing signs of dementia and Gusta's granddaughter got married, so Gusta moved in with Pooh. Maynard Spence, curator of the Hope County Historical Museum, bought Gusta's place and turned it into an antique store — yielding to Gusta's request that he call it Wainwright House Antiques. He'd have called it Augusta's Antiques for her, he wanted it so badly.

Maynard got married about that same time, so his daddy — our closest neighbor — moved out of their old homeplace and in with Pooh and Gusta. The three of them had calculated they could pay Pooh's cook and yardman and Gusta's housekeeper and still come out a good bit cheaper than if they all went into retirement homes. Not that they needed to be frugal. The two women each had more money than a third-world country, and Hubert had done well with Spence's Appliances over the years. Still, none of them had gotten rich *spending* money.

"It will serve you right if I see something real expensive at Maynard's I can't live without," I warned as I headed to brush my teeth and fetch my pocketbook.

I wish I could tell you I went to work and didn't give Burlin Bullock another thought. However, I'd long ago discovered that lying generates more complications than it solves. All day long, I found myself sitting at my desk, staring into space, muttering things to myself like, "How could you be so dumb?" and "Is there *any* way to leave town for a few days?"

I was sorry I had to meet Martha at the track. Martha notices other people — really notices them. Sure enough, about the time we had walked a quarter of the way around, just as I was fixing to announce I was happy with the way I looked and ready to give up walking, she asked, "What's buggin' you?"

I gave an airy wave. "Oh, nothing. Taxes, stuff like that."

"Seriously, what's wrong? Is Pop having memory trouble again?"

Joe Riddley had made a remarkable recovery from getting shot, but he tended to be a bit forgetful at times and his temper wasn't as dependable as it used to be. I was tempted to say "Yes" and let it go at that, but my conscience kicked in. Besides, Martha has had all sorts of training in counseling. I found myself admitting, "He's fine. But I've got a little problem. You know that Joe Riddley and I have been together all our lives."

"Since your daddy took you to his daddy's hardware store when you were — what? four? And he was six?" I nodded. "And Joe Riddley swaggered over, hitched up his brown corduroy britches, and asked, 'You wanna go count nails?' You've been counting nails ever since."

"Yeah. But what you don't know" — I had to feel my way. Confession comes hard to Presbyterians — "is that I once also dated somebody else."

That cut off her water. She didn't say a word.

"Now he's come to town, and —" I sighed. "It's a mess."

She went about ten strides before she demanded, "When did you have time to date anybody else?"

No wonder she asked. Joe Riddley and I started "going steady" in elementary school, which meant he carried my books and I saved him a seat at lunch. We dated through junior and senior high, which meant I wore his letter sweaters and he wore out a set of tires coming home from college while I finished my last two years. We dated all the way through college and got married the weekend after I graduated.

"The year after Joe Riddley finished college. I didn't think he loved me anymore."

"Pop? He worships the ground you walk on."

"Maybe so, but he was real slow popping the M question. Everybody expected us to get married after he finished college, so the Christmas before, I figured he'd give me a diamond. He gave me a necklace. That was okay — I didn't want to get married until I graduated, anyway, and I thought he'd ask me that summer. He didn't. In those days, a girl could hint, but she waited to get asked. I waited and hinted all summer. He didn't say a word. Even worse, he didn't come up to school that next semester. Kept saying he was busy. Heck, he was working for his parents. They'd have let him off for football games if he'd wanted to come, but I didn't see hide nor hair of him, except a couple of times when I drove home. We never went anywhere then, just sat around at our folks' houses. He even worked the two Saturdays I was here. He said he was learning the business, but we'd both worked in that store for years. Annie Dale was working for his daddy that year, and she was mighty pretty. I figured I had been a phase, and he was ready to move on."

"You never. You were just trying to justify what you did." Martha has always been willing to call a spade a shovel. She moved ahead. "Walk faster, or we won't lose an ounce."

"Joe Riddley loves me the way I am," I insisted. "He says I'm not fat, I'm voluptuous."

She didn't slow one iota. "But he really didn't pay me a speck of attention that fall," I added, hurrying to catch her.

"He wrote, didn't he? And called?"

"Not often. He never was much for writing, and neither one of us was comfortable talking long distance. Our calls were generally things like, 'I passed my differential equations exam' or 'Daddy's thinking of expanding the nursery side of the business. What do you think?'"

"If he wanted your opinion about the business, didn't that tell you something?"

"Yeah. That he was tired of counting nails. Let's stop a minute to catch our breath." While I rested, I said, "It may not make sense now, honey, but back then, I was mad. And hurt."

"And lonesome," she guessed, jerking her head to say it was time to get going.

I tromped along, trying to keep up. "That, too. And having second thoughts about settling down before I'd sampled what else the world had to offer. So I started dating somebody else."

"That was probably good for you and Pop both. Now, walk faster. We aren't snails."

"We aren't jet planes, either. We don't have to walk off all our weight tonight."

"In case you haven't noticed, everybody else is passing us. We're not exactly flying." She waited for another speedy duo to whiz by, elbows working as hard as their legs. Then she asked, "So what if the guy is here for a few days? It's been years since you saw him, right?"

"Yeah, but —" I hated to tell her the real reason I was worried. It sounded so petty. "I never told Joe Riddley about him, and I don't want him to find out now." She slid her eyes my way, so I hurried to add, "He could be so hurt, and you know he's been unpredictable since he got shot."

She laughed. "Expecting Pop to shoot him? It's not likely. They may not even meet."

"Oh, yes they will. Gusta's having a Do tomorrow, and he's bound to be there."

"I thought that was for Lance Bullock." She stopped so suddenly that I took two steps ahead before I noticed. She was standing dead in the track, hands on her hips. "It wasn't Burlin Bullock you dated, was it?"

"For a little while. And you know how Joe Riddley admires him."

I didn't mind watching my stock go up in her eyes. However, that didn't last long. Martha is nothing if not a realist. "He's probably forgotten all about it by now. He may not even remember your name." She marched on. I had to nearly run to catch up this time.

"He came by the house this morning to see me," I said, miffed both at what she'd said and at being left behind.

She raised her eyebrows. "What did Pop say to that?"

"Nothing. We talked out in the yard. But I don't want Joe Riddley getting any ideas."

"Getting jealous, you mean. Burlin Bullock's a mighty handsome man. I might have cheated on Ridd if somebody that good-looking had asked me out."

"No, you wouldn't. You're nicer than me. But he was handsome back then, too. Girls swooned whenever he swaggered by and thought up all sorts of reasons to talk to him."

"Including you."

"Not at all. The only two words I ever said to him before he asked me to a football game were 'You're wrong.' He'd given a report in history — we had class together — and claimed the Confederate treasury wound up near Macon. I set the class straight that it is supposed to be buried somewhere around here."

"And he asked you out after that?"

"Probably because of it. He wasn't used to people correcting him. I was a novelty."

I hadn't planned on telling her about Burlin, but I'd never discussed him with a single soul since my sorority sisters, which seemed like a hundred years ago. Now, the story poured out like somebody had wound me up and pressed the "on" button.

"After the next class, he sauntered up and

said, 'You got a date for the football game this Saturday? Because if you don't, I've got an extra ticket that's got your name written all over it.' I said, 'Who's been writing on your ticket?' and he said, 'I wrote on the ticket. I've been scribbling all over it while I worked up my courage to ask you. Will you come?' I don't know which of us was more surprised when I said, 'I guess so.' "

"Smooth." Martha tugged my arm. "Keep talking, but walk faster."

"Slave driver," I muttered. "But Burlin was the smooth one, not me. I was flustered. I was twenty years old and had never been asked for a date. Can you believe that? Joe Riddley always said something romantic like, 'I'll pick you up at seven for the prom. Be ready, now.' "

Martha gave a gurgle of laughter. "I can just hear him."

While she was waving and calling to another walker who passed us, I was remembering what Burlin said on our way out the door after class. "I thought you were engaged to that tall drink of water with the dark hair and the smoldering eyes, but I don't see a ring, and I haven't seen him around lately."

To my eternal shame, I replied, "Oh, he's just a friend from home."

"Earth to Mac. Come in Mac," said Martha. "You're still mooning over Burlin Bullock."

"I never mooned! In fact, I figured he asked me that first time because he'd wanted to take somebody else and she couldn't go. I told myself it wasn't exactly a real date — we were merely going together to enjoy the game."

"That's one way to assuage guilt. But because you didn't swoon all over him, he figured you were playing hard to get, which piqued his interest even more, right?"

"You are too smart to live. Of course, I didn't take time to analyze it back then — life simply happened. But Burlin had no way of knowing I was totally unfamiliar with the dating game. Heck, I didn't know how to play hard to get — or anything else."

"So, how many times did you go out?"

"That whole semester."

Now it was Martha who slowed down. "Four months? What did Pop say?"

"Pop wasn't there, and I couldn't turn around without stumbling over Burlin. The more I told him he didn't need to walk me to class or buy me Cokes, the more he showed up. We went to all the football games and dances on campus, to concerts and plays in Atlanta, and on picnics where he brought wine and cheese — which seemed real sophisticated to me. Joe Riddley and I generally threw together some bologna sandwiches and a six-pack of Cokes. Burlin was like a stream of water falling over soft rock day after day.

45

'Wouldn't you like to drive to Atlanta to see a play?' 'There's a concert down in Atlanta next weekend you'd like.' 'My parents are having a dance in Buckhead in October, and I'd like you to go.' Hey — when did we pass the finish line and start a second lap?"

"Keep walking. Did you say Buckhead?"

"That's where the governor's mansion is," another walker said helpfully as she whizzed by. I motioned for Martha to drop back a little so we couldn't be overheard.

"So you went to a dance . . ." she said, waiting for the rest.

"It was a fantastic dance," I admitted. "I borrowed a dress and shoes from sorority sisters, so I looked presentable. He looked fabulous in his tux. All my friends hung out the upstairs windows to watch us leave. We danced well past midnight, then drove back in the crisp autumn night air with his convertible top down. It was more romantic than anything I'd ever known. I was beginning to think I was falling in love."

Martha stopped dead again. "You never. Poor Pop!"

I was glad to rest, but I looked over the grass in the middle of the track because I was too ashamed to face her. "Joe Riddley wasn't *there*, honey. Burlin bought me books when Joe Riddley didn't even buy stamps. He sent orange mums on Halloween when Joe Riddley didn't even send a funny card. He bought me corsages for football games and records of music we'd heard the Atlanta symphony play, and Joe Riddley didn't call for two weeks in a row. And it wasn't just the convertible or the posh dance or the gifts. I'm not that crass. We talked — a lot. Joe Riddley and I knew each other so well, we talked in a kind of shorthand. Burlin didn't know a thing about me and seemed to find every detail fascinating. I started to find him pretty fascinating, too."

"Time to walk again," Martha ordered. "We're almost halfway around again."

"Can't we cut across the middle and go home now?"

"Walk. You can't stop in the middle of your story."

I huffed and puffed. "I should have talked faster. I'm not cut out to be a power walker."

Martha wasn't the least bit compassionate. "We aren't even power strolling. Pick up the pace and talk faster. You were saying you were beginning to fall in love."

"I said I was beginning to think I was in love. That's not the same thing at all. I was walking around in a happy glow, feeling cherished." As we rounded the end of the track and started down the other side, I was remembering how rosy life had seemed back then.

"You're dragging your feet again," Martha finally said. "So what happened then?"

47

I didn't tell her about Burlin pressuring me to go to bed with him. I have limits to what I discuss with my daughters-in-law. Besides, I didn't want to confess that the only thing that saved me was not my love for Joe Riddley but some shred of self-preservation that whispered in my ear that Burlin only wanted what he couldn't get. I didn't tell her about little things that had begun to annoy me, either. The way he always wanted to guess what I was thinking and know if he was right. Frequent references to his family's importance, and a sort of expectation that Georgia owed them something because of all they'd done for the state. We were both young. Since then, he'd established himself as a politician of some integrity. I didn't need to tarnish his reputation. Only one thing would I admit. "When I went to meet his family —"

"He took you to meet his family? It was that serious?"

I had managed to shock Martha, Queen of Unflappable. Another time, I might have preened. Now I was sorry I'd said a word. Who knew what she might let slip to Ridd? I backpedaled like a circus clown. "They were getting together up at their lake house to celebrate his sister's birthday, so he invited me along." I couldn't resist bragging a little, though. "My sorority sisters were real impressed. One told me, 'That house was featured in *Southern*

Living a couple of years ago.' I went to the public library and looked up the article, so I could say a few intelligent things to his parents about it."

"His daddy was a state senator, right? And his mother was an heiress, or something?"

"They were important people," I agreed, "but that weekend they acted like anybody else — well, like millionaires with a huge house on a lake. We all went around in casual clothes and made sandwiches together for lunch. However, they did keep looking at me funny."

"Like they wanted to inspect your back teeth and test your wind, to see if you were good breeding stock?" Martha grew up on a farm, too.

"Sort of. To make things worse, Burlin's sister Georgia, who was a year younger than me, looked like a model. She was real friendly, but so gorgeous and glamorous, I kept wanting to go back to my room to put on lipstick and check my hair. And her roommate from Agnes Scott kept asking questions like 'Do you all ever go to class up at Georgia, or just party all the time?' The only person I felt comfortable with besides Burlin was his little sister, Binky. She was eight, intense, and plain as mud. We went for a walk through the leaves, and she told me she hated politics and was going to become a rancher out West, where she wouldn't have any people around for miles and miles — and she would never, ever vote. But she said I could come see her if I wanted to."

We laughed, then both grew solemn, because it hadn't really been funny. Martha voiced my thoughts when she said, "Poor little thing. It's hard to be a plain child in a beautiful family."

"Especially a family that talks nothing but politics morning, noon, and night. It began to really annoy me that they all presumed they had some God-given right to decide what's best for the whole state, when anybody could see the only part of Georgia they knew a thing about was Atlanta."

"So you finally got your eyes opened, right?"

"Sort of. At least, I began to cool off toward Burlin a bit. But I was trying to forget Joe Riddley, too, since he seemed to be cooling off toward me. When I came home for Thanksgiving, he worked Friday and Saturday. We didn't do a thing the rest of the time except watch television or go for rides, and all he talked about was the store. I couldn't talk about the Buckhead dance, Atlanta symphony concerts, or my weekend at the lake house of a state senator, so I didn't say much, either. It was, without a doubt, the most boring, miserable Thanksgiving of my life. I considered giving up men for life and becoming a missionary to Africa."

Martha laughed so hard I gave her a light smack. "Hush, or you'll have everybody on this track coming over here to see what's funny."

"I was picturing you as a missionary. For your kids' sake — and mine — I'm sure glad you didn't. Africa is probably glad, too. But what happened to Burlin? And what got you and Pop back together?"

I didn't answer right away. I needed to edit the next part. I couldn't tell Martha that Burlin bought me an enormous teddy bear for Christmas, had a shoe-repair man put a zipper in its chest, and filled the hole with a blue box holding an enormous diamond ring. "Marry me," he'd pleaded. "I want you so bad I can't stand it."

I still cringed to think about that moment. I had been surprised, shocked, and confused. Surely Burlin had noticed I was pulling back. Why would he think I would marry him? And did he really want to marry me, or did he only want to sleep with me?

On the other hand, Joe Riddley was vanishing as a marriage prospect, and I wanted to marry somebody. Burlin was charming and fun. If I married him, I could become a lady bountiful, a patron of the arts, a terrific political wife. Should I marry him and spend my life doing good?

I opened my mouth to say "Yes," and found I couldn't. So I stared at the ring and didn't say any of the things a girl is supposed to say.

Burlin finally laughed and gave me a hug. "Surprised? I thought you might be."

I thrust it back at him. "Keep it for a day or two while I think it over. Okay?" I jumped up and ran away.

Behind me, I heard him calling, "What's to think over?"

I headed back to my room, praying frantically. "Help! What do I do? What *should* I do?"

Since no angels showed up with an answer, I laid my problem in the laps of my best friends, who had gathered for what we called a "we aren't going to study tonight anyway" party. Most of them equated hormones with love, and considered a glamorous future every girl's God-given right. They squealed, giggled, jumped up and down, and assured me it was time to "get over" Joe Riddley and "do what your heart tells you is right." One of them suggested we go celebrate.

We drove across town in a downpour to a favorite campus dive. They spent hours discussing my wedding, down to what color my bridesmaids should wear — rose pink or yellow — and where I should go on my honeymoon. Bermuda won.

Then a quiet girl in the corner asked, "When will you tell Joe Riddley? It's sure hard for me to picture you without him."

With no warning whatsoever, I started to cry. I was a sopping, sodden mess by the time we started back to the dorm. That's where I picked up the story for Martha.

"Well, I'd gone out for pizza with some friends one night before Christmas break, and on our way home, a car turned in front of us. Our driver slammed on her brakes, and I hit my head so hard against the side window, I wound up in the hospital, unconscious. When I came to in the middle of the night, Joe Riddley was sitting by my bed. As soon as Daddy had called and told him about my accident, he'd driven two hours in blinding rain to get to me. When he saw that I was awake, he started saying all the things I'd been wishing he would say. Then he explained that he'd been working hard to pay for my diamond, so he could ask me to marry him. He hadn't wanted to give me a ring attached to debt."

"That's sweet," Martha said.

"Yeah, but I told him I didn't care what the ring was attached to, so long as it was attached to him. I felt like I'd come home. And that was that."

Sneaky woman. While I was talking, she had steered me past the finish line again and partway around a third lap. But at least she had slowed down. I started eyeing the grass on the sidelines, looking for a comfortable spot where I could collapse and spend the night. She, on the other hand, was still fresh enough to have a theory. Or so she said. "I believe that whatever age you are when you fall in love, you continue to relate that way for the rest of your life, unless something drastic happens. You and Pop fell in love when you were children —"

"No, it was in junior high."

"You were still young. So you acted like teenagers until the night of your wreck, right? I'd guess that's when you fell in love as grown-ups."

I told you Martha was smart. But I didn't fill her in on any of the juicy details about all that happened that night in the hospital. Like I said, I have some limits on what I discuss with my daughters-in-law.

My feet felt like we'd covered half the distance to California. I couldn't talk anymore and keep walking, so I shut up. Besides, I wanted to relive that wonderful night. Unfortunately, memory is not a biddable thing. Mine jumped ahead to the next morning when, as Joe Riddley was about to go, Burlin showed up, upset because he'd heard about the accident. I asked him to fetch me a Coke, and while he was gone, I persuaded Joe Riddley to go on back to Hopemore, since I'd be coming home for Christmas in few days anyway. He gave me one last kiss and stumbled out of the room half-asleep, not suspecting a thing.

When Burlin came back, I intended to tell him gently that I couldn't marry him because I was going to marry Joe Riddley. He didn't give me time. Thumping the Coke down on the night stand beside my bed, he scowled and demanded, "You love that son-of-a-gun, don't you?" I was too astonished to do more than nod. "Why didn't you tell me sooner? Why did you — hell, Mackie, why didn't you say something?"

I burst into tears. "I didn't know." I rummaged around for a tissue and finally wiped my nose on a corner of the sheet. "I mean, I used to know, all my life, but I didn't know later. I mean, I didn't think —" By then I was blubbering and incoherent, but it was from embarrassment and shame, not indecision.

Burlin turned and pounded the wall next to my bed, uttering a stream of language he had never used in my presence before. When my son Walker turned out to be a swearing wall pounder, I had to wonder if children can inherit traits from old boyfriends who leave an indelible print on your life.

Neither of us said anything for a few minutes. Burlin's back was to me, but when he turned, his face was red with anger and his eyes were full of tears. "I had such *plans*," he said huskily, still scowling. "We were going places, Mackie. What can he offer that I can't?"

I just shook my head. None of my answers would make sense to a Bullock.

He bent down so he could look straight into my watery eyes. "You sure? Real sure?" I nodded. "That's it, then." He headed to the door, then turned and uttered one small bit of spite. "You owe me a Coke. And I hope that every Christmas you'll think of me, and how you broke my heart." Burlin always did have a good instinct for exit lines. And I'll confess that every Christmas season since, he has floated through my mind once or twice.

I'd forgotten I was walking around a track with Martha until she interrupted my memories to ask, "So what's worrying you? I mean, all that was years ago."

"Yeah, but I've never mentioned any of this to Joe Riddley. He really admires Burlin. He watches him on television, quotes some of the things he says. I don't want him to find out that while he was faithfully slaving away to buy me a diamond, I was out with Burlin painting the town at least a deep shade of pink." I didn't add that Burlin made me nervous, because the buffalo on my front lawn felt like a trumpet announcing he didn't plan to ignore me.

"Pop could get upset," Martha admitted. "He's not always as steady and reliable as he used to be. Maybe this would be the perfect week for you all to rent a house at the beach."

"We can't. Joe Riddley has a workday tomorrow morning at the church, and he promised Gusta we'd come to her Do in the afternoon. We both have a dinner meeting

Monday night, and I have traffic court in the south of the county Thursday morning. Not to mention those blasted quarterly taxes I have to prepare. Believe me, I've thought about this for hours, and there's not a way we can leave town right now. The only good news I've had all day is that we are finally at the end of this blasted track."

As we headed toward our cars, Martha reached out and felt my forehead. "No stretch of my imagination can order you to bed for a week with a fever, and it looks like there's no way you can avoid seeing the Bullocks at least tomorrow. Maybe you ought to go ahead and tell Joe Riddley tonight that you all dated a few times. It's been years, after all."

"Honesty is the best policy," I said glumly. "But I'd rather go have a root canal."

When I got home, though, Joe Riddley was just coming in from work, wearing his favorite cap, a red one with YARBROUGH'S stitched on it in white. He'd gone all the way out to Dad's BarBeQue to pick us up some supper, and he'd stopped and gotten us a video that was not a World War II movie. How could I hurt a man like that? If Burlin was going to be in Hopemore all week, I'd simply have to find ways to stay out of his path.

It was as simple as two plus two, and I was a math major, after all.

I failed to factor into that particular equation Burlin's personality and a murder.

4

Parking was so tight for Gusta's party Saturday that Joe Riddley left his car at the store. "You realize I'll have to walk two blocks through this humidity in new shoes and a silk pantsuit," I pointed out as we climbed from the car.

He pulled down the sleeves of his best black suit and ignored my complaints. "We'd better use the alley, or somebody will ask us about bedding plants, no matter how we're dressed."

A man sat on the ground with his back to our building and hands on the knees of a gray suit. He wore an old felt hat over a long gray ponytail and must have been sweltering in the heat. His nails were dirty and cracked, his hands broad with strong, stubby fingers. He was absently humming to himself, looking up at the clouds. As we approached, he shifted his head to peer at us. His face was lined from hard living and too much sun, and one of his front teeth was missing, but his smile was sunny — if a bit vacant.

Joe Riddley stopped. "If you are hungry, fellow, go to Myrtle's around the block, to the back door. Tell them you'd like a meal.

Our church is good for dinner every day for a week."

"That's nice. Real nice." His voice was a husky whisper.

Joe Riddley loped toward Gusta's and I panted along beside him. He's never figured out that I have to take three steps every time he takes two. About halfway there he said, "I never feel like I do enough for those folks. If we were real Christians, Little Bit, we'd take him home and give him a bed and a bathtub." I couldn't answer. I was too out of breath trying to keep up.

Traffic was extra slow on Oglethorpe Street that afternoon. Tourists usually drove slowly to look at the string of big lovely homes with wide porches and tall white columns. What attracted attention now was the huge buffalo grazing on Gusta's lawn. The skinny man called Sarge, again in jeans and a T-shirt, watched him lazily from under a magnolia tree.

As we started up the walk, the buffalo lifted its head. "He's winking at you," Joe Riddley told me. "I owe you an apology, Little Bit. Remind me to give you one someday soon."

"It better be a good one." I followed him up Gusta's wide, shallow steps.

On the front porch, Hubert Spence threw a cigarette into the bushes and came to greet us with a guilty look. We all knew his doctor had told him to quit smoking after his heart attack.

Joe Riddley jerked a thumb toward the small brass sign by the door: WAINWRIGHT HOUSE ANTIQUES. "I don't see how Maynard gets any business with that little bitty sign. Nobody can read it from the street."

Hubert stuck his thumbs in his waistband to hold open his jacket and stuck out his chest. "He does most of his business over the Internet or by word of mouth. He's not interested in hoards of tourists tramping over his fancy oriental rugs looking for bargains."

"How'd you get so smart?" Joe Riddley clapped his shoulder. Hubert punched his arm.

They'd been neighbors most of their lives, growing up on adjoining farms and eventually moving back into their parents' old homeplaces. They'd never agreed over politics, religion, or whether Georgia or Georgia Tech was the better school, but otherwise they'd been good friends. I, however, took an experimental sniff before I gave Hubert a hug and was delighted to find that living with Gusta and Pooh continued to improve his personal hygiene. He used to think deodorant was for sissies and two baths a week plenty for a man who worked indoors. Now he wore a starched shirt and a well-pressed suit, and smelled of a pleasant aftershave.

"Looks like Maynard wouldn't want hoards of Gusta's guests tramping all over his carpets, either," I told him.

He gave me the smile of a man whose only child has done far better than the parent ever expected. "He's rolled up the rugs. Don't set a glass down anywhere, though, except on the little trays he's got scattered around. He doesn't want water circles on his furniture."

"I'll set mine on the floor," Joe Riddley assured him. "Nothing can hurt heart pine."

"It'll break a termite's teeth," Hubert agreed. He waved us inside. "I'm gonna stay out here a little while longer. Too crowded in there for my taste."

Joe Riddley steered me through the front door before I could offer to keep Hubert company.

The hall looked a lot like it used to when Gusta lived there, full of impressive pieces of furniture and oil paintings.

"Welcome," said a woman near the door. She certainly wasn't Augusta Wainwright. She wasn't much taller than me, while Gusta was impressively tall even after shrinking an inch or two. This woman might have bought her navy dress at one of the expensive stores where Gusta shopped, but she wore it with comfortable Enzo flats Gusta wouldn't be caught dead in at one of her Do's. This woman's skin was tanned and lightly wrinkled, as if she enjoyed the sun. Vanity had

61

made Gusta careful of the sun long before anybody mentioned the ozone layer, and even in old age, Gusta was beautiful. This woman's nose was thin and pointed and she wore no makeup except for red lipstick that looked applied on the run. Her straight hair was blunt cut, parted on one side, and held back by a small gold clip. It had once been brown like her eyes, but was now frosted with gray.

Her prim mouth curved in a smile as she stepped toward us, fingering a string of pearls too long for the neckline of her navy dress. With the other hand, she handed us each a little red pin. "From Lance Bullock, with his compliments." Her voice was deep and gravelly, the kind that can make a grocery list sound sexy.

Before I could explain that I couldn't wear the pin, Maynard hailed us from a back corner of the hall.

"Where's the beautiful member of your family?" Joe Riddley greeted him, looking around.

"Working." Maynard's wife, Serena, was a nurse and worked with Martha.

"You're beautiful, too," I assured him, giving him a hug. He'd come a long way from the skinny nervous little boy next door. Of course, his sleek blond ponytail had given Hopemore a lot of trouble when he'd first returned from New York after his daddy's heart attack. That afternoon, tied with a brown velvet ribbon to match his coat, it looked downright distinguished.

"You know," I told him, "I'm even getting used to your earring by now."

"Watch out," he warned Joe Riddley, "or she'll be taking an ice pick to your ear while you're sleeping." He ran one hand under his collar and heaved a big sigh. "Sorry about the temperature. The air-conditioning is going full blast, but you don't notice unless you happen to be near a vent. I've raised the windows, hoping for a breeze."

"It's not that bad." I comforted him. "You must be nervous about folks walking off with one of your precious doodads."

"Not particularly. They are insured. But I am mad that we were brought here under false pretenses." He glowered toward the double doors leading to the living room. "I was a little surprised that Miss Gusta wanted to hold a party for Lance Bullock, since her politics run in the other direction, but she said his aunt is an old friend of hers, and I was willing to do my part for my party. She neglected to mention that Lance plans to announce in the next few weeks that he's switching parties."

"You're joking, of course."

I really thought he was, but he shook his head. "Miss Gusta told me herself, when she first got here. Said this way he avoids the primary and picks up a lot of votes. I cannot for the life of me figure out how a politician can let one party boost him or her up, then step over to the other party if the pickings look better. What do they stand for? And who'd trust them after that? No matter which party he switched from or to, who'd be dumb enough to vote for a traitor? Except my dad," he added with a grimace.

Before we could reply to that, I heard, "Yarbroughs, is that you? I want you to meet someone." Gusta sat on her usual throne by the living room door. She beckoned with one long bony finger sparkling with diamonds. And although she looked a little shrunken in her purple linen dress — she'd aged a lot since her only son died the year before — she still sat regal as a queen and expected people to obey when she called. We moseyed in that direction.

She reached for one of my hands. "Mac, Joe Riddley, I want you to meet my very dear friend Georgia Bullock Tate, Burlin's sister. Georgia, this is Judge and Judge Yarbrough."

I blinked. Georgia was only a year younger than I, so what had she done with her crow's-feet? She didn't look a day over forty-five. She was still slender, but filled out her black linen shift in a way I could find it in my heart to envy. Nothing sagged, and her hair — that light yellow that only good salons

64

can achieve — was cut short with long pixie bangs that brushed her forehead above eyes the same dark gray as her brother's.

I resolved to see about getting myself a makeover as soon as I got some free time.

Thank goodness, she didn't recognize me. She put out a hand and greeted us with the comfortable charm that comes from years of being with the right people in the right places. "I'm delighted to meet you and so happy to be in Hopemore. It's a lovely town." As she clasped my working paw, I was glad I'd thought to ask Phyllis for a manicure that morning, but Georgia wasn't the least bit interested in me. She was looking up at Joe Riddley with an earnestness that made him hold her hand a lot longer than was necessary.

He had to clear his throat before he could speak. "We're real glad to have you here, Mrs. Tate. I've admired Burlin for a long time."

Georgia's face crinkled into a beautiful smile. "Why, thank you, Judge. What a sweet thing to say."

Normally I'd have stepped in about then to be sure Joe Riddley didn't get carried away. He's not real skilled at handling pretty women who smile up at him. However, Gusta's deep voice distracted me. She spoke behind her cupped hand, but in a normal voice that defeated the purpose. "Georgia's husband, Edward, is Lance's campaign manager. She's down here helping Lance run his campaign."

"Lance is going to be our next governor, you know." Georgia nodded proudly toward the windows where a tall stocky man in a black suit was talking enthusiastically to a group of men. His hair was black and very thick, his shoulders powerful. He looked like the kind of man I wouldn't want to cross. And he didn't look more than ten years younger than Burlin.

I'd gotten that far when the woman in navy came up behind me. She must have heard Georgia and noticed where I was looking, because she murmured in my ear, "Not the man in black. That's Edward, Georgia's husband. Lance is talking to the large woman in red. He's prettier than Edward." Her smile was still prim, but her brown eyes danced. Suddenly I knew who she was. I almost exclaimed "Binky!" without thinking.

Georgia reached out an arm to draw her into our circle. "This is my baby sister, Abigail." Nobody who saw the two of them together for the first time would believe that, but Georgia didn't give anybody time to say so. "She's worked as Burlin's secretary for years. Now she's helping Edward run Lance's campaign."

"What happened to the ranch out West?" I wanted to ask.

Instead, I looked at the real Lance. He was

thirty-six, I remembered, and nothing like his daddy. He was as tall as Burlin, but stocky, with dark hair curling down to a thick neck. His navy suit looked rumpled, like he'd done some living in it, and the lines in his pink face seemed to have been drawn by laughter. As I watched, he threw back his head and laughed so hard I could see fillings in his back teeth.

What on earth could he find so funny, talking to Chancey Carter? Chancey was circulation manager for our local paper, and a front-runner for Hopemore's most boring woman. We were too far away to hear their conversation, but I went to school with Chancey from first grade on and had yet to hear her talk about anything except herself, Georgia history as it pertained to her own family's genealogy, or her mother — who, at ninety, was a hellion over at the nursing home. Burlin would have chatted with her briefly and excused himself, I suspected, but Lance bent over her and listened like he enjoyed it. When Edward Tate touched his elbow and seemed to want him to move on, Lance gave a little wave to say, "In a minute."

"That's his wife behind him — Renée," Binky said with pride.

Renée must be ten years younger than Lance, but stood almost as tall, with narrow hips, a long face, and a strong nose. Her eyes were large and green, her mouth wide with a full lower lip. As I took her in, from the tips of her taupe pumps to the top of her almost black hair, I couldn't help thinking that these Bullock women were expensive to keep. Renée's haircut was so ugly, it had to have cost a fortune — cut long to brush her collar at the back, chopped unevenly at the bottom, tucked behind her ears. Her green suit was raw silk and exactly matched her eyes.

She wore what looked like a practiced smile as she listened to Chancey. I didn't get the feeling she was as involved as Lance. Still, when Chancey paused for breath, I saw Renée ask a question that set Chancey off again. I wondered if the cotton shell had come with Renée's outfit or if she was just unconcerned with dressing to please Hopemore. In contrast to Gusta's diamonds, Binky's pearls, and Georgia's necklace of chunky black rocks set in heavy silver, Renée wore no jewelry except simple gold hoop earrings. In that crowd of folks who had hauled up their socks to look real nice on a Saturday afternoon, she looked exotic, casual, and comfortable. I eased one foot out of my dressy shoes for an instant and wished I had that much gumption.

When Renée turned away to stifle a yawn, Binky murmured, "Poor thing, she's asleep on her feet. She flew in yesterday morning from Paris so she could come on this trip."

"She and Lance are a great team. When they get to the governor's mansion —" Georgia began, but Binky touched her forearm.

"Let's don't talk politics right now. We're here to enjoy the hospitality of Mrs. Wainwright."

Georgia nodded. "Of course we are." She turned back to Joe Riddley. "And we are enjoying Hopemore so much. Have you lived here long?"

"All our lives," he told her.

I'd lived in Hopemore long enough to be a flower girl in Gusta's wedding — the one who tripped going down the aisle and showed the world her ruffled underpants. Gusta would be mentioning that any minute unless I headed her off. "We just moved out of the house Joe Riddley's great-granddaddy built," I told them. "How many families can make that claim?"

Gusta huffed, miffed at missing another golden opportunity to embarrass me. Georgia, of course, didn't know that. She asked in the bright, interested voice of somebody trying to warm up to strangers, "And you are both judges?"

"I used to be. Mac, here, replaced me." Joe Riddley stood there with a silly smile on his face, caught like a moth in Georgia's sparkle.

When she turned to greet somebody else, I nudged him toward a waitress making her way through the room with a tray of little sandwiches. "Go get something to eat. I'll see you in a bit."

As he loped away, I watched anxiously to make sure he didn't run into Burlin. The way he admired the man, it would be like him to take Burlin into the corner for a long chat. Fortunately, Burlin was nowhere in sight.

That's because he was right behind me. I jumped when he murmured in my ear, "Hey, Mackie. You look wonderful. I wondered if you'd be here." I shivered in spite of myself as I felt a puff of his breath on my neck. Then I blushed. I had to admit at least to myself that I hadn't put on my most gorgeous outfit and made sure Phyllis did her best just so I'd look nice for my husband. Nobody wants an old boyfriend wondering, "What did I ever see in her?" But I had the grace to feel ashamed.

Gusta's old eyes looked from one of us to the other with a most calculating expression.

Georgia raised her eyebrows. "Why, Burlin, do you already know the judge?"

"So do you," he told her. "Remember MacLaren Crane? She came to a dance the year you came out and up to the lake house for your birthday that year."

Binky's hand flew to her pearls. "I didn't recognize you, but I remembered you used to live in Hopemore."

Georgia reached for both my hands and gave them a squeeze. "Mackie! How marvelous to see you again."

From the way Gusta's lips tightened, I'd have a few questions to answer later. Burlin must have noticed, because he leaned toward her and said, "This sure is a great party, Miss Gusta. You must be a lot like Georgia — she's the organized one in our family and the one who knows how to throw a party. I sure thank you for having us." Gusta preened to be getting so much attention from a political celebrity. He chatted with her for a few more minutes, then said again, "This sure is a nice party you've thrown for Lance. And speaking of Lance" — he took my elbow — "I want Mackie, here, to meet him." He pulled me gently away and led me across the room.

I had to congratulate him. "Neatly done. She's not generally that easy to leave."

"It's taught in politics training school, under the care and feeding of dragons."

"That dragon feeds on scandal and gossip, so be careful." I retrieved my elbow and put distance between us.

"Duly noted." He raised his hand and beckoned to Lance.

Lance excused himself from Chancey and headed our way. His wife stayed long enough to listen to a few more words, then moved after him with the long-legged grace of a giraffe.

71

She, like Burlin, looked cool and collected, but Lance had beads of perspiration on his forehead. One curl had come loose and was dangling over one eye. Renée wiped it back gently as Burlin said, "I want you all to meet somebody. This is an old friend of mine, MacLaren Crane."

"Yarbrough," I amended, shaking the hand Lance shot out.

"Of course, Yarbrough," Burlin agreed easily. "I forgot for a minute how old we all are."

"Speak for yourself," Lance informed him, giving him a fond punch. "I don't think Ms. Yarbrough's much older than I am."

Burlin draped one arm around my shoulders and his other one over Lance's. He drew us both close and murmured, "Boy, if things had worked out the way I planned, this woman would have been your mother and I'd be governor of this state."

That's how we were standing when the flash went off.

5

I pulled away from Burlin's arm. He waved at the photographer. "Not now, Carstairs." The reporter gave him a mock salute and disappeared.

A voice asked behind us, "An old flame of yours, Burlin?" It was the big man in black, Georgia's husband. He came around me to offer a huge hand. "Glad to meet you. Any friend of the Bullocks is a friend of mine." But behind rimless glasses, his dark eyes looked down at me like he was the judge in a fishing contest, trying to decide if I was the prize catch.

I stepped farther away from Burlin. "I'm not an —" I began, but Edward Tate was the type of man who seldom listens to an older woman unless she's offering a contribution or calling him to dinner. He was already turning back to Burlin to speak in a low voice.

"You didn't mention you had friends in Hopemore." He sounded like he was accusing Burlin of a crime.

Burlin beamed at me. "We go back to college days, but I wasn't sure she still lived here."

What I wanted to say wasn't fit for polite

company, and saying it might get my name in the newspaper — that reporter was still hovering in earshot — so I took another step away and said, "Good to meet you, Lance. You, too, Renée." I headed toward a group of people I knew.

I heard Edward ask Burlin in a low voice, "So you two were an item — when?"

Still in earshot, I slowed to a snail's crawl long enough to hear Burlin say in an offhand way, "I told you, college days."

"Well, we need to be circulating, not standing here. Lance, you go to the hall. Burlin, you take the sunroom, and I'll work this room some more." I heard them moving off.

I glanced back and saw that Renée had remained where she was, watching me with an odd look in those enormous sage-green eyes. Could she possibly feel sorry for me?

I could feel sorry for her. Edward hadn't included her in his instructions, and Burlin had scarcely bothered to introduce her. I suspected she might be lonely at times in the Bullock clan.

What I needed to cheer me up was food, even Gusta's feeble offerings. But Gusta had either stretched her budget this time or one of Lance's political parties was paying. The table nearly creaked under the weight of shrimp, little pastries filled with lobster, exotic cheeses they hadn't gotten at the Bi-Lo, tiny rolls to fill with sweet pink ham or rare roast beef with horseradish sauce, and enough vegetables to feed a rabbit for a year. I filled a plate, then wandered — glad to see Joe Riddley at the back of the hall with a bunch of men, probably expressing their doubts that Georgia's football team could carry on that afternoon without them there. I kept one eye on Burlin, who was circulating, but so far he had been nowhere near Joe Riddley's corner.

Gusta was having a marvelous time playing hostess in her house again. I heard her tell several different people, "You cannot imagine what I feel, coming back to my precious home and seeing it like this. And moving is so disastrous to your things. Mother's dining table got scratched, Granddaddy's clock has run slow ever since, one of Grandmother's Limoges plates got chipped — she bought the set on her honeymoon, you know — and I still haven't found that Tiffany lamp my husband's father gave us when we married."

I knew for a fact that the table scratch was under the edge, the Limoges plate had been chipped for years, and the lamp had resided in her attic until her granddaughter took it home with Gusta's blessing, but why mess up a good story with facts? As I well knew, it *was* hard to leave your old home. Let her find comfort anyplace she could.

I moseyed over to one of Maynard's fancy

tables and asked for white wine. Renée glided up beside me and said, "Perrier, please," in a pleasant, husky voice. As the bartender filled her glass, she turned to me with a confidential murmur. "So — you used to date Burlin?"

The bartender — a former student of Ridd's who now played with him on our church softball team — perked up his ears. I said, "Burlin greatly exaggerates. We took history together back in college." Please note that both statements were absolutely true.

She shrugged. "Whatever. It would be nice to discover he was once interested in something besides politics." She sipped her water while her eyes roved the room. When they stopped, I followed her gaze and saw she was looking at Lance, who was in the arch to the hall talking with several people. He had one hand resting on the doorframe and was stroking it.

"It's in their blood, I guess." I sipped my own wine and wondered what it took to look as sophisticated as Renée. Had she been born elegant?

I was surprised when she said forcefully, "It's not in Lance's blood." She flared her nostrils like a nervous horse. "If the others didn't keep his nose to the grindstone, he'd happily go back to work."

"What does he do?" I hadn't read or heard much about Lance since he was a child.

"Restores old houses for new uses. His degree is in architecture. He'd much rather be wandering around looking at this house than talking politics. And if he was, I could be dozing on the dock of the lake house this afternoon." She stifled a yawn, then gave me what passed for a smile. "Sorry. I am just so tired! I guess that's why I'm telling you all this. But Georgia would have a fit. Please forget what I said." She smiled down at me and sipped her water.

Georgia spoke brightly from behind me. "You two aren't talking politics, I hope? Abigail says it's off-limits this afternoon." She put her arm around Renée's waist and gave her a squeeze. "You're too jet-lagged to think straight. Why don't you go out on the porch and get some air?"

"That's a good idea. Excuse me." Renée drifted through the crowd like green smoke.

Georgia picked up a glass of red wine and sparkled down at me. "I can't believe we've run into you again after all these years. What have you been doing with yourself since college?"

I was wishing I'd gone with Renée. Georgia had so much energy, it wore me out to stand next to her. Besides, the story of my life was going to sound pretty tame. "The usual. Husband, two sons, four grandchildren. I help run the family nursery and agricultural supply store."

She inclined her head and managed to look interested. "And how did you become a judge? Did you go to law school, like Burlin? He graduated from Yale, you know."

I did know, but I was surprised Georgia *didn't* know you don't have to be a lawyer to be a magistrate in Georgia. They do in big counties like those around Atlanta, but down here, we don't have that big a pool of honest lawyers to choose from. How could that information have slipped past somebody so involved in politics?

Georgia didn't care whether I went to law school or not. She was already giving my arm a little squeeze and saying, "I was so sorry when you and Burlin broke up. I'd have liked to have had you for a sister."

Now what is a woman supposed to say to that?

I knew what this woman had to do. I had to shift us both away from the bartender's big ears. I took her elbow. "Let's find a quieter corner." When we got there, I suggested, "Tell me about you." I resigned myself to ten minutes of glamorous achievements.

She surprised me. "Hardly a thing worth mentioning. I play a lot of tennis and serve on a lot of committees and keep both our house and Burlin's." Somehow, I didn't think that meant she cleaned the toilets. "Edward's my second husband, you know." She put up a hand to hide her lips as she whispered,

"He's a bit younger than I, but don't tell anybody. My first husband was a lot older, and after he died, I decided I deserved some compensation. Edward and Burlin are in business together, you know — lobbying and political consulting. Edward started out lobbying for the timber industry. Now he and Burlin represent a number of Georgia interests, both in Atlanta and in Washington, but mostly they serve as political consultants. I help out by planning and hosting dinner parties, planning events, writing thank-you notes, things like that. Abigail manages Burlin's office — she's the real organized one in the family, no matter what Burlin says — and he's her whole life, bless her heart. But Burlin likes for me to plan his parties and serve as his hostess, because" — she lowered her voice — "Abigail is not exactly a firecracker at a dinner table."

She wouldn't be the adornment Georgia would, either, but neither of us said that.

"Burlin's lucky to have you," I told her. "He mentioned that his wife died."

Her gray eyes grew sad. "Yes, bless her heart. She died in a fire at a rehab clinic. It was very tragic." We paused for a few seconds of respect.

"Was it in the papers? I never read it."

"No, we kept it quiet. Burlin didn't need those old stories raked up again, so Abigail and I made sure the press didn't get even a whiff of it. Poor Sperra." She sipped her wine and seemed to be thinking. "I've been helping Burlin out for — golly! It's twenty years now." She leaned closer. "Don't quote that figure to anybody. I don't admit to a day over fifty."

"You don't look even that."

"Thanks. I try to keep fit. And now that Lance is running for governor and Edward's running the campaign, I won't have a minute to call my own." If she glowed any brighter, Maynard could cut off all his chandeliers.

"You look like you don't mind."

"I don't. I love politics. And if we can get Lance in as governor — well, who knows where he might go after that?" Clearly she had some idea of where she wanted him to go, and I suspected it involved a large white house. But right now a small frown creased her forehead. I followed her gaze and saw that Renée had come back inside and was standing behind Lance. As the businessmen he'd been talking with moved away, she leaned over and spoke urgently into his ear. He shook his head. She narrowed her eyes, flared her nostrils. He gave her a pleading look and stepped forward to greet a couple who'd been looking like they were working up their courage to speak to him. Renée glared at his back.

Georgia spoke very softly. "Do you think it would be terrible if I told Renée she can go on back to the inn for a nap? She is plumb worn out, bless her heart."

"I doubt if anybody would notice. The only person she might possibly offend is Gusta, and she's got a granddaughter . . ."

Georgia smiled to show she'd picked up my hint. "Thanks." She went straight to Renée and put a hand on her shoulder. Renée listened to what Georgia said and gave a relieved nod. Georgia drew her toward the living room arch and spoke in a voice audible from where I stood. "Renée just got back from Paris yesterday in time to drive down here with all of us, because she wanted to be here for this week's round of events, but she hasn't gotten her time zones straight yet. Would you mind if she went and took a nap?" She gave a little laugh that implied, "You know how these young women are — no stamina."

Gusta reached out and patted Renée's hand. "You go stretch out on your bed and catch up on your sleep. We'll take care of your husband."

"Thank you." Renée started out, then grabbed Lance's elbow and tugged. "I need to talk to you a minute before I go." He followed her to the porch.

Georgia moved back into the living room. Conversations dwindled as men watched her walk past with a confident little sway to her hips.

I talked to a few other people, but I was beginning to feel warm and sticky. Maynard was right — the air-conditioning wasn't up to that kind of crowd. I headed for the porch, trying to walk like Georgia, but I didn't hear any conversations stop as I passed.

The porch was empty except for Hubert, Lance, and Binky, who were leaning against the railing like cronies. Hubert and Binky were both smoking. "Those things have already almost killed you," I murmured to Hubert as I joined them.

"You sound like Burlin," Binky told me. "He's always on to me about quitting, but I tell him we all need one vice, and this is mine." She slid something into her pocket with her free hand. "Well, Hubert, it's been good talking to you, but I'd better get back to the party. You coming, Lance?" She stubbed her cigarette out on a small plastic plate and picked the plate up to carry it inside.

"In a minute." He craned his neck and peered at the ceiling of the porch. "I wonder if those are the original boards."

"Gusta would be proud to tell you they are," I informed him.

"Don't be long," Binky warned him as he strolled down the porch looking at siding. The front door closed behind her with a click.

Hubert looked at his cigarette in disgust. "It's an addiction, Mac. You know that."

"Fight it," I advised. "You're a grown-up."

"I know." He fished in his pocket and brought out a book of matches. "But see that? I just got 'em this week. Aren't they pretty? I had 'em printed for my fortieth anniversary celebration next month. Here, Lance," he added as Lance headed back our way. "Take home a souvenir."

The cover was bright cherry red, with SPENCE'S APPLIANCES, HOPEMORE, 40 YEARS dropped out in white. "Thanks." Lance pocketed it absently, still looking at the ceiling.

"They are nothing but temptation at my fingertips," Hubert grumbled, taking out another matchbook and frowning at it. "I keep picking up a few and carrying them around, and whenever I want a smoke, there they are."

I reached for it. "Let me relieve you of temptation, then."

He snatched it back. "I'm not handing them out in town before the celebration. You can have as many as you want then."

"Maybe you ought to advertise on packs of gum instead," Lance suggested, leaning against the rail again to examine the front of the house.

"Didn't think of that." Hubert took one last puff and tossed his lit cigarette over the rail.

It landed in the grass with a little flare. "Maynard won't have to worry about rings on his furniture if you burn the place down," I told him.

He huffed, but he trotted out onto the grass and ground the butt under his foot.

"Not again," Lance muttered, looking toward the street.

The homeless man in the gray suit was shuffling past. At the front walk, he paused to give us a jaunty wave. Lance shook his head and made a small, amused sound. "I don't know if we're on his circuit or if he's on ours, but that man has been in almost every town we've been in these past two months. He even shows up at some rallies — the ones that give free food. Watch out, or he'll be mingling with Mrs. Wainwright's guests."

"Not if she sees him, he won't. Maybe he's a very loyal supporter."

He chuckled. "Registered to vote in every county? I could use some of those."

Before I could reply, Hubert shouted, "Hey! Git out of here! Git, you hear me? Git!" He ran across the lawn, arms flailing. "Git out of my barn, too, and stay out. You hear me? Go back where you came from." Too busy looking at the homeless man to watch where he was going, he tripped over the buffalo's chain and fell sprawling onto the grass.

The buffalo gave an angry snort and jerked its head.

"Hey!" shouted Sarge, the keeper. "Watch where you're going."

Hubert hauled himself to his feet and trotted on across the lawn. The homeless man had stopped at the corner of the lot to watch him. "Git!" Hubert waved his arms.

He wasn't getting much reaction from the homeless man, but the buffalo was fascinated. He trotted after Hubert. I guess his chain wasn't sufficiently anchored, or maybe Hubert had dislodged it, because it came loose and dragged along behind him.

"Hubert!" I yelled in warning. He looked back, and panic spread all over his face. He started running faster. The buffalo picked up speed.

"Oh, Lord," Lance breathed as Hubert dashed toward the street. The buffalo loped after him. Sarge ran after the buffalo. Lance pelted after Sarge.

Tires squealed. People shouted. I hardly dared to look.

Hubert was safe on the other side of the street, but the buffalo and a Toyota had collided. Thank goodness, nobody had been going very fast. The buffalo shook its head as if clearing flies. The Toyota's front end had a buffalo-shaped dent.

An angry man got out of the car, waving his arms. "Get him out of here," Lance shouted to Sarge, gesturing at the buffalo. Sarge grabbed the animal's chain, shaking his free fist at the driver. Lance went to talk to the driver, who was shouting the kind of words I won't bother to repeat. Your imagination is at least as good as his.

The homeless man was nowhere to be seen.

People streamed from Gusta's party to fill the lawn, discussing what might have happened as if they'd been there. Lance continued to talk to the man in the car. Edward hurried out to join him, and pretty soon he and the driver were both writing something down. I saw Edward motion to Sarge, and he led the poor buffalo to a truck parked down the block.

Hubert limped to join me, his face redder than a man's ought to be after a heart attack.

"That was real smart," I greeted him. "Just what Gusta expects of her guests. Sit down."

He was wheezing in a way I didn't like. He collapsed into a porch rocker. "Dangnabit, that bum is camping out in my barn, and I can't get rid of him. Leaves out food to attract mice, uses my woods for a toilet —" He obviously wasn't planning to discuss the buffalo.

"How do you know it's him?"

He gave me a look that said I didn't have the sense I was born with. "How many homeless people we got in Hopemore?"

He had a point. We had poor people, of course, but most of them had relatives somewhere around who could squeeze them in during a financial crisis.

"Besides," Hubert said, pulling out a handkerchief to wipe his face, "I saw him once. I've run down several times trying to surprise him, and once I saw him out on the edge of the woods, but he saw me, too, and scuttled away before I could catch him." He stopped to do some more wheezing. "How can I sell the place with him hanging around?"

"Poor Hubert," I commiserated. "But Lance said the man is following him around, so just wait a week. He'll leave with the Bullock campaign."

Lance mounted the steps as I spoke. He had been looking worried, but now he chuckled. "That's me, Pied Piper of the Homeless."

I liked this fellow. That didn't mean I would vote for him if he changed parties, mind, but I liked him. He didn't take himself too seriously, which I always regard as a virtue.

He pulled out his own handkerchief and wiped his flushed face. "I'd better get back inside and soothe Miss Gusta. We've spoiled her nice party."

"You've made it a success," I assured him. "She'll talk about nothing else for days."

He sighed. "Maybe so, but it looks like I'm gonna need a lawyer."

When he'd left, I asked Hubert, "Have you asked the sheriff to get rid of the man?"

Hubert gave a snort. "I told Charlie Muggins at our Thursday-night poker game, but you know Charlie. He loves strutting around in his police chief's uniform, but he sits there and tells me he doesn't have the manpower to stake out my barn."

"It's not his jurisdiction anyway," I pointed out. "It's the sheriff's."

Hubert glowered. "I may take my shotgun, climb up in the loft, and just wait for the fella to show up. Then I'll blow him to kingdom come."

Guests who were returning to the party looked at him oddly.

I put a hand on his shoulder. "Don't. I don't want you appearing before me on charges of murder. And think how Maynard would feel if his children's grandfather was in jail for life."

"There is that," he admitted, "but I gotta do something. I'm getting desperate. The Realtor said the last family was pretty interested in the house, but when they got to the barn and saw signs somebody was bedding down, they said they didn't want to live so far out."

"Huh," I grunted. "Folks want to get away from it all, but once they get half a mile from streetlights, they get antsy."

Hubert gave a bitter laugh. "You got that right. Every city slicker's dream: a private, gated five country acres smack dab in the

88

middle of town." He rocked a few minutes, then said, "I'll tell you what, Mac. Do some of that detecting you're so good at. Sneak up on him, get him to talk to you. Tell him I'll buy a bus ticket to anywhere he wants to go. One way."

Hubert knew I wouldn't do that, but talking seemed to have helped him let off steam. We were quiet for a spell after that. We'd been neighbors so long, we didn't need to talk. I don't know what Hubert was thinking, but I was thinking how terrible it must be not to have a safe place to sleep or a modern bathroom when you needed one.

Out of the blue, he asked, "Did you see the little lady I was just talking to? Her name's Abigail, and she's Burlin Bullock's sister." He smoothed his hair, which was a bit thin but still wavy. "She's coming over to our place for dinner tonight. Would it be proper for me to ask if she'd like to go for a little spin afterwards, to see the sights? Gusta and Pooh generally shut down pretty early —" He was looking at me just like Lulu did when she hoped I had a treat in my hand.

I didn't want to spoil his party. On the other hand, I didn't want Hubert courting Abigail. Hubert wasn't any older than us, and he had a sizeable bank account. Now that Pooh and Gusta had taken him in hand, he even smelled good. Georgia hadn't mentioned any romance in Abigail's life. Had anybody even mentioned her last name? What if she were susceptible and married Hubert? Could I live in Hopemore with the constant threat that Burlin might come back? Was that reason enough to stand in the way of Hubert's happiness?

"You'll have to ask her," I said.

Maynard's phone rang just inside the open window. "I'll get him," I heard Maynard say.

I heard Joe Riddley's voice. Next thing I knew, he was striding through the door waving me to follow him. "Come on, Little Bit. That was Bethany. The barn's on fire, and she can't get either Martha or Ridd."

6

"Lulu!" I gasped the word as I hared after Joe Riddley, who was practically running down Oglethorpe. In my mind I saw my dog as I'd found her the year before, lying in a blood-soaked nest of pine straw in the woods after she and Joe Riddley had both been shot. The would-be murderer had left her for dead, but although her left hind leg was mangled beyond saving, that plucky little beagle had burrowed into the pine straw and managed to survive until I found her.

Save her and her pups, I begged God. *That poor dog has suffered enough.*

"Did she get Lulu and the pups out?" I called after Joe Riddley's back, clutching my stomach to keep my insides from falling onto the street.

He looked around, his mouth grim and set. "I don't know. Cindy's horse, either."

"Did she call 911?"

"The fire trucks were already there. Stop yapping and run."

I'd barely gotten my car door slammed before he had zoomed out of the lot. All I can say about Joe Riddley's driving is, it was a good thing he'd driven those roads for fifty years. He'd never have made it home at that speed, otherwise.

We saw smoke above the pines before we even reached the gravel road. "I'll bet it was Tad," I muttered.

"What was Tad?"

"Who started the fire. Smoking."

"He's smoking?" Joe Riddley didn't sound as upset as I was, but when we grew up, all the boys smoked. It was their contribution toward the Southern economy.

"Martha said the girls caught him smoking in the woods. Ridd gave him a talking to, but that probably just drove him to the barn."

"If he set a fire, I'll give him more than a talking to." His hands tensed on the wheel.

"Don't be too hard on him. He's just ten." I leaned forward in dread to peer at black billows filling the sky.

"He's also spoiled rotten," my husband muttered.

"The sins of the grandparents visited on the children," I replied. When he threw me a questioning look, I explained, "We haven't helped Walker and Cindy raise their kids. We hardly know that little boy."

Until this past year, we and Walker's wife had kept each other at a polite distance. Her family had land, money, and pedigrees going back to the English aristocracy. Her dad bred hunters and was a bigwig in foxhunts that are still held in that part of Georgia. Cindy hunted every year, and she and Walker lived in the kind of elegance *Southern Living* implies is normal throughout the South. Their kids had grown up spending more time at the country club than they did down at our place, and we never went to their house unless invited. It was only in the past few months that Cindy and I had discovered we had several things in common and begun to appreciate each other. I regretted those wasted years.

Joe Riddley reached out a big hand and covered mine. "It's not your fault, honey."

He turned onto the gravel drive one handed, but had to take back his hand to grab the wheel as the car fishtailed on the turn.

I waited until he'd straightened us out before I said, "But if Tad and Jessica had grown up like Ridd's kids — swimming in our pool, playing in the barn, riding around with you on a tractor or the forklift —" I sniffed back tears. We were passing the first of three houses on our road, and I was terrified of what we'd find when we got home.

"Tad's always been more interested in tennis and golf," Joe Riddley reminded me. "When he comes to the store, he wrinkles his nose like he's afraid he'll get dirty. The only two things I've ever seen him show interest in are animals and video games."

"He's still our grandchild."

"Which he's gonna find out, if he set that barn on fire." His face was grim.

By the time we got to Hubert's old house, the smell was so strong I could taste it. In spite of the heat, I put up my window.

I heard somebody behind us and looked over my shoulder. Sheriff Bailey "Buster" Gibbons was following us in his cruiser. "Buster's gonna bust you," I warned, but I knew it wasn't true. Buster and Joe Riddley had been best friends since kindergarten. He wasn't there to make an arrest. He was there to stand by us if the house burned down.

Joe Riddley squealed into the driveway and stopped up near the road. Buster screeched to a halt right behind us. He jumped out of his car and yelled, "I thought you were driving, Mac!" Then he called after Joe Riddley as he ran behind him, "Is the tractor still in there?"

Every muscle in my body froze. Of course the tractor was in the barn. Two mowers, too, and an edger, all full of gas. Ridd kept them that way, plus an extra can of gasoline or two. Before I'd finished that thought, Buster had caught up with Joe Riddley and they'd picked up speed. Surely those men weren't fools enough —

Of course they were. That unfroze me real quick. "Don't you go in there!" I yelled, leaping from our car. One of the firefighters heard me. He left the others, who were directing streams of water against the house, and ran to bar the way, motioning angrily for the men to get back. His face streamed sweat and was streaked with soot.

Joe Riddley waved his arms. The firefighter pointed to the backyard. Buster nodded and practically dragged Joe Riddley to the shade of an oak beside the drive, out of the range of sparks. I figured the firemen had gotten the tractor and mowers out and safe.

But where were the children? "Bethany? Cricket? Tad!" I yelled.

"Me-mama! Oh, Me-mama!" Bethany dashed from the porch to fling herself into my arms, sobbing. Her soft brown hair smelled smoky. Tears dripped down my neck. I held out an arm to her friend Hollis, who had pounded after her across the lawn. We stood there in one big hug.

Finally I had to draw back to cough. My nose burned and my mouth was full of the taste of smoke. When I looked at the poor old barn, I shivered in spite of the heat. Flames were shooting out its windows and roof. Anybody could see there was no hope of saving it. The house stood a good distance away, so flying sparks were landing short of it, but I appreciated the firefighters' caution in wetting it down — especially when I felt a breeze lift my hair.

The strong streams of water were doing a great job of dislodging the house paint, though. Poor Ridd would have a lot of work to do when this was over.

Down in their pen, Joe Riddley's three hunting dogs were lifting a chorus. I stopped to listen, but couldn't hear Lulu's soprano among them. I couldn't hear the screams of a frantic horse, either, which was good, but it was hard to hear anything clearly with the thud of water against the house, the deafening crackle of flames, and an occasional sound like a shot when fire hit a pine knot. I strained my ears and hurried nearer the barn, to be sure I didn't hear animals caught inside.

"Did you get the animals out?" I called back to Bethany. She nodded, then jumped as the barn roof caved in with a *whoosh* and a volcano of sparks. As far away as I was, I felt tiny sparks sting my cheek and arms and saw a little flame spurt from my pants just below the knee. I slapped it out, yelping with pain as I felt a burn.

Hollis took a swipe at my hair. "You're on fire!" She hit my head twice, hard, and I felt a stab of hot pain. "That got it," she said.

"That's one time you won't get smacked for beating up an old woman. Thanks." I tried to grin, but my lips felt parched.

I hadn't noticed before that Hollis's freckled face was streaked with soot and her copper eyebrows, lashes, and hair were singed. She nursed one hand where a long burn had raised a blister halfway up her arm and looked anxiously around the yard. "We're still missing one pup."

"How'd you get burned?" I demanded.

She shuddered as she considered the blazing barn and spoke in short gulps punctuated by tears. "I went in for Lulu and Starfire. But they were gone. We don't know how they got out. And we haven't seen Starfire. We've rounded up Lulu, though. And all the pups but one. I locked them in the downstairs bathroom. We're still missing Feisty."

"He probably got out on his own." I comforted her. Feisty was the first pup to master climbing out of the box, and he'd been exploring ever since. But if he'd been exploring a dark corner of the barn when the fire started —

I refused to finish that thought, but could tell from her eyes that we shared it. "Maybe he went toward the dogs' pen," she said hopefully. "I'll go look there." Hollis had never been good at standing still. She thudded away.

Bethany clutched me tighter. Her teeth were chattering and her body shook all over. "I couldn't go in, Me-mama. Not even for Lulu. But Hollis did, and she's terrified of horses. I feel like such a coward!" She shook and cried until her knees buckled and she fell to the ground. She flung herself in the grass, sobbing and coughing smoke.

I knelt beside her and patted her back. "Nobody expected you to go in, honey. You called 911 and got the fire trucks here. That's enough. And the horse and Lulu got out in time."

Her voice came in short bursts. "I didn't call 911. And I don't know how the animals got out. Starfire must have kicked open her stall and the door." She burst into stormy weeping again.

"How'd you discover the fire?" Maybe talking would calm her down.

She sat up and wiped her eyes on one biceps, leaving a streak of soot down her cheek.

"The fire trucks came screaming down the road. Hollis and I were by the pool —" She looked down in surprise at her bathing suit and bare feet.

Our pool, now their pool, was behind the house and protected by a high wooden fence. I'd had Joe Riddley install a mirror so I could see who was coming down our drive and decide whether to greet them in my swimsuit. I could imagine the girls' fright when they heard sirens and looked in the mirror to see fire engines barreling toward the house.

Still, there was too little of her suit to be out there in front of a bevy of firefighters. The younger ones were eyeing her appreciatively. "Go get something on." I struggled to my feet. "Where are Cricket and Tad?"

Bethany gave a big sniff and jumped up. "Omigosh. Cricket was napping, but he can't be sleeping through all this. Heaven only knows what he's getting into."

I grabbed her before she sprinted away. I'd done all the running I planned to do in one day. "Where's Tad?"

I could tell she wanted to go to Cricket. Bethany is very responsible about keeping her little brother. I tugged her arm again. "Where is Tad?"

She frowned, as if trying to remember. "He played video games all morning, and we all swam and worked on our tans for a while after lunch, then I took Crick up and read him a story before his nap. Tad wasn't at the pool when I got back, and I haven't seen him since. Daddy told him to weed the garden. Maybe —" She looked across at Ridd's vegetables.

I stared, too, willing a slender little boy to stand erect after pulling too many weeds.

Silly us. As if any boy in hearing distance would be weeding with fire engines in the yard. Talons of fear gripped the base of my spine. "Could he be around back?"

She shook her head. "Hollis and I were back there looking for Feisty." Her gaze darted a look at the smoldering remains of the barn and she gasped. "Oh, no! You don't think he was in there, do you? Smoking?"

"He wouldn't have stayed once the place was burning. You go get dressed and find Cricket. If he wants to come out, tell him I need him to look after Lulu and her pups, to calm them. That ought to keep him inside. Call your folks again, too. I'll look for —"

A lump in my throat cut off the sentence.

Bethany gave me a desperate look and ran barefoot across the yard, leaping when she stepped on a spark. But instead of going inside, she headed toward the firefighters. She asked a frantic question, waving her arms toward the barn. They shook their heads and said something that seemed to reassure her. She came running back, again leaping as she stepped on sparks. "They said there wasn't anybody in there." She hurried back toward the house.

She didn't see the firefighters give the barn worried looks and aim a couple of their hoses back in its direction. A plume of steam rose as they sprayed the raging fire, then subsided with the defiant hiss of a fairy-tale monster.

Except this was no fairy tale.

"Don't let Tad be dead before I get to know him better," I prayed into the smoke-laden air. But where could he be?

I looked around the yard, trying to think like a child. A match dropped in the barn, a flash of flame, an attempt to stamp it out or beat it out with something. But what then?

Would he run away and leave Lulu and his mother's horse? I didn't think so. Tad loved animals.

That was probably how the dogs and horse got out — shooed or led by a frantic boy who must then have darted into the house to call 911. But where would he have gone after that?

My dressy shoes and silk pantsuit weren't designed for wandering around the countryside, but they weren't going to be good for much after today, anyway. I looked at the drive, full of fire trucks and hoses and decided I'd start looking on the other side of the house. Halfway around, I saw a child's T-shirt lying on the grass, too small for Bethany and too big for Cricket.

I picked it up and carried it with me, a talisman that he was not in the barn. "Tad?" I called. "Honey, where are you?"

Only an oriole replied, from Joe Riddley's orchard out behind Ridd's cornfield. It sounded a whole lot happier than I felt. "Oh, shut up," I snapped. "Tad? Tad! God, help me find him!"

The only answer I got was the deep print of a horse's hoof over at the edge of a perennial bed. I knew it hadn't been there the day before, because Ridd had been thinning his beds while Martha and I walked. He'd have throttled anybody who let Starfire near his flowers. The prints continued toward Ridd's fields.

I headed for the corn with hope. I couldn't see anything for the tall dry stalks, but ten acres of dying cornstalks would be a good hiding place for a small boy and a nervous horse.

For an hour I followed that horse's tracks. As far as I could read the prints, Starfire first crashed through rows of corn every which away, then went straighter for a time, doubled back, ran parallel with the gravel road for a while, and finally turned through a little plantation of pines we'd put in for pulpwood. The tracks were real deep sometimes, less deep other times, and middle deep toward the end. I deduced that it had first been running, then slowed down, then — hopefully — Tad had climbed on its back. But I knew that was all conjecture. Why hadn't I taken less math and at least one course in tracking animals?

Dust and pine resin collected over my layer of soot. I was so sweaty, my clothes stuck to me from all directions. I progressed from worry to anger to plumb weariness. By now, I didn't care what Tad had done, if I could only find him and go back home to sit down.

I shoved my way through the little pines muttering things I'd learned from Bo. When I got to the gravel road, I didn't know which way to turn. The horse might have gone on back to the barn, or it might have headed for the highway. I saw some scuffs on the side of the road like it had headed toward the highway, so I decided I'd walk as far as the house at the corner. It stood empty now, but used to belong to old Amos Pickens, an ornery, smelly old geezer and a dreadful neighbor. I doubted he was playing a harp where he'd gone, for he didn't have a kind bone in his body. He would never have permitted me to walk up his drive looking for a lost horse.

I walked wary of snakes in the tall weeds. "Starfire? Starfire!" No answering whinny came from the back, and the weeds were too high for me to go farther. The place had stood vacant since Amos died, except for a few months when a hot-shot young doctor bought it with grand ideas he couldn't carry out. He hadn't even gotten around to removing the galvanized stove pipes Amos had attached to his roof. They were beginning to come loose and leaned crazily in all directions. Poor Amos. He'd spent his last years terrified that alien forces were massing on Venus for an imminent attack on earth and had believed the pipes would mess up their radars if they planned to land in Hopemore.

I headed back up the road toward our place. If I hadn't been bone tired and scared for my grandson, it would have been a pleasant walk. Birds were twittering to each other about northern summer vacations. A rabbit wiggled its nose at me from the verge.

This far from the fire, I could smell hay and cotton dust, and it wasn't smoke that made my eyes smart. I remembered walking down that road with Joe Riddley on moonlit nights after the kids were asleep, walking down it with two tiny boys to see if blackberries were ripe, and strolling down it with various dogs just for the exercise. I also remembered how often I'd thought about taking a walk, then given up the idea to do something else. I wanted to shout at somebody, "Wait, I can't move away yet — I haven't gone for enough walks!"

Just as I reached Hubert's pasture between his house and ours, I heard a whinny. Whether it was Starfire or not, I couldn't see until I'd got through the barbed wire and climbed a little rise, because the pasture rose from the fence, then dipped again to a small cattle pond. Down near the pond, a black stallion grazed. He lifted his head and whinnied again when he scented me. Heaven only knew what I smelled like by then.

I knew him at once by the blaze on his nose. "Tad?" I called. "Where are you, honey?"

A clump of trees stood just beyond the pond. The child had to be there, unless he were in the pond. I refused to think that. I'd jumped in that filthy pond to save somebody once and didn't want to repeat it. "Tad? Come here!"

I saw a motion beyond a thick oak trunk; then Tad came out wearing dust-smeared sneakers and cut-off jeans. In his arms he cradled Lulu's pup Feisty.

Tad was a slender, almost delicate child, with his mother's dark brown eyes and her daddy's blond hair. He was striking now and would be a real heartbreaker when he grew up — especially since, like his mother, he always looked good. Even with his hair tousled, dusty, and stuck to his forehead with sweat, his chest bare, and his arms scratched with bloody welts, he looked ready to pose for an upscale kids' magazine.

Until he got closer. His face was coated with what looked like a mixture of dust, snot, and tears, and his eyes looked so sorrowful, I wanted to hug him forever. I figured, though, that if I was sympathetic right away, he'd bolt. I let him come closer, then held out his shirt. "So," I said in my most matter-of-fact voice, "you set the barn on fire?"

"I didn't mean to." It was Walker's quavery voice, Walker's whine. This kid might be part of our family after all. He handed me the pup and pulled on the shirt, muttering, "It wasn't *exactly* my fault."

"Whose fault was it?"

"I — uh — I had a match and Lulu jumped up on me, and I dropped it into the hay."

"Don't you blame this on Lulu. You were

smoking in the barn and set it on fire. Let's keep that in the forefront of this conversation, all right?"

"I didn't mean to do it," he protested, reaching again for the pup and cradling it under his chin.

I gave him the look I send down from my bench when a prisoner is trying to make excuses and we both know he's guilty. "But you did cause the fire."

He looked at his filthy sneakers like they were the only interesting thing on his horizon. "Yes, ma'am." He swiped his eyes with one arm.

I forced my voice to be stern. "And you were smoking again."

"Yes, ma'am." That was almost a whisper. "But I won't anymore. I've quit."

"Your daddy's insurance company is going to have to pay a lot of money to build Uncle Ridd a new barn. Do you know that?"

His eyes flashed. "Daddy had nothing to do with it. I'll pay Uncle Ridd back. I've got lots of money in the bank."

"That's your college fund," I reminded him. "Insurance will pay for the barn, but your daddy isn't going to be happy."

He stuck out his lower lip and sulked.

"And Uncle Ridd's going to have to repaint his house where the fire hoses have knocked off the paint. He may want you to help him."

The lower lip jutted out a little more. Work

and Tad had never been friends. He scuffed the grass with one toe and didn't look at me. The pup reached up and licked his chin.

When I saw a tear glisten and fall to the toe of his sneaker, I relented a little. "But thank you for saving Lulu and the pups. And Starfire. That took a lot of courage. Horses are generally scared of fire. How'd you manage it?"

He looked up with a flicker of pride. "I took off my shirt and covered his head; then I led him out. I tied him to the railing by the steps while I called 911, but then — then —"

"Then you got a little scared of Uncle Ridd and decided to ride off into the sunset."

"I didn't get scared! It was Starfire. He was real jumpy because of the fire, so he was plunging all over the place. I was afraid he'd pull down the porch. I untied him to ride him across the yard, but he jerked the rein away and bolted into the field. I been looking for that dratted horse all afternoon." His eyes were stormy, not the least bit repentant. Before I could reply, he added, "Mama would die if I lost her horse."

His daddy would have said, "Mama would kill me if I lost her horse." I gave him points for that distinction. "So what did you do then?"

"I took off after him, but I tripped over Feisty, who was waddling across the grass. I didn't have time to put him in a safe place, so I dropped my shirt, grabbed him up and took him with me. It took ages to catch Starfire, and by then we were lost. We must have walked a hundred miles. I thought we'd never get out of there!" His eyes flickered with the memory of what must have been very real fear. Tad had never ridden tractors like Bethany and Cricket. I doubted if he'd ever been in the cornfield before, and ten acres can seem like the whole world to a child.

"How did you get found again?"

"Starfire finally got calm, so I led him to a rock and climbed on his back. I didn't have a saddle or bridle, so I rode bareback." Again, that flicker of pride. "We rode around for a while until I saw trees that looked like the ones beside your road and headed that way. It was hard getting through them" — he looked ruefully down at his scratches — "but when we came out, we were across from Mr. Spence's pasture. Starfire was real thirsty, and I knew the fishing pond was over here, so I brought him for a drink. We were coming back as soon as he'd rested a little."

I didn't say whether I believed *that* or not. I had another worry right then. "You didn't drink that water, did you?"

He screwed up his face. "No way. It's full of cow poop." He sighed. "I sure am thirsty."

"Let's go back, then." I nodded toward

Feisty. "Hollis is out looking for him. She rounded up Lulu and the others, but she's worried that Feisty got stuck in the barn."

"Is the barn real bad?"

"It's gone. The roof caved in before I left."

He took a step back, eyes wide. "I can't go back there. Uncle Ridd will kill me!"

"I doubt that. He'll be mad, sure, but Pop and I won't let him kill you. My guess is you're in for some serious weeding and paint scraping in the next few days, though."

"I'm not going back! I won't!" He flung the pup at me and dashed toward Starfire, who was taking a drink down beside the dock. Tad pelted along the dock, clutched Starfire's mane, and flung himself on the horse's back. The next minute, horse and boy were galloping toward the far horizon.

"Tad! Wait!" I was calling to the wind.

Furious and exhausted, I headed home. I wasn't sure I could walk another quarter of a mile in my fancy shoes, but I sure couldn't walk a foot on gravel without them. I was relieved to hear a vehicle tearing down the road.

Barely able to lift my arm, I flagged down Ridd's truck, plopped the pup on his front seat, and climbed up after it. "Are you just getting here?"

"No, I've been here for an hour. There's nothing more we can do right now, and since I was blocking his car, Daddy sent me looking for you." He frowned. "Where the Sam Hill have you been? You look like you've been through the wars."

"A couple," I agreed, slamming my door. "I was looking for Tad."

"You couldn't find him?" Ridd sat there without putting the truck in gear. He looked real worried, and no wonder. This was the first time Walker and Cindy had ever gone off and left their kids with anybody except her parents.

"Oh, I found him, over yonder by the pond. We had a nice little chat. But he refused to come back to your place. He's run off on Starfire."

Ridd shrugged. "He won't go far without somebody to wait on him hand and foot."

"Honey!" I chided him. "Granted he hasn't grown up as rough as you two did —"

Ridd snorted. "I doubt if he's ever had to lift a finger for himself. He has to be reminded every morning to make his own bed and hang up his clothes, and when I asked him to weed the garden this morning, he told me he'd rather not, he doesn't like getting dirty and he's 'a bit nervous,'" — he sketched quotes — "around bugs. How can any boy of ten be scared of bugs? And when I told him it was an order, not a request, he pulled up a whole row of leaf lettuce and told me he thought lettuce only grew in balls." Ridd pounded the steering wheel in

110

frustration. "Face it, Mama, the kid's sweet, but he's a loser — and now he's burned down my barn!" He laid his head on the wheel and sobbed.

I touched his shaking shoulder. "You're scared and worried, and that's okay, honey, but don't take it out on Tad. He's scared, too. Scared you're gonna kill him for burning the barn, scared Walker will kill him because he carries the insurance on it." I peered across Ridd toward the pasture. "I just hope he comes back."

Ridd put the car into gear and started down the road. "Oh, he'll come back when he gets hungry or sleepy. I can't see His Highness scavenging food or sleeping rough."

But Ridd was wrong. Tad did not come home.

7

We hung around Ridd's kitchen drinking iced tea and discussing what ought to be done about the barn, but we didn't start worrying about Tad until it began to get dark. That's when I got ready to call Buster and have the entire sheriff's department scouring the county for my grandson.

Ridd, Joe Riddley, and even Martha voted me down, willing to wait a while longer for him to come home on his own. "We don't want to embarrass him any more than we have to," Martha reminded me.

"Nail his hide to what's left of the barn, maybe, but not embarrass him," Ridd agreed sourly.

You may be wondering why we weren't frantic. An out-of-state friend assures me, "If my twelve-year-old granddaughter disappeared for several hours, with or without a horse, I'd have the police, the National Guard, and the Royal Canadian Mounties out looking for her, and her parents would never forgive me if I didn't involve them."

If it had been one of our granddaughters, we'd probably have done the same. If we'd lived in a city among strangers, we'd have been terrified. And if Tad had disappeared without the horse, we'd have worried that he would thumb a ride with the wrong person.

As it was, three of us around that table could remember that Ridd and Walker had each taken off in a huff around Tad's age. Ridd slept all night in the cornfield and crept in to make breakfast as an apology. Walker bedded down with a friend, then called us the next morning to demand, "Are you ready for me to come home yet?" — having given *us* time to straighten up our act. We all figured Tad was just running off his temper and putting off the time when he'd have to come home and accept his punishment.

Still, even though he had Starfire with him, I kept picturing him trying to jump a fence and breaking his neck, the horse stumbling in a hole and falling on him, or a stranger trying to steal that gorgeous horse and child. When I mentioned each of the possibilities, Joe Riddley reminded me that it's hard to kidnap a child with a horse; Hope County is small, rural and basically still a safe place; and Tad has ridden horses since he was six and was a good, careful rider.

Joe Riddley was ready to call Walker, however, until Ridd disagreed. "You know what would happen, Daddy. If we tell him Tad's run away, we'll have to explain why, and you know exactly what Walker would do."

We certainly did. Walker would hop the

next plane so furious that Tad burned down the barn, he might forget that the boy was ten years old and scared. Walker was just learning to be a good daddy to Tad. None of us wanted Tad coming home to a furious father who'd say things he would later regret.

"We could at least go out looking for him," I suggested. So Martha started putting together a scratch supper while Ridd and Joe Riddley went driving up and down logging roads and tractor trails. I drove over to Walker's, thinking maybe the boy had gone home. He wasn't there, but I did see crumbs on the counter and a smear of peanut butter that indicated he'd swung by for something to eat. The pantry had no bread or peanut butter, so I figured he'd taken them with him. I hurried upstairs to his room and saw that his sleeping bag was also missing from the closet shelf. The little rascal — his whole family were seasoned campers. He had come home long enough to provision himself for at least one night of sleeping rough.

I did take time, though, to use Cindy's directory to call her friends, thinking maybe Tad had gone to one of them. He hadn't. I made them promise not to alert his parents, explaining that he had camping supplies with him and promising we'd call Cindy and Walker if Tad weren't home by the next day.

I returned to Ridd and Martha's. Joe Riddley came back at dark, and Ridd half an hour later. We all sat on the side porch not eating much, exhausted and drained. A gentle rain had started falling. "He's gonna get wet," Ridd said, and sounded downright satisfied.

I understood that he was still mad at Tad for putting us through that horrendous day, but grandmothers have more patience and sympathy than parents and uncles. "I hope he doesn't catch a cold or get bitten by a snake," I worried aloud.

"Is Tad gonna die?" Cricket asked, looking at our long faces.

"We don't think so, sweetheart," Martha told him, "but nobody knows where he is."

"God knows," he reminded us. "Time to pray."

I don't know how families get through rough times without praying together. We all felt better after we'd spent time asking Tad's third parent to take special care of him that night. But when I asked God to help Tad find a dry place to sleep if he was outdoors, Cricket interrupted, his lower lip stuck out like a plate, "You mean Tad gets to camp, and I don't?"

"Camping without your parents can be scary, tiger," his granddaddy reminded him.

Cricket thought that over, then closed his eyes. "Don't let him be scared, but don't you let him have fun without me." That ended the prayer.

Joe Riddley stood up and headed for the

115

phone. "It's too early for a missing persons report, but I am gonna call Buster." We heard him explain the situation and could tell that the sheriff was promising to alert all his deputies to watch for Tad and the horse.

It was late when Joe Riddley and I finally admitted Tad might not be coming home, and left. He gave a little laugh as he walked me to our car. "I was sitting there," he confided softly, "wondering why those folks didn't go home so we could go up to bed." His voice sounded a little wistful.

"Do you miss this place?" I asked, keeping my voice down.

"Yeah," he admitted. He turned and I knew in spite of the darkness, he could see every inch of it in his head. He pulled me close to him under one arm and spoke into my hair. "We did the right thing, Little Bit, but it's gonna take some getting used to."

I turned and threw my arms around his chest. "I'd rather get used to it with you than anybody else." We stood there a minute, enjoying the closeness, then I pulled away. "This place smells awful. Let's go home where we can breathe."

When we got there, I had so much smoke and soot in my hair, I had to wash and dry it before bed. Phyllis wouldn't be open again until Tuesday, and I couldn't lay my head on the pillow reeking of smoke. As I slid in beside Joe Riddley, he murmured sleepily,

"Know what? That *was* Burlin Bullock admiring your roses this morning. I ran into him at Gusta's party. If you'd known, you could have invited him in for coffee. He's real nice."

I'd been enjoying the cool sheet beneath me. Now an unpleasant chill slid all the way up my body. I gave a quick little shiver. "You talked to him?"

His voice grew drowsier and drowsier. "Just for a little while. Mostly about Georgia's football team. He was at the university when we were, but he and I never —" He slid into sleep.

I lay awake for ages, alternating between worrying about Tad and concocting reasons I could give for leaving town that week.

Neither of us slept well until nearly dawn, then we both slept like dead people until Ridd called at nine. "Tad's still not back. Martha's got to work, but I'm going out looking for him and leaving Bethany here in case he comes home. One of Walker's associates is coming, too, to assess the damage. Can you all eat on your own?" We usually went to their house for Sunday dinner.

"We were eating on our own before you were born," I reminded him. "We'll go out somewhere." Joe Riddley was still snoring beside me. He hadn't even heard the phone. I hung up and closed my eyes, promising myself I'd snooze just one more minute. When I woke again, we barely had time to dress and sling the Sunday paper into the living room on our way to church.

In the narthex, a friend greeted me. "That was a good picture in the paper, Mac."

"Thanks," I told her. "We were all having a great time." Of course, she was a little late with her compliments. It had been a couple of weeks since I'd been in the *Statesman* with a bunch of middle-school kids who were conducting a mock magistrate's court.

The woman gave me an odd look and walked away.

Joe Riddley and I took our usual pew, with him on the center aisle. A lot of people turned around to look at us. They must have heard about the fire and wanted us to know they were sympathetic. It wasn't our barn anymore, but it had been for thirty-five years.

I was checking my bulletin to see what the first hymn would be when I heard a light wave of whispers coming from the back. About the time it slapped the back of my neck, I heard Joe Riddley offer, "Why don't you join us? There's plenty of room."

I looked up to see Burlin Bullock hesitating by our pew. I wished he were somewhere else — Outer Mongolia, for example — but figured the two of them couldn't come to much harm in church, so I slid down. I took Joe Riddley's arm to pull him after me, though, so Burlin had to sit on the aisle.

That was the most restless service I've ever attended. Maybe Burlin was used to it, being in politics all his life, but I was distracted by all that whispering and craning of necks toward our pew. In addition to praying for Tad, I added a special prayer of thanksgiving: "Thank you, Lord, for saving me from life in the political fishbowl."

I was scared to death Joe Riddley would ask Burlin to join us for dinner and relieved when Burlin turned to Joe Riddley during the last hymn, shook his hand, and slipped out before the benediction. He had ignored me the whole service, for which I was grateful.

A lot of folks craned their necks to get a glimpse of the famous man as he left. We don't often get worshipers who've appeared on national TV.

Celebrity dust must have rubbed off on us, because when Joe Riddley and I came through the doors and started down the church steps, everybody down on the sidewalk stopped talking and stood looking up at us. When they saw we'd noticed, they quickly turned away.

We stopped by the house on our way to the restaurant. My feet were still sore from the day before, and I wanted to put on some everyday shoes.

As soon as we got in the door, Joe Riddley called Ridd's — with me standing at his elbow so I could hear. Bethany said they still hadn't heard from Tad, but added, "Mama told Daddy that if Tad hasn't come home by night tonight, we have to call Uncle Walker and Aunt Cindy. They may have some idea where he would have gone."

I was ready to skip lunch and start driving around the county again, but Joe Riddley refused. "I'm starving, woman, and we both know that kid's inherited the Crane temper from your family, just like his daddy did. But Tad's also got common sense. He's either hiding with a friend whom he's sworn to secrecy, or he's loitering on Ridd's property somewhere waiting to build up his courage to come back home." He pulled me close to him. "And I promise you, Little Bit, if he's not back by nightfall, Buster will start combing this county inch by inch, and Ridd and I will be right beside him."

Satisfied with that, I hurried down the hall to switch my shoes.

I heard Joe Riddley opening the newspaper in the living room. Next thing I knew he was slamming it down on our bed. "And I thought he was different. Those politicians will say anything to get elected. Look at that."

I stared down into the faces of Lance Bullock, Burlin Bullock, and MacLaren Yarbrough, close together in a huddle. Burlin had his arms draped around both our shoulders, and we were obviously having a great time. Numb, I assessed the damage.

Front page, center of the page, picture four inches square. The headline read "Unexpected Ally" and the caption said *Burlin and Lance Bullock share a private moment with Burlin's college sweetheart, Judge MacLaren Yarbrough.*

I couldn't read the rest right then. My eyes were too blurry with tears. How could Burlin do that to me? Now I'd have to tell Joe Riddley.

I was trying to get my voice to work when he growled in disgust, "Dangnabit, I thought I'd finally met an honest politician, but if Bullock would make up a story like that just because we were all on the campus at the same time —" He shook his head and stomped back down the hall.

I couldn't face anybody after that, so I pulled out the week's leftovers and set a microwave buffet out on the counter. We each filled a plate and heated it up, but I wasn't really hungry and Joe Riddley isn't fond of leftovers. He looked at his plate, bowed his head, and said, "Lord, you've already been thanked for all of this once, so I just thank you that we had enough before to serve it twice. Amen."

While we were eating we got three calls from excited friends wanting to say they'd seen my picture in the Atlanta paper, the

Macon paper, and the Savannah paper. Joe Riddley put the dishes in the dishwasher while I took the third call. I hung up and told him, "This is the most embarrassing thing that's happened to me since I tripped at Gusta's wedding because she ordered my dress too long." My voice wobbled and angry tears streamed down my cheeks. "And you know what? This is Gusta's fault, too. If she hadn't thrown that dumb party —"

He pulled me to him. "It's gonna be all right, honey. The Bullocks will leave in a day or two, and you know how quickly folks forget. Just watch your step while they're in town. I know I keep telling you to keep up with politics, but that doesn't mean you need to jump in whole hog." He gave me a little squeeze. "And don't be too hard on Gusta. She's probably hopping mad that you got your picture in the paper with the Bullocks and she didn't."

He reached for his cap. "I'm going down to Ridd's to see if we can think of someplace we haven't looked for the boy. Why don't you take a nap? Ignore the phone." He knew as well as I did that I couldn't ignore the phone. Tad might call, or a deputy needing me down at the jail.

National news must have been slow that day, and Burlin was news anytime. During the afternoon, I talked to people from all over the country who called to say my face was on their front page. My brother in Montgomery suggested I sue somebody for libel. A woman I'd met at our church's general assembly called all the way from Albuquerque to gush, "I hadn't realized you were Burlin Bullock's wife. It's an excellent likeness of you, and your husband is a real handsome man. Is Lance your older or younger son?" I told her what I'd told everybody — that it was a big mistake — but she asked, "Would your family like to have this clipping? I don't have your address."

I hung up and went outside to spray my roses. Killing Japanese beetles and black spot fit my mood. Wouldn't you know I'd step in a lump of buffalo doo? A fitting comment on the day.

About five that afternoon, Martha and Cricket showed up. "You ready to walk?" she asked. "Ridd and Pop are putting up a new shed for the lawn mowers, but I can't stand the smell of smoke for one more instant." We both knew she also couldn't stand waiting at home for Tad.

I checked my watch. Two hours until Joe Riddley and Buster would start looking for the boy. "I'd rather go to Myrtle's," I said. Martha and I are old pie buddies, and if there was anything guaranteed to make time pass and me feel better, it was chocolate pie with three-inch meringue at Myrtle's Restaurant.

"Myrtle's, Myrtle's." Cricket seconded my motion by jumping up and down.

"You know that's why we're in the shape we're in," Martha reminded me.

"Yeah, but today, honey, I need all the support I can get."

"Me, too," she agreed. "And we can at least walk over there."

"Did you see today's paper?" I asked as we headed that way, trying to sound casual.

"Haven't had time," she replied.

"We had a big fire down at our place," Cricket informed me. "We nearly all got burnt up."

"I was there," I reminded him. "I asked about the paper," I continued to Martha in a low voice, "only because there was a stupid picture of me in it taken at Gusta's party, so folks may look at me funny."

Her eyebrows shot up. "With you and you-know-who?" When I nodded, she grinned. "I'll have to go home and look. My mother-in-law the celebrity."

"Your mother-in-law the fool."

We ambled along listening to Cricket chatter and talking of this and that. When we were almost at Myrtle's, Cricket suddenly pointed. "Look! There's Mr. Spence with a *woman!*"

Hubert came down the sidewalk looking real natty in tan linen slacks and a short-sleeved blue shirt. Holding his arm, Abigail was plain but neat in khaki pants, a white knit top, and a navy cotton sweater tied around her shoulders by its sleeves. Hubert held the door like she was royalty.

"Gusta and Pooh must be conducting good manners and hygiene classes," I murmured to Martha. "Shall I send Joe Riddley down for a few sessions?" She gave a gurgling laugh, then broke off to exclaim, "Half the town must be here today. I hope we get a table." Hubert and Abigail were still waiting near the front.

As we got inside, Cricket beamed up at me. "You're famous, Me-mama. Everybody stopped talking when they saw you come in."

Georgia Bullock sat at a corner table with her husband, looking like a Southwestern belle in tan jeans, a turquoise-and-tan shirt, and several pieces of silver-and-turquoise jewelry. She stood as soon as she saw me and came toward us with both hands outstretched. "Oh, Mackie." Her voice carried all over the room. "I was just sick about that awful picture in today's paper."

Anybody who hadn't already seen it was sure to scurry off and find one. Down in front of me, Little Big Ears was staring up and demanding in a voice that carried at least as well as Georgia's, "Why does that lady call you 'Mackie,' Me-mama?" He informed Georgia, "Her name is Little Bit." Georgia laughed, then turned to speak to Abigail.

Hubert came to give me a friendly pat.

"Been running around on the old boy, have you? Just what I'd expect to happen up in Athens. At Tech, now —"

"At Tech in your day, there was nobody to run around with," I snapped. "But speaking of running around —" I nodded toward Abigail's back.

"I've been showing Miss Abigail some of the sights," he admitted. "Even ran by the house to see if that bum was still there, but I didn't see any sign of him."

"You aren't to hurt him," I reminded him. "Call Buster if you see him."

Hubert's face grew pink. "I'll shoot him dead if I catch him in that barn."

Abigail turned and stared at him in surprise. Hubert gave an embarrassed laugh. "Sorry to be breathing fire, Miss Abigail, but MacLaren here was asking about that homeless man who's set up camp down at my place. It's nothing you need to worry about."

"Abigail never worries," Georgia assured him. "But I'd better. Edward's about to eat my pie." She gave us a brilliant smile and headed back to her table.

How did she manage to look so gorgeous at her age? Did anybody have any idea she was almost as old as me? I thought about mentioning that in a carrying voice, but Myrtle hurried up just then. "I've got two tables. Mac and Martha, you all take the one in the corner. Hubert, you all follow me."

She led Hubert and Abigail to a center table like that was standard procedure.

The fact is, Myrtle is apt to skip the niceties. She embarrasses members of the Chamber of Commerce to death by calling to tourists as they hesitate near her door, "If you can see well enough to drive yourself here, you can see well enough to find yourself a table. Come on in." It tickled me to watch her hovering over Hubert's table, saying things like, "You all take your time. The pies are just out of the oven. I'll bring you some water while you make up your minds. You want something else to drink with the water?" When they ordered sweet tea, she hurried to the kitchen like they were her only customers.

They were certainly the only customers she was paying attention to. My coffee cup was still empty. I regarded the bottom and consoled myself that it wasn't Abigail or even Georgia who was causing all that stir. Any woman with Hubert would do. Myrtle is a romantic at heart.

I owed her a favor for interrupting us when she did, too. It had eventually dawned on me that if I had announced that Georgia and I were close in age, folks wouldn't wonder why she looked so good, they'd wonder why I didn't. Besides, I couldn't let on I knew how old Georgia was without confirming everybody's suspicions that I'd known her — and

127

her brother — before.

Cricket climbed into his chair with a worried frown. "Mama, Mr. Spence wouldn't really kill anybody, would he?"

That was the question we would all be asking in a couple of days.

8

I considered taking Monday off. For one thing, although the sheriff had actually started a search for Tad the afternoon before, the child had not been found. Joe Riddley and Ridd joined the search when Joe Riddley called at sundown and found Buster already had his deputies on the job. They looked until midnight and came home tight-lipped and anxious. Even though Buster agreed Tad was most likely in no danger, but simply hiding out and enjoying a few days of un-usual freedom, neither Joe Riddley nor I got a wink of sleep. We just lay in bed trying to think where that child could be.

For another thing, after yesterday's paper, I preferred to avoid people. I was planning to make a list of places to search for Tad until Clarinda put one fist on her ample hips and commanded, "You leave the searching to the sheriff. But you and me can unpack all those boxes in the guest room." That got me moving.

It was because I was trying to remember what was in those boxes as I pulled into the parking lot that I didn't notice Burlin lounging against one of our trucks until I got out of my car. He looked as good in that pale blue shirt as he had in the yellow one Friday and the gray suit he'd worn to Gusta's party. He and Georgia had both aged well.

A Spence's Appliances bag dangled from his arm — and if you wonder which appliance would fit into a plastic bag, you've never lived in a small town. Hubert sold radios, CD players, radio-controlled toys, watches, cameras, toasters, and those gizmos you put under your cup to keep your coffee warm. Anything electric or electronic. His was the only place in town to get that stuff, although that side of his business would suffer when the new superstore opened in December.

I slammed my car door and informed Burlin, "We aren't hiring right now. That superstore that's getting built outside of town is putting a damper on the local economy. If you political types want to do something to help us out, do something to boost our economies and tax national corporations out the kazoo. However, I'm not speaking to you after yesterday's paper."

He pushed away from the truck and brushed off his backside. "I was afraid you weren't. You hadn't seen it before church, had you? I could tell, because you didn't look daggers at me, like you are now. But believe me, I didn't talk to any reporters about you. I suspect Edward — he's a wizard at knowing what will get somebody's name in the papers to help get them elected."

"It was my name," I reminded him, "and I'm not running for anything. And how could Edward have told them anything unless you told him first?"

"I didn't. I swear it." He held up both hands in protest.

"You didn't help things by showing up at church."

"I didn't know it was your church. And when your husband invited me to join you, I didn't know what else to do except sit down, shut up, and pretend we were all friends. I hope we are, actually. We may need your help with yesterday's buffalo incident."

"I don't do buffalo," I informed him. "And you aren't asking me to fix a trial, are you?"

"Of course not. But if you could keep it from coming to trial —"

"I can't, and you ought to know that." I turned to leave.

"Wait." He grabbed my arm. I pulled away as if he'd given me an electric shock. "Sorry. But listen, I heard about your grandson, and I'm sorry. I brought you something." He held out the bag. "It might cheer you up."

I stepped back and held up both hands. "I can't take anything from you. I'm a judge and you're a politician. After what happened Saturday, I don't even want to be seen with you. Who knows when the next photographer will show up?"

He put the bag behind him and shook his head sheepishly. "When I saw this, I forgot you were a judge. I'll take it back and get a refund, and I'll try to make sure you don't get in the papers again. I won't hang around waiting for you to come home or come to work. I won't stake out the local café waiting for you to show up for ice cream. I won't serenade your window late at night. I won't —" He was grinning again.

"Stop it," I said crossly. That was a list of things he used to do. I blushed just thinking about those songs outside my sorority house window. Burlin wasn't an actor for nothing. He'd shown up in a sombrero with a guitar to sing Spanish love songs in a sultry accent and came in a cowboy hat with a ukelele and sang like Roy Rogers. My sorority sisters thought he was very romantic. I pretended to think him silly, but for a while I found him romantic, too. Right now, I wanted him to go sing his songs somewhere else.

He ducked his head, but I knew he wasn't the least bit repentant. "I'll go, but I want you to know something, okay? You've aged well. Are you happy with this fellow you married? Because if you aren't, by gum, I'll stick around and give him a run for his money."

"He'd probably say, 'Take her — you're welcome to her,' but I have every intention of sticking around to torment him for a number of years to come. Now go away and let me work. I've got quarterly taxes to do this week."

"Okay, if you say so." He gave me a little salute and sauntered across the parking lot. I was idly wondering what he had in the bag when he started to whistle "I'll be seeing you."

The rest of the morning, I felt like a corpse. People kept coming in to view my remains.

Three deputies showed up, one by one, with warrants to sign. All our employees found reasons to come to my office for a minute. Every single person assured me Tad would be found, but they all also managed while leaving to mention my picture in the paper. Each of them, like the Cheshire cat, left a big grin behind.

Buster had told Ridd to go on to school. However, he didn't have a third-period class that semester, so he came over around ten. "I'm getting pretty frantic, Mama. We've called every friend Tad has, and I've been by their house again. He's vanished. You don't reckon somebody's kidnapped him, do you?"

I'd had one idea in the night I hadn't followed up on yet. "Have you called Cindy's parents? Maybe he rode up there."

Ridd was dubious. "Thomson's pretty far — fifty miles or more."

"Tad was pretty desperate." I reached for the phone, then stopped. "What shall I say?"

He shrugged. "Think of something." He slapped his cap against his leg, just like his daddy did when he was worried.

I thought as I dialed. When Cindy's mother answered, I said, "Hi. We want to have a welcome-home supper for the kids next Saturday at our new house and wonder if you all would like to come."

"Why, that would be nice. Let me check my calendar." She sounded astonished, and no wonder. I'd never invited her for a casual meal before. "We'd love to," she came back to say.

I gave Ridd a sour look as I hung up. "I achieved our object. If Tad had been there, she'd have said something. But now I'm stuck with throwing a party, and it has to be nice, since they're coming down. Heaven only knows where I'll put everybody in our little bitty house." He gave me a sharp look, and I was sorry I'd said it that way. "We'll manage," I added quickly. I didn't want him or Martha ever suspecting I wished we were back in the homeplace.

He heaved a sigh as he stood to leave. "I just hope Tad's back by then."

"I do too, hon. Buster thinks he's fine, and I keep reminding myself that the kid knows how to camp and there's all sorts of places he could be hiding out that we haven't looked yet, but then I start imagining things."

That at least got a chuckle from him. "And when it comes to imagining awful things that can happen to people, you are the world's most creative. But Walker's almost as bad. Buster said to give them until tomorrow morning to turn up the kid, but if they haven't found him by tomorrow, I've gotta call his daddy. Walker's gonna be furious that we've waited this long, and Cindy will kill us all if anything has actually happened to him."

"I know," I agreed. "Still, Walker was going to be furious anyway, and it was a joint decision not to call them right away. We'll all stand behind you on that."

He bent to give me a hug. "I love you. Do you know that?"

"I've suspected it a time or two, son. I love you, too."

Joe Riddley searched with Buster's men that morning, but he came in around ten thirty, ushering Georgia Bullock ahead of him. "Look who I found wandering around in the street." He sounded downright gallant.

"I can't believe I got lost," Georgia said with a rueful laugh, "but I'm terrible about that. I once got so lost in Lavonia, I drove past the post office three times before I found the road out of town. Thank goodness your husband found me, Mackie." She beamed up at him like he'd personally escorted her to the moon.

If so, she could pose for the flag. She wore a navy blazer with matching slacks, and a silky white shirt with a red-white-and-blue striped scarf around her neck. Even her long, slim shoes were red and navy. Every wisp of yellow hair was in place, her makeup hadn't wilted in the heat, and her lipstick was fresh and flag red.

I'd forgotten to refresh my own lipstick after standing for ten minutes talking to Burlin in the parking lot, and my hair was probably windblown, but I reminded myself she was still only one year younger than me.

"I hate to bother you all," she went on in a hurried, breathless voice, "but I'm looking for Burlin and Renée. We're all supposed to be going down to Dublin for a luncheon." She looked around the office like I might be concealing somebody behind the filing cabinets.

"They're not here." I stood up so she could see they weren't under my desk, either.

She tapped a thumbnail against her upper front teeth. It wasn't an attractive habit, but it made her seem more human, like the rest of us. Joe Riddley must have thought so, too, because he came down off the clouds to say, "I have a bone to pick with your brother. My wife doesn't need rumors getting around about her and anybody."

I held my breath. Here it came . . .

Georgia gave a disgusted sigh. "Nobody

does. The way reporters twist things around is terrible. You never know what they'll print, which is why I am always telling Lance and Burlin that the less they say, the better. I'm so sorry, Mackie." She actually had tears in her eyes.

All that unexpected sympathy made me admit, "I did see Burlin briefly in the parking lot when I came in about an hour ago. He was on his way to Spence's Appliances. I don't know where he was going after that."

"Thanks. Maybe Hubert will know where he is, then. Nobody else is worried except Abigail and me. Lance is answering mail, Burlin's wandering, and heaven only knows where Renée is — she went for a walk just after breakfast and hasn't come back yet. That woman has no sense of time. I hope she doesn't make us late." She turned to Joe Riddley with an anxious frown. "It won't take us more than half an hour to get down there, right?"

"If you drive like MacLaren, here. Otherwise, you'd better allow forty-five."

"Especially on these roads," I added. "It's two lanes all the way, and you never know when you'll get caught behind a timber truck or a tractor."

"And it looks like it might rain." She checked her watch and sighed. "So we'll need to leave in less than an hour. Edward likes us to be early. But thanks." She turned to Joe Riddley and her frown dissolved into a radiant smile. "Thanks for rescuing me, Judge Yarbrough." She tripped out in her patriotic shoes.

Joe Riddley grunted as he sank into his leather desk chair. "Hubert, is it? Not Mr. Spence? I was Judge Yarbrough."

"Hubert's practically family," I consoled him. "He took her younger sister to Myrtle's yesterday and was wondering Saturday night whether to ask her to take a drive after dinner with Gusta and Pooh."

He reached for his mail. "After dinner at Gusta's he ought to have taken her to a restaurant."

He settled back with a catalogue and I returned to our taxes, but I knew he wouldn't stay long. In a few minutes he got up. "Might run down to the south of the county. There's a fishing pond down there I'd forgotten about." We both knew he was itching to be out looking for Tad.

"Go ahead," I told him. "I'll hold the fort."

For another few minutes the office was quiet and I got a little work done. Then I heard a tentative knock on my door and Abigail Bullock poked her nose in my door. "May I come in?"

I considered asking if the Bullocks were planning to set up headquarters at Yarbrough's, but Mama didn't raise me to be rude. "Sure. Glad to have you."

She gestured toward the dark green wing chair by our window. "May I? For just a second?" When I nodded, she sat and adjusted her khaki skirt over her knees. Her shoes were sturdy loafers, and I recognized her brown blazer as one I had almost ordered from L.L. Bean. She clasped her hands in her lap and gave me a hesitant smile. "I doubt that you really remember me —"

"Of course I do, except I keep thinking of you as Binky. We went for a walk and you said you were going to have a ranch and never get involved in politics or even vote. What happened?"

Her gravelly voice was wistful. "Life happened, I guess. I got married right after college, but that didn't work out. Then I was a secretary for a while in Atlanta, but I hated it, so when Burlin's wife had a bad accident —" She paused, in case I wanted to say something. When I didn't, she seemed grateful. "She had to be hospitalized for a while and Lance was only five, so Burlin needed somebody to take care of him. Since I hated my job —" She raised one hand and twisted her wrist to show how obvious the answer was. "I started as Lance's nanny, but when he began school, Burlin kept giving me more things to do. Like he said, he isn't the organized one in our family, and I'm a good secretary, I just disliked my first boss. I've been working for Burlin ever since."

"I guess politics is in all your blood," I teased.

She shook her head. "I don't really care for politics, any more than I used to, but I believe in Burlin and Lance. They are fine men, Mackie."

I made some agreeing noises and changed the subject. We talked about this and that for a bit, the way people do when they don't know each other well and don't expect to see much of each other in the future. I did notice that she worked Hubert Spence's name into the conversation several times. The only real surprise in our conversation was when I asked if she was comfortable down at the Annie Dale Inn.

"Oh, sure. I've known Annie Dale for years. We met on a bicycle trip from Savannah to Atlanta" — That's the kind of thing serious bikers toss out. I've never known whether it is supposed to overwhelm the rest of us with our lack of physical stamina, or merely normal, for them — "and we've been on several tours together since. We did a couple of weeks at bed-and-breakfasts up in Delaware several years ago. I think that's when she decided to go into the business. Since then, we've done the wine country of France together and two weeks in Spain. Do you bike?"

"Not often," I said, meaning, "Not in the past forty years."

A silence fell between us. Binky looked down at her lap, then directly back at me. "I have a favor to ask. Of course, you may not be real fond of any of us after that article."

"Was it your fault?" She shook her head. "Then what can I do for you?" I expected a pitch for Lance's campaign.

She surprised me. "I overheard part of your conversation with Hubert on the front porch Saturday. I didn't mean to eavesdrop. I was standing right by the window, and it was open because the room was a little close —"

She paused and gave me an encouraging look, as if to say, "Your turn."

"That's all right. We weren't saying anything private."

"No, but I heard Hubert mention something about you having detecting skills. I asked him about that yesterday, and he told me all about you. So I ran your name through the Internet —"

Again she gave me a chance to speak, but nobody had given me my script for this play. Besides, I was mulling over the fact that my name was on the Internet. I'd looked up all sorts of things, but never thought to look up myself. I could hardly wait for her to leave.

When I hadn't spoken for a several seconds, she said, "Since you have experience in finding things out —"

"Just local things," I interrupted. I didn't mention that it was because of Police Chief

Charlie Muggins's incompetence. I might not like Charlie, but I didn't want Hopemore's dirty laundry strewn from Hopemore to Atlanta.

"This *is* local." She shifted so she was leaning toward me, resting one elbow on her knee and her chin on that hand. "There's a homeless man who seems to be following us. A short plump man in a gray suit."

"He's the one who caused all the commotion Saturday afternoon," I reminded her. "Lance joked that he must be registered to vote in every county, and shows up where there's free food."

"Lance isn't worried, but Georgia and I wonder if we should be. He's been in Augusta, Savannah, Athens, and Valdosta. I haven't actually seen him — I'm generally handing out name tags or buttons at the door, and he comes in the back. But Georgia's seen him several times. She says he stays at the fringes of crowds, gets something to eat afterwards, then fills his pockets. I've asked around, but nobody seems to know who he is. And we don't know if he's following Lance or Burlin." She gave a rueful laugh. "Georgia said maybe he's even stalking her. Men tend to do that." Before I could decide if she sounded bitter, she'd hurried on. "But he may just be hungry. I don't want to bother Burlin if he's harmless."

"You don't think he's a terrorist, do you?"

The man we saw in the alley didn't look anything like my notion of a terrorist, and I couldn't think of a single reason why terrorists would be interested in a governor's race, particularly before the primary, but the same kind of people who started witch hunts in the sixteenth century and communist hunts in the twentieth have begun seeing terrorists behind every bush in the twenty-first. Walker got so disgusted after Cindy was frisked three times in the airport security line on their way to New York that he suggested we change our national anthem to "Land of the no longer free and the used to be brave."

Binky laughed. "Heavens, no. And neither Burlin nor Lance have made enemies who would send a hit man after them, either. Besides, if he'd wanted to hurt them, he's had several chances. He's more of an annoyance than anything else. But I want to add my vote to Hubert's that you find out who he is and send him on his way." She stood and stuck out a thin tanned hand. "It is good to see you again." At the door she turned, and I braced myself. Joe Riddley claims that most people say what they came to say when they're about to leave. She gave me a fleeting smile. "Would you call me Binky? I've always liked it better than Abigail."

Through the glass pane in our office door, I watched her head for the front door and wondered what it had been like for her, growing up thin and plain with two gorgeous older siblings, and wondered when she'd developed her interest in the subject that consumed them all.

"We've had the Bullock campaign. Now we can get to work," I told my computer. But before I did, I went online and ran my name through a search engine. To my astonishment, there were scads of listings. The first ten I pulled up, however, were all that same dreadful picture. It made me sick to think people in China could put my name in their computers and that's what they'd find. I was wondering if it were possible to delete things from search engines when there was another knock at my door. I looked over my shoulder and saw Lance Bullock peering in my door. "Do you have a minute?"

I turned bright pink and punched off my monitor. "Sure. Come in. You and Renée are the only members of your family I haven't seen today." I hoped he hadn't seen what I'd been looking at and thought I was admiring myself.

He looked appreciatively around the office. "Are those the original beaded board walls?"

"Sure are. And the original unfinished floorboards, too. Have a seat," — I indicated the wing chair under the window — "although that chair has been there only thirty years. Are you taking a historical tour of Hopemore? We also have our original tin

144

ceiling and oak counter out front."

He grinned and adjusted his red-and-blue striped tie. He had on a navy suit that matched Georgia's, but his was endearingly rumpled. "I'd rather see the historic sites of Hopemore than go make another speech, but that's what I've got to do. Right now, I'm looking for Renée. She went for a walk early this morning and hasn't come back, and our crew is getting antsy. Georgia suggested you might suggest some walks around town." He shoved back his cuff and looked at an expensive gold watch. "We have to leave in less than an hour to get to Dublin."

"Georgia told me. We don't have any special walks around here, but maybe Renée wandered around and got lost. We aren't a big town, but it's possible."

He shook his head. "Renée never gets lost. She's a legend. Travels all over the world and finds her way around places she's never been in before." His pride was evident. "She works for her daddy, you know. He has an international PR firm in Houston, and she's one of their best account executives." He must have remembered I was part of the electorate, because he added, "Of course, when I'm governor —"

Hillary Clinton, Princess Di, and Fergie sprang to mind. I wondered why nobody taught budding politicians, "Marry an adoring, mindless woman who will devote her life to being your wife. If she is intelligent,

145

strong, and/or competent, you will both get crucified."

". . . completely supports my campaign," Lance was assuring me when I tuned back in. "We are a team in everything we do. But campaigning — well, it wears her out. And she just got back from a meeting in Paris and hasn't adjusted to the time change yet."

"She looks like she's used to doing important things, not watching other people do them," I said bluntly. "No wonder she takes long walks. It's better than climbing walls."

He gave me a rueful grin, but all he said was, "Well, I'd better get back to where we're staying. We have to go, whether Renée shows up or not." He added, under his breath as he left, "But if she doesn't, Edward will kill her."

Somebody would get killed very soon, but it would not be Renée.

9

I tried to bow out of our seven o'clock dinner meeting at the community center, sponsored by one of the business groups in town. "If I eat two big meals a day, Martha will make me walk more," I told Joe Riddley. "She already walked my legs off this afternoon. And I want to be home in case Tad calls."

"Tad would call Ridd, not us. And you gotta come. Hubert said Saturday that he's got our state representative coming to talk about how upcoming legislation is going to benefit small towns. As much as you dislike the man, you're bound to have questions you'll want to ask."

We arrived early enough to claim seats at a round table right up next to the head table and speaker's platform. I did dislike the speaker, but I was real put out when somebody across the table informed us that Hubert had put him off a month "to take advantage of having Burlin Bullock here in town."

I was also disgusted to see I was getting some mighty sly looks.

The Bullock men arrived in twin navy

suits, but Burlin's looked newly pressed and Lance's looked even more rumpled. Both joked and glad-handed folks all the way to the head table, up on a low stage. Georgia had changed her outfit though. The *Statesman* would later describe her as "radiant in a red pantsuit with a jaunty patriotic scarf and silver pumps." Like her brother, she smiled and charmed folks like there was nowhere she'd rather be.

Hubert walked beside her, staying so close to her golden head that Joe Riddley leaned over and asked, "You reckon Hubert's gotten bitten by a love bug?"

"Not with that sister — she's married," I told him. "He was with the younger one Sunday at Myrtle's."

"The sad sack?"

I was annoyed at the description, but poor Binky did look sad, trudging along behind Georgia and Hubert. She was wearing her navy and pearls again, and the comfortable flats. She'd tied a red, white, and blue scarf around her hair like an Alice-in-Wonderland band, but the effect was childish rather than dashing.

Renée slouched beside her in a drab khaki suit that was downright ugly, but looked like it could be the latest thing in New York City. She smiled most of the time, but I caught her watching Burlin, Lance, and Georgia's royal processional with a curled lip, and figured she was put out about something.

Edward brought up the rear, again in black. He looked like he was making an effort not to wring somebody's neck. He kept clenching and unclenching his fists, moving his jaw from side to side, and taking deep breaths. Finally, when they all got past the crowd and up at the stage, he grabbed Burlin's elbow and spoke with urgent gestures. Lance shook his head with a frown. Burlin also shook his head, but bent to listen to something Georgia was saying. Burlin nodded, Lance finally nodded, and Edward relaxed. From across the room, it was like watching a silent movie.

For some unfathomable reason, Gusta was sitting at the head table, splendid in a gray voile dress with a white collar. She had never worked a day in her life, so in spite of the fact that she ran almost every other organization in town, business groups had been blessedly free of her meddling until now.

Gusta waved Burlin to one seat beside her and patted the chair on her other side for Georgia. Hubert took the remaining seat on that side, so Edward, Lance, Renée, and Binky went to the other end of the head table. As other folks were finding their seats, Burlin caught my eye and gave a little wave. Folks at our table smiled and gave me peculiar looks, but I turned to Joe Riddley and asked, "You want the beets off my salad?"

like I didn't have a clue what they were smiling about. Still, Burlin was in my direct line of vision, so each time I looked up, he was there — generally smiling right at me. They don't make medicine for that kind of indigestion.

Lance didn't seem to feel well, either. He kept pulling out soft pieces of his roll and pilling them between his fingers, until his bread plate must have had a fair-sized pile of dollhouse biscuits. Sometimes he'd whip out a pen and jot down something. I saw him pick up his fork a few times and dab at his plate, but never saw him carry a bite to his mouth. And he kept looking at his watch like he was timing the proceedings.

Renée kept watching him and chewing her bottom lip.

Between dinner and the speaker, Hubert roamed around the room talking to various people. When he got to my table, he leaned over and said, "Don't worry about the bum in my barn. I'm taking care of that situation." I didn't have time to reply, because he had to go to the mike to introduce the program.

Burlin took the podium with a smile. "We sure are having a good time in Hopemore, folks. This afternoon we men got in a great round of golf at your lovely country club, my sister Abigail took a ten-mile bike ride through your pretty countryside, and the other women got well-deserved naps."

"Not me," Georgia called. "I was writing thank-you notes."

He chuckled. "See? At any time of day or night, there's always one Bullock working for you." I don't know why, but the audience laughed. Burlin went on. "But the one who's planning to do the most for you in the near future is my son, Lance. Hubert, here, asked me to speak tonight on the changing economic face of Georgia, but Lance is the one with the facts at his fingertips. So, Lance? Come up here and tell these folks what you know."

Hubert looked real put out. Lance got up slowly, like he wasn't sure how he'd be received. But Edward started clapping, and Binky, Georgia, and Renée followed his lead. In another second, all the sheep in the room were putting hands together like they'd wanted Lance all along. I knew they'd rather have had Burlin than his son, so I didn't clap, even though Georgia gave me a bright smile and clapped above the table so I could get the hint.

Instead, I looked around the room — a sea of white faces dotted with a couple of black ones and one Mexican restaurant owner — and figured that no matter what Lance had to say, the economic face of Georgia still had a lot of changing to do.

Lance had some changing to do, too, if he planned to make memorable public speeches.

He was long on statistics and short on humor. Or maybe his speaking had been a late idea, and he'd had to write his speech during dinner. Maybe that's what they'd been quarreling about, and why Lance had failed to eat.

If it had been Edward's idea to stick us with Lance, he should have at least stuck around to hear the speech. Instead, he'd pulled out his cell phone almost as soon as Lance started talking, listened a second, then hurried out. He didn't return until Lance was winding up half an hour later. I was surprised to see it was only 8:15. As long as the speech had seemed, I'd thought it was well past my bedtime.

Hubert took the mike again. "Lance, Burlin, are you all willing to stick around here a little longer to answer any questions about the upcoming election?"

Lance looked up like he was going to refuse, but Burlin had already called, "Sure. We'd be glad to." People applauded, on cue. I saw Renée touch Lance's arm and say something. He shook his head.

"You want to stay?" Joe Riddley asked.

"I need to walk Lulu." We'd brought her and the pups home after the fire and installed them in a basket on Bo's porch.

"I walked her before we came. Had plenty of time while you were primping."

I started to insist that I hadn't been

primping, but the truth was, I'd been spending more time in front of my mirror since the Bullocks came to town. Women like Georgia tend to do that to me. So I said, "I'd still like to go home."

Joe Riddley knew my mind was on Tad. He handed me his keys. "Go ahead, then. Take the car. I'll walk home. I need the exercise." I hurried out before he could remember it was his new car he'd just handed over.

Near the front door, I ran into Gusta, Georgia, and Renée surrounded by a cluster of other women. Binky hovered in the background. Gusta stuck out her cane to bar my way. "Good evening, MacLaren. I was hoping to catch you. Georgia, here, is driving me home and stopping by for a little while. Lottie's made a special dessert. I want you to join us."

"I'm sorry —" I began.

She leaned so close I could smell the fixative she used on her back bridge. "You'll be sorrier if you go home. This whole crowd is coming. If you don't join us, it will look like you're avoiding the Bullocks because of that silly picture — or mooning over what might have been. Come on. Act natural and show the world you don't care what the papers say."

Gusta had a point. She also had considerable experience in acting natural no matter what the papers said. They'd been brutal to her granddaddy when state funds went missing while he was governor, to her brother while he drank his way through three terms in the Senate, and to her husband after somebody discovered how many slum properties he owned in Hope County. If Gusta went through all that with her dignity intact, she could certainly teach me a thing or two.

Besides, Joe Riddley had eaten my dessert. "For a little while," I agreed.

Georgia took a couple of steps and winced. "Augusta, do you mind if we run by the Inn first so I can change shoes? These are too tight." That ensured that everybody looked down at her silver pumps. She lifted one shoe, splattered with mud. "To make matters worse, I wore them on a little walk this evening and got them filthy. I'll hurry right in and be back before you know it." She turned to Binky, who was hovering at the edge of the crowd. "Abigail? Will you drive Gusta?"

Abigail shook her head. "I'm not going to be able to go. I've got work to do."

"I'll drive Gusta," I offered.

Gusta frowned. "You drive like a maniac."

Georgia, though, turned to me with a grateful smile. "Would you? Thanks! Renée and I will be there almost as quick as you are."

The other women giggled as they hurried to their own cars. Few of them ever got invited to dessert at Gusta's, and potential

First Ladies don't often come to Hopemore — although I didn't see much future for Renée as First Lady of Georgia if she didn't learn to occasionally say a civil word to some of the electorate.

I pulled all the way down Gusta's drive so she could use the ramp at the back door, and other cars pulled in behind me. We trooped into the living room where Pooh waited in a wing chair, wearing a pantsuit of soft pink knit with a scarf to match. Lottie always made sure she looked pretty for company.

When she saw us all, she clapped her hands in childish delight. "A party! How nice of you all to come." Then she turned to Lottie, who was hovering in the dining room doorway and murmured anxiously, "Do we have anything to serve?"

Lottie's tan face looked worried, but that was her natural expression. Nobody in the room doubted that we'd get something delicious. "Pecan pie and ice cream. It's all set out here in the dining room. Miss Gusta and I thought that's what you'd like to serve."

Pooh dabbed at tears with a wisp of white handkerchief. "You are both so good to me."

"Will you please bring her a plate, Lottie?" Gusta's voice wavered a little. I knew she hated to see her old friend like that.

"I sure will, Miss Gusta. I've already fixed it for her." Lottie would never let on to Pooh that her own pie had been made without sugar, to help control her diabetes.

None of the rest of us would eat until Georgia and Renée arrived, so we sat there chatting of this and that. I moved over by Pooh and told her about our fire. "Did you get the cows out?" she worried, fork halfway to her mouth.

"It was Daddy who kept cows, Pooh. Joe Riddley and I used our barn for tractors."

"Oh. Did the tractors burn up?"

"No, we got everything out. Even Lulu and her new pups."

"Oh, does Lulu have pups? I don't know what I'd do without my Saint Bernard." She told me something her dog had done that very afternoon, forgetting he'd been dead five years.

As I sat there wondering what else we could discuss, the hall clock boomed nine. "That clock sounds much grander than ours," I told her. "I don't remember it being here before."

"It's Gusta's," she confided. What leap of brain waves took her from that clock straight to lucidity? She leaned over and patted my hand and said in the clear voice we seldom heard anymore, "And it's telling you it's time to stop worrying about that silly picture in the paper. It will do Joe Riddley good not to take you so much for granted."

She *would* have to speak in one of those times when the whole room had fallen silent.

The eyes of every woman there flocked to me faster than flies to fresh-cut watermelon.

I had never been rude to Pooh in my life, but I can't answer for what I might have said if Georgia and Renée hadn't arrived right then. Georgia rushed in breathlessly, wearing her patriotic shoes. Her face was flushed and excited, and she was laughing at herself. "I know you all won't believe me, but we have been *so lost*. Renée *told* me to turn left at the light, but I didn't listen. So I don't know where we've been, but it took me fifteen minutes to find the courthouse, didn't it Renée?"

"At least." Renée raised one hand to hide what looked like a yawn. Then she gave us an embarrassed smile. "Sorry for holding everybody up."

Southern women jealously guard our right to bear the guilt of the world. None of us can stand for other people to think *they* are at fault.

"We didn't mind waiting — we were talking," said one.

"It's easy to get lost in this silly town," said another. "All those new subdivisions with winding streets."

"Even our old roads wander along tracks where it used to be easiest for wagons to go," put in a third.

"Or cows," chimed in a fourth. "I sometimes think the whole place was laid out by cows."

"We aren't as bad as Atlanta," another said regretfully, "where every street crosses every other street two or three times, but you sure can't turn right three times in Hopemore and expect to come out where you started." She sounded like that was something the Chamber of Commerce ought to advertise as a tourist attraction.

Comparing Hopemore, population thirteen thousand, with Atlanta was carrying things a bit far, so I said, "At least in Hopemore you can find a familiar landmark in a few minutes. The important thing is, you got here."

Gusta gave me the closest she ever came to a smile and said graciously to Georgia and Renée, "Won't you come to the dining room and try some of Lottie's pecan pie?"

Coffee was always served from a silver pot at Gusta Wainwright's, and between them, she and Pooh had enough china and silver to serve a quarter of Hopemore. We balanced fine china on our laps, enjoyed Lottie's excellent pie, set our cups and saucers on marble-topped mahogany tables, and listened to Georgia. Amazingly, Gusta let her preside.

To give her credit, Georgia didn't start talking politics right away. First she admired Gusta's dishes and talked about her own porcelain collection. Then she asked intelligent questions about Hopemore and listened to the answers. Only gradually did she start telling us how great Lance was and some of his impressive ideas for bringing Georgia up to Bullock standards.

Every now and then she would turn to Renée and ask, "Isn't that right, honey?" and Renée would smile and nod. Georgia could have brought along a doll with a bobble head and achieved about the same results. Renée must not have found Lance's political opinions quite as fascinating as Georgia did, either. I caught her stifling a couple of yawns.

Still, at one point when Georgia paused for a breath, Renée looked around and said, "You all have the prettiest walks around here. I went down a gravel road this morning and found a real nice pond with a little dock. It was the most peaceful place I've seen in a long time."

"Must be Hubert's pond," one woman suggested.

"Just down from your old place, Mac," another said — as if I might have forgotten, having been gone from it for a month.

"This state needs a lot of peaceful places," Georgia picked up, quick as a whip. "Lance has ideas for parks you wouldn't believe. I hope you all are going to turn out to vote for him, so he can get busy putting some of his marvelous ideas into practice, for the good of us all."

The way she said it, we were a group of her most special friends who would, of course, vote for Lance as a personal favor to

159

her. I even flirted with the notion for a second. I'd never known a governor personally. But I felt we ought to get something on the table and settle whether it was true or not. "Did I hear he's thinking of switching parties?"

Renée shifted in her chair and bent over her cup, so I couldn't see her face. Georgia beamed like I'd just asked the right question. "I'm so glad you brought that up. Lance feels that party isn't as important as issues, and that he is uniquely qualified to work with members of both parties for the good of the state."

"Is that a 'yes'?" I persisted.

She shrugged. "You'll have to ask him. *You* know, Mackie, that all I do is follow Burlin around and do whatever he says."

That stewed my goose as far as the others were concerned. If Georgia Bullock called me "Mackie" — especially with that "*you* know" and the intimate way she said her brother's name — I must be privileged to know things about him the others didn't. Every married woman in that room would go home and tell her husband that what the paper said was true. One of those husbands would mention to Joe Riddley that he'd never realized I was so friendly with the Bullocks. I didn't want to think what might happen then.

I started to get up from my chair to leave, then caught Gusta's eye. If I didn't stay there and tough it out, she would never let me hear the last of it. So I swallowed my pie and said, "I don't know you all that well, Georgia, but I sure will be asking Lance that question." Then I got up and went for more coffee.

The women were so enjoying their evening with celebrities — and their rare invitation to Gusta's — that nobody made a move to leave before eleven. When the clock chimed, Georgia gasped. "We may be locked out! Annie Dale locks the door at eleven and goes to bed, and she gave Burlin the front-door key for all of us. Unless he's already home and waiting in the hall, we'll have the dickens of a time getting in. I guess we'll see how good we are at tossing pebbles at a window." She laughed, but I could see she was anxious.

"Lance will be up," Renée assured her.

"And I'll call Annie Dale." Gusta went to do so immediately. She returned to assure them, "She'll wait up for another half hour."

"Can you find your way back that fast?" somebody asked. The others laughed, comfortable enough to tease the Bullocks by then.

Renée gave us a wink. "I'll drive this time."

I left in the middle of that hilarity. Georgia struck me as the kind of Southerner who might have to talk awhile at the door after she'd said she was leaving. Only when I got outside did I remember that my car — Joe Riddley's car — was blocked. I didn't want to have to go back and organize several women to back down the drive to let me out, so I walked home. I figured that Joe Riddley would either be out hunting Tad in one of our business trucks, or be engrossed in the eleven o'clock news when I got home, and I'd get up before him, so with any luck, I could get the car back in our garage before he missed it.

As it turned out, only Lulu, Bo, and the pups were there to greet me. The pups snored softly in their basket. Bo opened one eye on the back porch and asked in a sleepy voice, "You and who else?" Lulu danced around my feet with great joy, having already given me up for dead. That's how beagles always welcome you, being the most fatalistic creatures God ever made.

I gave her a treat and let her curl up beside me on the couch while I watched the tail end of the news. Then I went to bed. By the time Joe Riddley started banging around just after midnight, getting ready for bed, I was fast asleep.

At least, that's my story. I'm sticking to it.

10

Tuesday, Lulu started barking on the back porch before sunrise. At the old house, I'd have simply let her out. Here, she'd need a leash, so I might as well get dressed and take her for a walk. Joe Riddley was burrowed under the sheet, good for another hour. I figured Lulu and I could walk over to Gusta's and bring his car back. I took the keys and my cell phone, in the unlikely case some deputy needed me before I got home. Crime is slow around here at dawn.

It was a gray pearl morning, with no color in the sky yet except a smudge of peach to the east. The air lay on my shoulders like a damp blanket — it was, after all, Georgia in September — but there was none of the scorching heat of a month before. The birds were having a fine old convention before humans got up. Up on Oglethorpe, a few cars were carrying folks to work in distant towns. A couple of buzzards circled lazily, high in the sky.

I couldn't remember walking around town that early before, and was happy to live in a town so small that I could smell country even in the heart of it. I headed up

Oglethorpe to fetch Joe Riddley's car, but got distracted by our new window display. Bethany and Hollis were working for us after school and had filled the window with gift baskets of garden implements for women. They'd done a real good job. I might want one of those myself.

Our store was a block west of the courthouse and Gusta and Pooh lived a block east. As Lulu and I moseyed through the square, I noted that the buzzards must have found something. Six now floated in wide spirals overhead. I got so busy wondering how exactly it is that they spot a small dead animal from that height and send out invitations to their friends, I scarcely noticed when Lulu steered me down a side street toward the tracks.

The area by the railroad tracks is not a part of town I frequent. Years ago, when the train passed through Hopemore and stopped twice a day, we had a station, several warehouses, and a cotton gin down there. Now, the tracks were overgrown with weeds and the buildings deserted, except for a cotton warehouse Meriwether DuBose had recently refurbished for her new catalogue business. The Chamber of Commerce talked about revitalizing the area, but nobody else had caught the vision yet.

Still, I wasn't nervous. Lulu is a fierce bodyguard, and every criminal and drunk in town knows who I am — and that if he or she harms a hair of my head, they'll have Joe Riddley to deal with. Besides, with the whole town asleep, that area looked no more deserted than the rest. I could easily imagine that in a couple of hours the cotton gin would crank up, laborers would stack merchandise for shipping, and old men would start to congregate on the station porch.

"We'll go to the water tank and turn around," I told Lulu. The tank sat at the end of the buildings lining the tracks, in the middle of a large parking lot. Some towns, of course, surround their tanks with a chain-link fence, three strands of barbed wire, and a padlocked gate. Hopemore had simply planted a privet hedge around the base. After all, the ladder was too high to reach without another ladder and nobody had designs on our water. For years the tank had performed its invaluable function without anybody giving it a thought unless some intrepid high schooler scaled the ladder to blazon a message above the town.

What people neglect, however, nature takes back. The tank had originally been painted to blend with the sky. Now, as the sun rose and changed the sky to a light, clear blue, I was appalled at how faded and tired the poor tank looked. I couldn't remember the last time it had been painted. Recent crops of teenagers must have been too busy with video games and television to mess it up.

The once-trim hedge around its base had sent up shoots that sprawled high and unkempt. Outside the hedge, the asphalt was pitted with holes where the pavement had cracked and broken, and the whole lot was littered with flattened cans and the glint of broken bottles, dotted with clumps of high grass and small bushes.

Where I saw desolation, though, Lulu saw ecstasy. She took one whiff and strained on her leash. "You want to run?" I bent and released her. "Watch out for broken glass."

She dashed here and there, sniffing bushes and grass, then headed for the tank itself. "Five more minutes," I called as she wriggled under the hedge.

She raised a storm of what I thought was protest. I let her bark for a minute, then called, "Okay, come!"

She continued to bark.

"Lulu! Come!" That tone generally gets instant obedience, but she kept barking. I looked up and saw that the buzzards were directly overhead and descending. I didn't want them to mistake her — or me — for breakfast. I waved my arms. "Lulu, do I have to come get you?"

She set up a howl they could hear in Augusta.

I picked my way gingerly across the lot, watching for potholes, snakes, and buzzards.

"You're fixing to get a switching," I warned, although I had never hit that dog in my life. Lulu shoved her way through a gap in the hedge and danced, still yapping. When I stopped, she bounded out of reach, awkward but still agile on her three legs. "What have you found?" I demanded. "I'll come, because you don't usually get into fidgets over nothing, but I don't like the looks of that hedge." She turned and wriggled back under.

I looked for the best place to push through. Because they had been planted to deter kids from the tower, the bushes were real close together, their branches as sharp as the switches Mama used on our legs when my brother, Jake, and I were little.

"If you've just waked up a snake," I warned, shoving through the only hole I saw, "or are making all this racket over a dead possum, we're gonna both be sorry."

I cut both arms and got several rips in my shirt, and my hair didn't bear thinking about. I hoped Phyllis could work me in as soon as she got to the beauty parlor. "When I get to work," I informed Lulu, who was sticking so close to my feet, I was in danger of tripping over her, "I'm going to call the city and tell them to send somebody down to clip these bushes." She whined her disagreement.

It wasn't a snake or a possum she had found. It was the man in the gray suit.

He lay sprawled on his face beside one leg

of the tank. His gray ponytail was slung across one shoulder. A knapsack lay several feet away, spilling clothing and a hairbrush onto the ground. A battered guitar lay as if it had been tossed aside.

He wouldn't be needing it anymore. Not with that hole in the back of his head.

11

I have no idea how long I stood there. Long enough to think that nobody born of woman through labor and pain should wind up dead on a deserted asphalt lot. Long enough to say a prayer for whoever he was, confident that a God mindful of sparrows would know his name. Long enough to notice a lot of things I'd rather not have seen.

Flies crawled around his gray hair, feasting on dark dried blood. The stench that always accompanies death polluted the soft fall air. His hat lay beyond his head. A length of rusted galvanized pipe lay beyond it, with ominous stains at one end. A soft muddy spot several yards from the body, where the pavement had sunk and gradually filled with dirt, showed the clear print of a woman's shoe. A man's print lay in a similar depression — but he had worn pointed shoes, not the unexpectedly small sneakers with round toes worn by the victim.

Why was I looking at the dead man's shoes instead of calling the police? Because I didn't want to think about a red matchbook from Spence's Appliances that lay three feet from the victim's hand. It was too clean and fresh

169

to have lain there long.

Hubert had a temper when riled, and he'd been threatening this man in public for several days. Even though he had promised to blast him with a shotgun, might he have been willing to use a handier weapon if it presented itself?

Lulu pressed against my calf and whimpered, to remind me we had a problem here. I reached for my cell phone.

Royce Wharton was on duty again, at the end of his shift. As soon as he heard my voice, he chuckled. "Calling the police station early is getting to be a habit, isn't it, Judge? You got another buffalo?"

Royce wasn't a bad officer, just a mischievous one. When I said, "No, I've got a body," he sobered immediately.

After he'd taken the particulars about where I was and who I'd found, he said, "I'll send somebody right away. Go back to the street and find someplace to sit down until we get there."

"Seats are in short supply in this part of town," I informed him, "and I've got six hungry buzzards circling above. I'll just prop myself against the tank."

"Don't topple it," he warned. "We don't want you destroying evidence."

"If you see a deluge coming down Second Street, don't bother to come."

I'd scarcely hung up when Lulu started

whining. I looked where she was looking and saw that one buzzard now perched on a support halfway up the tank, watching me with a calculating eye. "Shoo!" I called. "Shoo!" He didn't budge, just crooked his head this way and that to see if the bigger predator would steal his meal.

"Scat!" I yelled, waving my arms to assure him I was alive. "Scat!"

Lulu added her voice to mine, a long mournful howl that sent chills up my spine.

The disappointed scavenger stayed just long enough to let us know he was leaving of his own free will, not because he'd been coerced. As he flapped away, the others — who had been circling lower and lower — followed. I watched them go, thinking that buzzards may be ugly close up, but they are beautiful in flight. Again I wondered how they find their prey.

Thinking about buzzards isn't my favorite way to spend an early morning, but it sure beats looking at a dead body and wondering who hit it over the head.

"Over here," I called to Lulu, who was sniffing toward the man. I snapped on her leash and kept her near me. "We don't want to mess up any more evidence," I explained. "Chief Muggins is coming. Hear his siren?" Not that a siren is necessary, going to a crime scene where the victim isn't going anywhere, but the chief had a new cruiser with a lot of fancy equipment, and he took every opportunity to share its glories with the taxpayers who bought it.

Charlie Muggins is in a class of his own in my book, at the top of a page headed "People I couldn't like if I tried." He struts around crime scenes like God's gift to detection, although his dignity is somewhat impaired by a constant need to hitch up his pants to keep from losing them to the weight of his belt. I don't dislike him for swaggering, or even because he treats women like we all secretly hope he'll make advances. I dislike him because he has never learned to shut his mouth or open his mind. The chief is bad about jumping to conclusions, then shaping facts to suit them. Only once, to my knowledge, has he picked the right murderer, and that was a lucky guess.

That morning, I heard his car stop and the door slam; then I heard nothing. The base of each leg of the water tank was set into a concrete support two feet high, so I managed to climb up on one, clung to the leg for support, and called over the hedge, "Chief? Over here. By the tank." Joe Riddley established a precedent I have continued. No matter how well we know officers of the law, we refer to them by their titles in public. They do the same.

"That you, Judge?" He shaded his eyes, since he had to look directly into the rising

172

sun. "I was heading in when Royce called that you'd found a body." He still stood on the curb.

"Right here," I shouted back, "through the hedge. I came in about there" — I pointed to the spot — "and he's lying down here." I pointed again.

Another cruiser pulled to the curb behind his. As the officers got out, the chief hitched up his pants and started strolling my way. "What are you doing in there?" he yelled. It didn't bother me that he sounded like he was accusing me of murder. Ever since Chief Muggins moved to Hopemore, he has lived in daily anticipation of catching me committing a felony. I'm not on the Favorite People page in his book, either.

"Waiting for you." I was getting tired of shouting and wanted to get down before he arrived to offer me a sweaty palm.

I hadn't planned my descent, however, when I climbed up. The ledge was too narrow to kneel or turn around on. The only thing I could do was jump backwards. I leaped like a gazelle, landed like a hippopotamus, and was nursing my right ankle when Chief Muggins pushed his shoulders through the hedge.

"You hurt yourself?" He sounded like that was proof positive I'd killed the victim.

"A little."

He lifted his hat, slicked back his yellow

hair, and put the hat back on. Then he stuck his thumbs in his belt and rocked back and forth as he surveyed the scene. "So tell me what's been going on here."

Two other officers, Buck and Dan, followed him through what was becoming a sizeable hole in the hedge. Both were once kids I handed out suckers to down at the store.

Dan moseyed over to look at the body. Buck took out a little notebook. "For the record, I did not kill the man," I said.

Buck wrote in big letters, saying the words aloud. "Judge Yarbrough reported she did not kill the man." Dan snickered. Chief Muggins glowered.

"I was out walking Lulu here" — I nodded to where she sat on her haunches regarding Chief Muggins without enthusiasm — "and she wanted a run in the lot. She went nosing around in the bushes and started making such a racket that I came to see what she'd found. I saw —"

I'd been all right until then, but as I looked back toward the body, my legs gave way. I'd have been lying beside the dead man if Dan and Buck hadn't dived in unison to catch me. Dan held me up while I caught my breath and hoped the world would stop spinning in a minute.

Chief Muggins scowled. "You ready to finish now?"

"Couldn't she come down to the station and

174

make a statement later?" Dan asked, still supporting most of my weight.

The chief didn't like it, but he gave a short nod. "Okay, come give us a report later. Buck, go call the homicide team." He was bent over, looking at Hubert's matchbook.

"It wasn't Hubert. You know it wasn't," I said. Chief Muggins ignored me.

I took a couple of experimental steps, but the pain was awful.

"You don't have a car?" Dan asked. When I shook my head, he turned to Chief Muggins. "I'd like to run her home, if you don't mind."

"Go ahead." Chief Muggins waved, but anybody could tell he thought it was a waste of an officer's time and the taxpayer's gas. As I hobbled through the hedge, he called after me, "Don't you let that dog leave a flea in the cruiser, now, and don't you be leaving town."

"I wish," I muttered.

Dan and I didn't talk on the way home. Even Lulu was quiet. My ankle throbbed, and I was thinking about that poor man and wondering if he'd left behind anybody who loved him. I got sad, remembering how cheerful he'd been Saturday. Tears dribbled down my cheeks, and I pulled a wadded tissue from my pocket to wipe them away.

Dan looked over. "Ankle hurting?"

It was easier to nod than explain.

As he helped me hop up the walk to our door a few minutes later, he urged, "Get that ankle seen to right away, now."

Joe Riddley heard him through the open window. As I hobbled in, he looked up from his newspaper. "What's the matter with you? Where have you been? And why the Sam Hill did you abandon my car last night?" Bo squawked his own protest.

The stuffing went out of me. I sank to the sofa and muttered, "You're as nasty as Charlie Muggins, except you provide a seat. I left the car at Gusta's because folks had blocked me in. As to where I've been, I took Lulu for a walk this morning — meaning to bring your car back when we came. Instead, I found a body, jumped off the water tank, and sprained my ankle." I leaned back against the sofa cushions and closed my eyes. "Oh, God, please let this be a bad dream. Let me wake up to an ordinary beautiful day."

"You got the beautiful day, but hell's bells, woman, can't you even go for a walk without getting in trouble? Come on, Lulu, looks like I'll have to get your breakfast."

Finding a body hadn't ruined her appetite, but I felt so wretched I started to cry again.

Joe Riddley can't stand a crying woman. He flung me a box of tissues, muttered, "I went ahead and made the coffee," and headed to the kitchen. While he banged around finding mugs in Clarinda's latest in-spired location, he called, "Sounds to me like you women did more carousing last night than the men. I thought you said you jumped off the water tower and found a body. But I know you didn't jump off the tank, because you'd be dead, and you didn't find a body, because you promised me after the last time you took off after a killer that you wouldn't meddle anymore in things that aren't your business. So, trusting that you are a woman of your word, you must be hung over. Here's your coffee. Get it inside you, then tell me what really happened."

The coffee was black and steaming, just the way I like it. "I was fixing to scramble me some eggs," he added. "You want some?" He headed back to the kitchen without waiting for an answer. Joe Riddley is a lot like Lulu in two ways: His bark is worse than his bite, and he ignores anything he doesn't want to hear.

While he was cooking, I called, "What did you mean about carousing last night?" I was surprised, because Joe Riddley has never gone out much with other men, except to business and church events. I couldn't re-member a time when he'd done what most folks call "carousing."

He didn't answer until he set a plate in front of me on the coffee table. "Eggs just the way you like them," he said, "toast the perfect shade of brown, butter and jelly on the side, and orange juice. What more could any woman ask for?" He set his own plate at the table and took his seat.

"An answer to my question. What did you mean about carousing? I left you at a respectable business meeting. What happened after that? And why are you sitting with your back to me?"

"This is my usual seat at the table."

"Yeah, but with me over here —" I sighed. "Who else went carousing?"

He named six other men, then added, "And Hubert and Burlin Bullock."

I was glad he wasn't looking my way. I dropped a forkful of eggs in my lap. While Lulu consumed the evidence, I asked casually as I could, "Not Lance and Edward?"

"No, Lance was tired and Edward had to run up to Augusta for a meeting. But Burlin said he'd like to see some of the nightlife around here, so we went looking for some."

"Where'd you go, the country club?" Except at the club, the liveliest nightlife in Hopemore is cockroaches.

"No, we went to that beer joint out on the Dublin road. Burlin and I wanted to show Hubert that Georgia men hold their liquor better than Tech ones."

"You never drank enough at one time in your life to call it 'holding your liquor.' How much did you drink?"

178

He hunched over his plate. "I didn't. I was a designated driver. But Burlin beat Hubert so bad, it wasn't funny."

"How could you be a designated driver? I had your car."

"I remembered that about the time Hubert started getting too drunk to drive, so I confiscated his keys. By the time we left, he didn't know whose car I was driving." He chortled. "Otis is going to find some peculiar footprints in Pooh's flower beds. Hubert couldn't stay on that three-foot walk to save his life. Burlin did real well until Hubert swayed up the walk, then he passed out like a light. Three of us had to carry him to his room and put him to bed. Annie Dale's done the place up real nice, by the way. You might ask her who helped her decorate it."

I ignored his slur on my own decorating skills, because he'd said something that relieved me considerably. "So Hubert was with you the whole time from the end of the meeting until you took him home too drunk to walk straight?"

He shrugged. "Mostly. He dropped Burlin by Annie Dale's while he went back to lock up. Then he picked Burlin up and they joined us about an hour after we got there."

Like I've said before, Hopemore is small. It doesn't take an hour to make a round-trip to Annie Dale's from the community center, turn off lights and lock up the building, re-

179

turn to Annie Dale's, and drive out to the roadhouse.

Joe Riddley didn't notice that he'd frozen me to the sofa. He swiped up the last of his eggs with his toast and added, "Burlin's as nice in person as he is on television, but after that sorry speech Lance made last night, I don't think he expects his boy to win any elections. Burlin was drinking last night like a man drowning his sorrows."

12

I spent the rest of the morning in miscalculation.

First, I miscalculated how busy Phyllis would be on a Tuesday. With celebrities in town, women were getting their hair done twice that week. I told her I'd come as early as she liked, but she informed me that she had two of the Bullock women to do that morning and couldn't possibly work me in until after four.

I also miscalculated the medical profession's reaction to a sprain. Because Joe Riddley insisted, I allowed him to carry me to "Doc in a Box" — a minor injury center — but I knew what a doctor would do: wrap the ankle in an elastic bandage, tell me to keep my foot up all day, and prescribe something for pain. But if it would make Joe Riddley happier to pay for that advice than to let me doctor myself, I was willing to go. I was hurting so bad, I'd have agreed to anything.

All the way there, Bo perched on Joe Riddley's shoulder and assured me, "Not to worry. Not to worry."

Less than hour later, a doctor who looked like a tenth grader had encased my foot and leg in a cast to the knee, told me not to put weight on the foot for a week, given me a pain shot and a prescription, and handed me crutches that, within minutes, did more injury to my armpits than jumping off the water tower had done to my ankle. When Bo saw Joe Riddley wheeling me back to the car, he flapped his wings and squawked, "Sic 'em, boy! Sic 'em!" I wished I could.

Joe Riddley wanted to take me home and dump me on the sofa for Clarinda to take care of. I pointed out that I could sit at my desk and prop my foot up, and if somebody didn't finish our taxes, Uncle Sam would get downright nasty. I was getting a bit foggy by then, but figured I could function so long as Joe Riddley kept bringing me cold co-colas. If I went home, Clarinda was sure to make more noises about those boxes stacked in the guest room. I'd rather work.

At the store, I couldn't climb the four steps from the parking lot to our office, so Joe Riddley drove along the old-fashioned double sidewalk to our front door, letting the whole town know something was the matter. I hopped in like some show-off kid while behind me, Bo perched on Joe Riddley's cap flapping his wings and yelling, "Little Bit! Little Bit!" He sounded so much like Joe Riddley that everybody laughed — everybody except me. My left leg wasn't used to hopping, or to supporting my whole weight. Sweat ran into my eyes and down under my arms, and I felt like I'd hopped a mile when, halfway through the store, my left leg started trembling, then gave out. I'd have fallen if a quick clerk hadn't grabbed a plastic lawn chair and shoved it behind me. I was so grateful, I forgave her for saying, "Oopsy daisy" in that silly tone grown-ups use when toddlers are learning to walk.

Joe Riddley and another clerk carried me the rest of the way in that dratted chair. They banged my other knee on the doorjamb going in, but I forgave them, too. They didn't do it on purpose. I refused to think about having to be carried back out at the end of the day. Or to the bathroom in an hour or so.

But I had miscalculated Joe Riddley's devotion. He fetched a five-gallon bucket for my bum foot, padded it with a small bag of potting soil, and informed me he had urgent work to do down at the nursery. "I'll walk over to Pooh's and fetch my car first." He took Bo and left me steaming. I looked at my poor bare toes sticking out of the cast and promised them I'd have Phyllis's manicurist put on a lick of polish. But how could I get to Phyllis?

I also miscalculated Chief Muggins's devotion to solving the murder of a homeless man. The chief gets right there when a wealthy person is robbed, but normally he could have found a hundred things to do before he bothered to investigate the death of a tramp. That week, however, with crime slow and the Bullocks in town, he called me before I'd booted up my computer. "I thought I told you to run by here to make a statement." Chief Muggins seldom employs those gentle introductory phrases with which most Southerners wade gently into conversation — how are you? how's your mother? how's your first cousin twice removed?

"I'm not running anywhere," I said, forgiving myself for a trace of smugness. "My ankle's in a cast to the knee. If you want a statement, you'll have to take it over the phone." I reflected that I was sure forgiving a lot of folks that morning. Painkillers seemed to be good for the soul. I thought I'd discuss that with Martha later — which reminded me of the single silver lining in my cloud: at least I wouldn't have to walk around the track for a while.

I'd forgotten that Chief Muggins was on the other end of the phone until he snapped, "I'll come over there." As I hung up, I looked down at my jeans and wished I'd changed more than my torn shirt before we went to the doctor. I like to look nice at the office. Still, Chief Muggins had already seen me that morning, and Mama used to say a true lady can entertain anybody, no matter how she's dressed, and make them feel that what she's wearing is the correct attire. This was as good a time as any to test that theory. I gave my hair a quick combing, added some lipstick, and greeted Chief Muggins like I lived in jeans every day — so why ever didn't he?

He brought a deputy I didn't know very well, who hovered in the doorway and waited for me to invite him in while Chief Muggins took Joe Riddley's leather desk chair. Then the deputy settled on the edge of the wing chair like he didn't plan to stay very long.

Our office is large enough for two big desks, several filing cabinets, and the wing chair, but it always feels small when Chief Muggins and I are both in it. He may have felt the same way, because he dangled his cap between his knees and got right to the point. "How did you come to find that body, again? Take notes, Jack."

I explained once more about taking Lulu for a walk, her wanting to run in the big lot, her barking, and my pushing through the bushes to see what she had found.

"Did you leave anything at the scene?"

"No. I took only a cell phone, a dog, and a leash, and I carried all of them out."

"May I see your right shoe please?"

I indicated my cast. "I don't have much use for it right now. I think it's still in the back seat of Joe Riddley's car, out in the parking lot. Why do you need it?"

"Where's Joe Riddley?" He peered around the office like he thought I was hiding him in an oversized file drawer.

I sighed. This could be a very long interview if Chief Muggins started suspecting not only me, but Joe Riddley as well. "He's gone to the nursery, but he takes one of our trucks down there because the trails stay muddy from irrigation and he doesn't like to mess up his car. Why do you want my shoe?" I reckoned it was time to get back to the matter at hand.

"We found footprints from a woman and a man who had been walking around the place. I need to see if one of them's yours."

"It's not. I saw them, too. But you can get my shoe if you like."

"You got keys?" the deputy asked.

"The car's not locked."

His face made it clear what he thought of that, but almost everybody is casual about locking cars in Hopemore. Car theft is not one of our major industries.

The deputy headed out, but stuck his head back in almost at once. "Er — what kind of car?"

"Silver Town Car," I told him. "In the spot by the back door marked 'J. R. Yarbrough.'"

When the deputy brought back my shoe, it looked lost and a bit shabby dangling from his hand. I sat there feeling so sorry for the shoe, it took me a minute to realize Chief Muggins was speaking to me. He sounded more impatient than before. "Judge? I asked if this is your shoe."

I had trouble connecting an answer to that question. Finally I said, " 'Course it's my shoe. What other woman would leave her shoe in my husband's car?" It was when I started giggling that I realized the painkillers weren't just making me forgiving, they were seriously impairing my ability to function. I felt so soft and cuddly, in another minute or two I'd be putting my head on Chief Muggins's blue shoulder and snoring like one of Lulu's pups.

That enlivened me enough to point to Joe Riddley's bottom drawer. "Take a couple of quarters from the cup in there and bring me a Coke. Take more quarters and bring everybody one." I laid my head on my desk and waited for somebody to obey.

A hand shook my shoulder. "Here's your Coke." It was the deputy, thank goodness. I'd hate for Charlie Muggins to lay a hand on me. Some kinds of slime are hard to wash off.

There's nothing like a cold co-cola to wake you up for whatever you have to face next. But I miscalculated Chief Muggins's ability to winkle information out of me. The only excuse I can give is that I was seriously T. U. I. — thinking under the influence.

"So what happened again after you got

through the hedge?" he asked, signaling for the deputy to take notes.

"I saw the dead man —"

"Would you repeat that, please? Be sure you get this verbatim, Deputy."

"I saw the dead man. He was lying on his stomach with one hand over his head and the other out to the side, and he had been hit hard on the back of the head. I could see that because his hat was lying off to one side. I also saw a long iron bar — a rusty bar — that looked to me like it could have been the weapon. I didn't touch it."

"Had you ever seen the victim before?"

I nodded, but it made me so woozy, I decided not to do that again. "Saturday afternoon. He was in our alley when Joe Riddley and I went —" I stopped. Chief Muggins hadn't been at the party, and the way he sucked up to important people, if he'd had an invitation, he'd have gone. I was feeling muzzy enough not to want to hurt his feelings. "We were going to an affair."

He snickered. "From Sunday's paper, sounds like it wasn't your first."

I glared. "That was not funny." I turned to the deputy. "Please write down his remark, verbatim, in case I sue for defa— defa—" Waving my hand didn't clear my brain, and "defamation of character" was beyond my tongue at the moment. "Oh, you know." I waited while he wrote something before I went on. "We were going to a party, and saw the man in our alley. Joe Riddley told him to go to Myrtle's for some dinner." That was so sad, I started to sniffle.

"So you actually spoke to the victim. Interesting." Charlie Muggins has a polecat's sharp nose and bright, suspicious eyes and a chimpanzee's flat face and wiry limbs. Right then the polecat was in the ascendency. His eyes almost glittered. "Did the two of you meet or speak before or after that?" He leaned forward like he was about to pounce.

I started to shake my head again — which was not a good idea — then I remembered. "Yes, he came by Gusta's during the party. I was on the porch and waved."

"Anybody with you? Burlin Bullock, for instance?"

"I'd throw something at you, but I wasn't raised in a barn. The people with me were Lance Bullock and Hubert Spence."

"Hubert, eh? Did he talk to the man?"

I swear, it was the painkiller that made me say, "He yelled at him and chased him down the block. But when the buffalo ran into a car, the tramp disappeared." Seeing that Chief Muggins looked confused, I hurried to add, "It was because the man was sleeping in Hubert's barn, and Hubert couldn't sell his house."

Chief Muggins leaned closer. "And Hubert was pretty anxious to get the man out of his barn?"

"Sure. It's hard to sell a house with a tenant in the barn."

"And Hubert threatened the victim."

"Sort of."

"Did he or didn't he?" In another minute, if he kept leaning forward, that chair was going to pitch him. I could hardly wait.

"Not exactly threatened. Just waved his arms and yelled. You know." I demonstrated.

To my disappointment, Chief Muggins leaned back and clasped his hands on his round little stomach. "I don't know what you know, Judge. That's why we're having this little chat."

"I know you found a matchbook from Hubert's store at the scene, but he'll have an explanation for that."

"He'd better." Chief Muggins's voice had an edge to it. "He's not giving those matchbooks to anybody, not even his old poker buddies, until his anniversary celebration next month. Which means he was at the scene of the crime. What did he say to you privately last night? And before you answer, you need to know I have two reliable witnesses who will testify that Hubert came to your table and said something about that man. What was it?"

Chief Muggins had the gleam in his eye of a polecat about to make a terrific stink. The deputy sat with pen poised, waiting for my answer. As an officer of the court, I was bound to tell the truth. "He said for me not to worry about the bum in his barn — those were his words —"

"Why were you supposed to be worrying about the bum in his barn?" Chief Muggins interrupted.

"Because Hubert asked me Saturday to see if I could find the man and convince him to leave town. But I'd been too busy, with the fire and Tad disappearing."

He snickered. "And being in the paper? So what did Hubert say Monday night?"

I sighed. "He said he was taking care of the situation."

Chief Muggins slapped both hands on his thighs and stood. "That's what I wanted to hear. Somebody else thought that's what he said, but wasn't quite sure. Thank you, Judge. I suspect I'll be needing you down at the sheriff's detention center sometime today for a probable-cause hearing. I hate to ask you to sit when the defendant is a close friend and former neighbor, but the other two magistrates are both out of town."

"I'm not supposed to put any weight on this foot for at least a week," I informed him. "You can slow down a bit and think things through before you rush into this."

"I've done all the thinking I need to do. But I'll leave you with something to think about until I see you again. That dead man you found and say you talked to? He was a woman."

13

After Charlie left, I tried to concentrate on the numbers on my computer screen. Instead, I kept seeing a person facedown under the water tank. My mind's eye roved over the long gray ponytail, the stocky body in the old gray suit. A woman? No wonder she had such small feet. What brought her to our town to die?

When the phone rang, I hoped it would be Charlie saying he'd found another suspect. Instead, it was Martha. "Have you heard from Tad?" I asked at once.

"Not a word. Ridd's coming home at lunchtime and we're going to call Walker and Cindy. But what's that I hear about you spraining an ankle? That's a pretty drastic way to get out of walking."

"I was desperate. How on earth did you hear that all the way down there?"

"Ridd sent me to the nursery this morning for chrysanthemums, and I saw Pop. He told me about it and said you are ensconced in your office like a queen, eating bonbons."

"Stuck here helpless as a baby is more like it, without a single bonbon in sight. I can't even get to the bathroom, and that's gonna be a problem in a little while."

"Didn't they give you crutches?"

"I can't get the hang of them. Besides, my left leg isn't used to carrying all my weight, and I'm not real good at hopping."

"You'll get used to them." That was the nurse speaking, not my sweet daughter-in-law. "Don't you put weight on that ankle, now."

"I won't, but I just thought of something. Back in the storeroom behind the utility room, there's a wheelchair J.R. used until he got his prosthesis." An accident crushed Joe Riddley's father's right leg below the knee a few years after we got married. He had a wheelchair especially fitted up to support his stump while he waited for it to heal, and one of the advantages of living in the same house generation after generation is that you tend to hang on to things because somebody is likely to need them again. Joe Riddley's parents hadn't bothered to clean out the attic or store room when they left the house, and neither had we.

"Will you find it for me?" I asked Martha. "Then, can you come take me somewhere?"

"You don't need a wheelchair. You can get used to the crutches."

"I could probably get used to Chinese water torture, but what's the point? It's just a week, and hopping is a skill I don't plan to need again. Will you look for that chair and come get me?"

193

I have often said Martha was God's best gift to this family. She proved it half an hour later when she showed up with a newly dusted wheelchair and asked, "Where to, madame?"

When she heard where I wanted to go, and why, her eyes widened. "Chief Muggins is gonna nail both our hides to his office wall."

"Maybe so," I admitted, "but I'm not going to touch anything, just look. Come on."

We headed back to Hubert's place. I pointed to a tractor track leading to the back of his barn. "There's a little side door down there. Pull as close to it as you can get."

As she came around the car to get me, I heard a scrambling inside.

"There's somebody in there," I whispered. "It's not Charlie, because his car's not here."

Her face brightened with hope. "You think it's Tad?"

"Could be. The little dickens, he could have been in this barn the whole time. Why didn't we think of that?"

"Ridd searched the place Sunday night and Buster's folks looked once, too. I guess he hid in the woods while they were here. Let me go in first." Martha abandoned me and went to the door. As she opened it to poke her head in, I heard a whinny. "Hello, Starfire," she said. "Tad? It's Aunt Martha. Where are you?" She listened, then repeated, "Tad? I know you're here." She stepped inside.

I waited for what seemed an eternity before Martha came back through the door holding Tad, defiant and filthy, by one elbow. His hair was littered with straw.

"Hey, Me-mama." His tone was sullen, and he was more interested in the tops of his shoes than in looking me in the eye.

"Hey, yourself," I told him. "Looks like you could do with a bath and a good meal."

He shuffled his feet. Before we could say anything else, we heard a car barreling down the road. Since it dead-ends into fields, it doesn't get much traffic. "I'm afraid I know who that is," Martha murmured.

Chief Muggins's cruiser roared up the drive and turned to block her car. He pulled off his sunglasses as he climbed out. "Well, well, well. What have we here?" Thumbs in his belt, he swaggered over to look Tad up and down. "I heard you were missing, boy. You been sleeping in this barn?"

"Yessir." Tad still hung his head. "A couple of nights."

"You have company?"

He hesitated, then nodded. "My mama's horse. He's still in there."

"That all?"

He jerked his head toward the door. "You can look." He still didn't look him in the eye.

Chief Muggins gave him a sharp look. "Well, it's a clear case of trespassing. We'll need to run you in and call Mr. Spence."

"Wait!" Martha and I said in unison.

"This isn't your jurisdiction," I added quickly.

Charlie had already turned to the deputy who came with him. "Cuff him, Jack, and call a sheriff's deputy to come pick him up. No need to bother Sheriff Gibbons."

He knew as well as the rest of us that Buster would never arrest Joe Riddley's grandson for sleeping in a neighbor's barn.

The deputy left off the cuffs and shoved Tad gently toward the car. Tad threw me a terrified look over his shoulder. "Don't say a word until we get a lawyer there," I called to him. "Not one word except your name."

He nodded as the car door closed behind him.

Charlie turned to me. "Now, what was it you wanted down here, Judge?"

"My grandson. He ran away after the fire, and we learned he was here." That was true — I merely neglected to mention that we'd learned it after we arrived. "My daughter-in-law's horse is still inside. May we take it on down to Ridd's?"

"Leave it for now. From what I under-stand, you all don't have a barn to keep it in." He raised his voice. "Jack, back the cruiser to let the judge out. She's leaving."

Martha took me to their house. We both needed a strong glass of iced tea. Thank

196

goodness she and Ridd had left the ramp in place at the back steps, from when Joe Riddley couldn't walk the year before. Otherwise, I'd have had to wait in the yard.

Calling Walker and Cindy to tell them to hire Tad an attorney was one of the worst calls I ever had to make. I called Walker's cell phone from the kitchen, with Martha backing me up on the den extension. He answered all elated, because they'd gotten tickets to a matinee they'd thought was sold out. They were on their way to lunch, and he sounded rushed. "Everything going all right down there?" he finally thought to ask. It went downhill from there.

First I had to explain that Tad was in jail because he'd been staying in Hubert's barn. Then I had to admit Tad had been missing for two days and we hadn't let them know. Then I had to explain that the child had burned down the barn and run away.

Walker said just before he hung up, "Not what I'd call one of our better family chats." That summed it up pretty well.

"He's probably pounding the side of a skyscraper right now," Martha said as she came back to the kitchen.

"But he's going to call a lawyer," I consoled her. "That was the important part, and he's coming home on the first available plane."

"Ridd's going to die. We've worked with

kids all our lives and never had a problem like this. Maybe Ridd was too hard on Tad about the smoking."

I touched her arm. "It's not all bad. Tad hasn't done anything illegal except spend a couple of nights in a barn, and I doubt Hubert will press charges, so Tad will get out as soon as a lawyer and judge talk it over. And maybe it will sober him a little — grow him up. If so, it may be one of the best things that could have happened to him."

She circled my neck with a hug. "I know you're just trying to make me feel better, but thanks."

I wished I could make me feel better. My ankle was throbbing, and Chief Muggins and his men were swarming all over Hubert's barn, looking for evidence that he'd killed the homeless woman who had been living there. I wondered what Tad might know, but there was no way I could find out right then. I just hoped he'd remember what I said and not tell Chief Muggins a thing until his lawyer arrived.

"Honey," I told Martha, "I need you to do me one more favor. Run me up to Hubert's store. It's real important. But can I have a glass of water before we go?" I fumbled in my pocketbook for my pain pills.

While she ran upstairs to brush her hair, I waited at our old kitchen table for the pill to kick in, but I didn't feel better. If anything, I felt worse. Heaven only knew what means

Chief Muggins would try to use on Tad before the sheriff's deputy or the lawyer arrived. And the chief would kill me if he found out I was talking to Hubert. But I had to. I could not believe Hubert had killed anybody.

Everybody knew he was a hothead, of course. When he was little, my daddy used to say, "God sure missed a good opportunity to put red hair on that child's head." But if Hubert had killed everybody he'd yelled at or poked in the chest over the years, the town would be strewn with corpses. Folks knew he had a temper, and made allowances. You make a lot of allowances in order to live in harmony in a small town.

I liked Hubert, in spite of his temper and past spotty hygiene. He could be real sweet. For instance, his hobby was growing watermelons in a patch between our house and his. We'd never bought a watermelon in our whole married lives. Every day or two all summer we'd find one on our back porch. We had even found a couple left on our new front porch. We'd never paid full price for an appliance repair, either. And when Joe Riddley was recuperating from getting shot, Hubert showed up one day with a big-screen TV for him to watch in bed and wouldn't take a penny for it.

I grabbed a tissue and swabbed my eyes. I wouldn't let anybody arrest the old buzzard if I could help it.

But I knew that any minute Chief Muggins would call to say, "Hey, Judge, I need you down at the sheriff's detention center for a probable cause hearing in this murder case. I know you can't drive, so I'll swing by and get you. You can have another ride in my fancy new car."

If I could think of any other pressing business — a sudden debilitating virus, a handsome stranger swinging by on a motorcycle to take me away in his sidecar — I would refuse. But when you get sworn in as a judge, you agree to put your personal preferences on hold and do what the law requires, so I'd probably have to let Charlie come get me and drive to the jail — which is what it is, no matter how many fancy signs they put up reading SHERIFF'S DETENTION CENTER. I would not, however, let him help me into the car.

I sniffed and mopped my eyes some more. Poor Hubert!

When we got to the jail, I wouldn't be able to stand on the box I use behind the bench. I couldn't stand at all. So I'd have to sit behind a table in my wheelchair, and poor Hubert would face a judge with bare toes sticking out of a cast under her robe and her hair sticking up in all directions, because Phyllis couldn't fit me in until after four.

My ankle would probably be throbbing again by then, too, because I wouldn't be

200

able to take any more pills if I expected Charlie to call. You can't have a judge presiding under the influence. What a dismal affair that hearing would be.

I tossed a wad of tissues into the wastebasket and grabbed some more.

Hubert would be furious, of course. He'd glare at me when I introduced myself and asked for his name and address, even though I am required to do that for the record. Maynard would come with his checkbook, expecting to sign away his house to get his daddy home for the night, and he wouldn't be real happy when I told him, "A magistrate can't set bail in a murder case. I am just here to be sure your daddy understands the charges against him. Then I'll write the superior court up in Augusta and they'll send a judge down next week to hear the case and set bail."

Hubert would splutter and squawk like Bo. "Next week? Who's gonna mind my store?" Except Hubert would use words that would make me have to threaten him with a citation for contempt unless he calmed down. Joe Riddley never tolerated swearing in court, and I don't, either. But I'd hate to cite Hubert for being Hubert.

My pain pill must finally be kicking in, because I had a happy thought. Chief Muggins might jump in and tell Hubert, "Wait until Joe Riddley hears what you've been saying to his wife," and I could threaten to cite him, too, if he spread a word of the proceedings beyond the courtroom. I could even threaten to lock him up. Maybe I ought to call Ike and ask him to lock Charlie up right now. That could solve a lot of —

That's the last thought I remember until Martha shook my shoulder. "You ready to go?"

I swam up from deep underwater. When I opened one eye, my cheek lay on the table, creased by the handle of an iced-tea spoon, and the clock over the sink had jumped half an hour. "Are you sure you don't want me to run you home?" she asked in her nurse's voice.

"No, get me to Hubert's. I can wheel myself back to the store." I hoped that was true.

Hubert's store was a lot like ours — high and dim, lit by dangling flourescent lights. The only daylight came in through plate-glass windows up front. It still had its original punched-tin ceiling and the wide unfinished floorboards his granddaddy had put in when the place was first built as Spence's General Store.

Hubert was behind his counter, ringing up a sale. When that customer left, he turned to help a young couple who looked younger than twenty and who both looked like they would jump if he said, "Boo!"

The woman murmured a soft question

about used freezers. Hubert shook his head. "Not right now. Come back later in the season and I might have one or two."

The man pointed toward a far corner. "What about that dusty old thing? I'll give you twenty-five dollars cash."

"Sorry." Hubert shook his head. "It's broken. I keep meaning to fix it, but I haven't gotten around to it. How about a new one, a little down and a little a week?"

The man and woman looked at each other and shook their heads in unison. "Not this week. Thank you," she said in a pale, tired voice.

I felt so sorry for them. They were mighty young to be weighed down by that much worry.

Hubert ushered them out the door, then came toward me with a disgusted look on his face. "Doesn't anybody want a *new* freezer this fall?" His disgust turned to malicious delight as he saw my ankle. "Boy, I'd sure like to see the other woman."

I opened my mouth to protest, but he warned, "I only got a few minutes. I'm running down to Wrens for a political meeting. What you need?"

"You're getting mighty political, all of a sudden. I guess Abigail Bullock will be there?"

"Probably. I'm driving Miss Georgia down." He rubbed his hands together. His nails, I saw, were clean. "Her husband had to go down early, and she needs a ride. We fixed it up at dinner last night."

I clearly remembered that Georgia had driven herself to Gusta's, and it seemed to me I'd seen as many Bullock cars as Bullocks in the past few days. They traveled as if afraid one of them might get abandoned somewhere with no escape. Still, Hubert's budding transportation service was not what I wanted to discuss. "I came to warn you that you're in a peck of trouble. Do you know that?"

He sat down in a customer chair and slapped both palms against his thighs. "I'm not in any trouble. I haven't done a thing. In fact, the only trouble I had has been taken care of."

"Not by you, I presume?" When he didn't reply, I said, "I guess you've talked to Chief Muggins today."

"Yep, he dropped by earlier to say that the bum who's been living in my barn got hisself killed last night. No skin off my nose."

"It was more than skin off my nose. I found him and sprained my ankle." I held out my cast. "Chief Muggins asked me what you meant last night when you told me to forget the situation down at your barn, that you'd take care of it yourself. I said I didn't know."

When Hubert didn't enlighten me, I added,

"I found myself wondering, though."

He huffed. "Okay, nosy. I meant that I'd bought a padlock. I'm going down on my way to Wrens to put it on the back door to the barn even though all the bums are gone." He glared from under bushy brows. "I understand Tad's been camping out down there, too. I don't want every Tom, Dick, and Harry in the county living in that barn."

"Don't be too hard on Tad," I begged.

He smoothed back his hair. "Hadn't planned to. I already told Buster I don't aim to press charges. And I plan to tell Ridd he can leave the horse there until Walker can make other arrangements. But I am gonna put on a padlock and give him the key. I don't want folks sleeping in my barn."

"That's fair. Did Chief Muggins ask where you were last evening?"

"He did, and I told him — at the same meeting you were. Lots of people know that."

"Did he ask about one of your matchbooks lying near the body?"

"Yep. I told him how it might have gotten there, too. He strutted and huffed a bit, but if you played poker with Charlie, you'd know that the worse his cards, the bigger his bluff."

"He might not be bluffing this time. How did that matchbook get there?"

"Not that it's any of your business, but I went for a little walk before the meeting and must have dropped it. I told you, I keep a pocketful. Besides, I have a witness." He smoothed back his hair and preened a little. "Miss Georgia was with me."

"Not Abigail?" No wonder Binky had looked sad last night. She wasn't even a glimmer next to her shining big sister.

"No, she had to wash her hair, and Miss Georgia said she'd like some fresh air."

"So you took her down to the water tank? It's not exactly one of the attractions in our Chamber of Commerce brochure."

He gave me a smug little smile. "We weren't paying much attention where we were going, to tell you the truth. We were talking. Georgia is a highly intelligent woman, knowledgeable on a wide range of topics."

By which I figured she had let him do most of the talking.

"We wandered down by the tracks, and when we got near the tank, she said she hadn't been that close to one before. I told her I hadn't been near it myself since —" He had a sudden fit of coughing.

I glared. "Was it you who climbed that tank in high school and painted Joe Riddley's and my initials up there with a heart around them?"

He shrugged. "It's been so long, I forget." A smile flickered at one corner of his mouth.

"I ought to call Chief Muggins right now and tell him to lock you up. You old reprobate. You know good and well the only reason I've put up with you all these years is because I liked your wife and felt sorry for Maynard." I calmed down enough to add, "I can't believe you made Georgia climb through that hedge, though."

"She didn't mind," he insisted. "That woman is game for anything. But she didn't get scratched. I held the branches back for her."

Once again I wondered if Gusta and Pooh were conducting manners classes, but I didn't want to discourage progress by commenting on it. I said, "And you were smoking again?"

"I been smoking again ever since they started building that superstore. It's gonna shut me down, Mac. Folks already take the interstate up to Augusta to buy their big appliances. I can't compete with chain-store prices. I only sell to those few folks who don't have a truck and want something delivered, or to folks who need something right away. What's keeping me open right now is repair work and sales of little stuff — televisions, radios, music equipment, stuff like that. Once the superstore opens and undersells me on that, what am I gonna do?" He looked around the store like he was watching all his stock go up in smoke.

"Retire," I suggested. "Maynard doesn't want or need the store, so you don't have to pass it along. Hold an enormous sale, rent out the building, and grow watermelons. I'll bet you could grow one big enough and sweet enough to win a prize at the county fair." When he brightened a bit, I teased, "You could travel, too — like up to Atlanta to visit the Bullocks. We don't have to work until we die, Hubert, just because our parents did."

He didn't say he would retire, but he reached over and gave my hand a little pat.

We were having a good old time until I went and spoiled it. "What about after the meeting last night? Where were you then?"

He snickered. "Ask Joe Riddley."

"He said some fellows took Burlin Bullock out, and the two of you tried to drink each other under the table."

He slewed his eyes my way. "I could have beat him, too, but I decided to quit. Didn't want to embarrass a guest."

"That's not the way I heard it. And it sounds to me like there's some time unaccounted for between the time you dropped Burlin off to change clothes and the time you went back to pick him up. The reason I'm here right now — and Chief Muggins will have my hide if he finds out I came — is to warn you that he's gonna want a pretty careful description of your actions during that period. If you can find any witnesses to where you were, line them up."

"I was closing up the building. That takes a while."

"Not half an hour. Where else did you go?"

I expected him to say he'd dropped by his house for something. Instead, he jumped to his feet, his eyes turned pink, and he lapsed into the countrified talk he grew up with — a sure sign he was getting his dander up. "I was takin' care of bidness, that's where I was. Nobody saw me, and I didn't see them." He stood up and shook his finger at me. "You've always been a meddler, MacLaren, and I'm sick and tired of it. You stick to your bidness, and I'll stick to mine. Now, I've got to go pick up Miss Georgia. You can wheel your own meddling self home."

"He wouldn't kill anybody," I assured myself as I rolled out onto the sidewalk and down to the corner, where the city fathers had finally obeyed the disabilities act and created an accessible curb.

"Not on purpose," myself agreed.

But that said it all. What if Hubert had run into the vagrant and his temper got out of hand? I hadn't thought to ask Chief Muggins if the woman had been killed under the tank or somewhere else and brought there.

Something else bothered me. Hubert wasn't usually much of a drinker. Why had he drunk so much last night?

I could think of only one way to distract Chief Muggins from Hubert.

I called him as soon as I got back to the

office. "I've remembered something that might be of use to your investigation. That vagrant had been stalking Lance Bullock — or at least following his campaign. Maybe somebody at one of the places where Lance has spoken recently will know who she was."

I thought of the call as a diversion tactic.

It turned out to be a bomb.

14

Have I failed to tell you that Chief Charlie Muggins thrives on publicity? Normally, his scope is limited to the *Statesman*, but he never resists a chance to branch out.

As soon as he hung up from my call, he went in search of the reporters who'd been hanging around the Bullocks. At Hardee's, he ran into a tenacious young newspaperwoman with a reputation for digging dirt from under any rock. He told her that the dead woman had been stalking the Bullocks and asked if she'd noticed the woman in the crowds. She asked, "Have you checked her fingerprints in the system?"

He hadn't, of course. Chief Muggins didn't consider a homeless person worth bothering about. But she told him, "You do that and I'll call some of my contacts around the state. This may be very important." Between them, she and Charlie would eventually create an uproar.

I didn't know any of that at the time, of course.

When Joe Riddley picked me up at noon to take me home for dinner, thunder was rumbling in the distance and I was plumb worn out. I told him as we drove home, "I think I'll stay home and rest this afternoon. I'm even going to call Phyllis and cancel my appointment. It's been a hard day, between finding the body, finding Tad —"

He slammed on the brakes so hard it's a wonder my air bag didn't pop out and smother me. "You found Tad? Why the Sam Hill didn't you let me know?"

"I guess I forgot." I filled him in on Martha's and my discovery and Charlie's absurd overreaction without wasting time explaining why Martha and I went to the barn in the first place. I finished, "Then Martha and I had to call Walker and Cindy, then I went to talk to Hubert —"

"Dangnabit, Little Bit, you leave Hubert to Charlie. I've told you and told you, I don't want you meddling in stuff like this. Where is the boy?"

"Down at the juvenile detention center, thanks to Chief Muggins. But Hubert says he's not pressing charges."

"Tad ought to have somebody with him. I'm gonna leave you at the door and run down there. I'll pick up a bite on my way back to work."

Clarinda and I discovered that the wheelchair wouldn't maneuver in our house without serious rearrangement of furniture, so I was back to crutches and hopping on one foot. My left leg got so trembly that she called Martha and told her, "Bring that walker Joe Riddley used while he was learning to walk again. We got another patient here who needs it." Martha had a meeting at church that afternoon, but said she'd run it down later.

Before Clarinda left at two, she turned back at the door to say, "You get you a good nap so we can start in on those guest room boxes tomorrow."

I stretched out on our bed, but I couldn't sleep. The thunder boomed closer and closer, like the approach of doom. When I closed my eyes, I saw that poor woman under the water tank; then I saw Hubert in his store, red and furious. Where could he have been that he didn't want to talk about? Had he started having those bathroom accidents that happen to some older men and needed to change his clothes? Had he needed to take medication and forgotten to bring it to dinner? Hubert always acted like taking medicine was equivalent to wearing a pink tutu.

I wondered who the dead woman was and why she'd been following the Bullocks around. She looked too old to be a groupie, too unsettled to have a voting registration card. I got to thinking about how she had once been a cute little kid with dreams and hopes, and wondered how she had wandered so far from whatever she could have become. As I stared at the low ceiling over my bed, I began to see a whole parade of people who never developed their potential. Which of them might have found the cure for cancer or come up with a workable solution to the Middle East crisis, if they'd blossomed like they should have? And was it their own fault they didn't, or something lacking in the rest of us?

A crash outside my window brought me bolt upright. I hadn't lived through a bad storm in that house yet, and we had two tall pines in our backyard. Pines are real brittle. If one of those fell, it would take our bedroom with it.

I obviously wasn't going to sleep. I might as well get up. To perk up my spirits, I combed my hair and put on a muumuu Walker and Cindy brought me from Hawaii — a flowing, flamboyant floor-length garment bright with tropical flowers and butterflies. They'd even brought gold slippers to go with it. I slid on the left one and hopped into the hall to admire myself in the full-length mirror Joe Riddley had attached to the linen closet door. "You look like a Hawaiian queen," I told my reflection.

Make that a hopping queen. I barely made it to the living room couch before I collapsed. I sure would have respect for anybody I saw on crutches after this.

Oddly enough, once I lay down on the couch, I got drowsy. The sky was so dark it

214

felt like early evening. The thunder now sounded like a friendly rumble. It surrounded the dim room like a cocoon. I closed the blinds over the couch. Then, wrapped in the afghan Mama made her last year on this earth, I fell fast asleep.

The doorbell woke me. Only half-awake, I yelled, "I can't get to the door. Come on in." We don't lock doors in the daytime.

I should have. I looked over my shoulder to see Burlin, holding a bouquet of autumn flowers in a yellow vase. Lightning backlit him in the open doorway. "You ought to lock that door. For all you knew, I could have been the Hopemore killer. And why are you in the dark?"

I yawned and blinked, trying to waken, then pushed myself upright. "You caught me dozing." I checked my watch. It was after three, so I'd slept an hour. I sure was glad I had on more than my bathrobe, and hoped my hair wasn't a mess. I refused to let my hands check, though. Who was I trying to impress?

"I came to bring you these." He carried the flowers over to the dining room table. "There. Is that okay?" He turned on the dining room light so I could see them.

"They're beautiful, but I wish you hadn't done that."

"I didn't. They're from Georgia and Abigail." He straightened the vase a little, and I

215

recalled that he liked things neat and tidy. He said, "Hubert Spence told us about the murder down in Wrens at a lunch meeting, but he didn't say it was you who found the body. We heard that after we got back from Dublin, and Georgia said, 'That poor thing. Go order her some flowers, Burlin, from all of us.' I'm just the delivery boy."

"The florist delivers," I pointed out.

He bit one thumb and grinned like a little boy. "I know. I asked if I could bring them. I took them by your office, but they said you were at home, so I hurried over to beat the storm." He paused, then added, "That's a real fetching caftan."

I was disgusted to find myself flushing. *It's not your ankle that's out of whack*, I told myself sharply, *it's your head.*

I must have frowned, because Burlin looked down at me in concern. "Are you doing all right? It must have been real traumatic, finding him."

Either Charlie wasn't releasing the news that the victim was a woman, or the Bullocks had limited access to the Hopemore grapevine.

"It was pretty traumatic, but that's not why I'm home." I lifted my hem enough to show off my cast. "I sprained my ankle."

His eyebrows came together in concern. "Does it hurt?"

"Only when the pain pills wear off or I try to walk. I'm not real graceful on crutches. I

216

thought you could be my son or daughter-in-law, bringing me a walker."

"That would have been more practical than flowers." He looked around. "Isn't anybody here to help you?"

"No, the cook leaves at two." All of a sudden the house felt very empty.

He must have felt it, too, because he headed for the door. "I just wanted to bring the flowers." He opened the door.

A tremendous flash lit the room. Thunder boomed. The skies opened and rain streamed down. Burlin peered out. "Looks like the good Lord's tipped over his rain barrel."

I resigned myself to the inevitable. "You may as well stay awhile. There's no need to get soaked."

He shut the door so promptly, I had a suspicion he'd timed his arrival to coincide with the downpour. "Put your feet up again. I'll sit here." He moved a chair so I could look at him without turning my head. Then he switched on a lamp, turned off the dining room light, took his seat, stretched his feet out in front of him and folded his arms like he was planting himself permanently.

"It sure is peaceful in here," he said when I hadn't said anything else. "Between the murder and the coming storm, everybody over at our place has gone nuts. Binky and Georgia had some kind of tiff, and Binky went to bed with a migraine. Georgia is like a self-rewinding tape" — he changed his voice to sound like a mechanical female, uttering one syllable at a time with no inflection whatsoever — "We ought not to stay here. It's not good for Lance's campaign to be in the middle of a murder investigation. We ought to move on. We ought not to stay here."

He was so funny, I chuckled in spite of myself. He joined me, then said, "She never says that when we're campaigning in Atlanta —" He stopped, leaving the sentence open.

"— where there's always a murder investigation going on." I wished I hadn't done that. Pausing to let me finish his sentences was a game he'd liked to play when we were dating.

"We're still on the same wavelength. I thought so," he said with satisfaction.

"Not often," I told him. "Where are Lance and Renée?"

"Lance is broody as a hen. I can't get two words out of him. And Renée — I think the woman has sleeping sickness. She naps every chance she gets."

"What about Edward?"

He grimaced. "One can get too much of Edward."

"You could always go talk to the buffalo."

"Not today. He's been impounded until Lance's lawyer and the driver of that Toyota come to some agreement." He gave me a

218

slight frown — I suppose to show I was supposed to do something about that. When I ignored it, he sighed. "I tell you, on days like this, I could give up politics. Lance is supposed to speak at a barbeque tonight in a park, but with all this rain, there won't be anybody there, and we'll all be huddled under a tree. I sure wish I had a cozy home —"

He saw the expression on my face and changed direction. "So how can I cheer you up? Want me to sing? Dance?" He held up both hands and shuffled his feet, then suggested, "Or shall I just sit here and keep you company, in case you want something?"

He sounded lonesome. And it wasn't his fault I'd been in love with Joe Riddley when we met. I could at least be nice to him while we sat out the storm. "Fix us both a glass of tea. There's some in the refrigerator. I'd get it, but I can't carry anything with these danged crutches."

Only when he rose and headed to obey did I remember that I was ordering around a former congressman. Oh, well, it was probably good for his soul.

"Where are the glasses?" he called from the kitchen.

"Your guess is as good as mine. We've lived here just a few weeks, and our cook is still letting things settle in where they feel at home."

He laughed. "We had a cook like that,

once." I heard cabinet doors bang, followed by a deafening crash of thunder. "That was a divine 'Voila!' I found them." Ice tumbled into glasses; then I heard him open the refrigerator. "Lemon?"

"Please."

He returned carrying two glasses of tea with a plate of peanut oatmeal cookies balanced on one. "I saw these in the jar, and they looked great." He picked up three, took a bite, and said with his mouth full, "I love cookies. My wife used to bake, but nobody does since she left. Smack my hand, though, if I reach for more. I could easily eat them all."

Clarinda's peanut oatmeal cookies have broken more ice than was between Burlin and me at that point. After all, we never did have trouble finding things to talk about. Besides, I would have found even Chief Muggins a welcome visitor with the light and noise show outside and rain drumming away like a boy with nervous fingers.

I couldn't believe it when Lulu started to bark and I heard the electric garage door going up. "It must be after five. Joe Riddley's home."

I was merely stating a fact, but he grinned. "Shall I run out the door, or hide in a closet?"

"That's not funny, you know."

He looked at his watch. "Actually, I do

have to go. We're supposed to be leaving for Augusta in ten minutes. I'm getting as bad as Renée — she has no sense of time."

He was heading for the door when Bo called, "Hello, hello, hello," and Joe Riddley greeted Lulu in the kitchen, "Hello, girl. I reckon we'll have to fix supper. That no-count wife of mine has paid off a doctor to say she has to lie around for a week."

"We're in here," I called. He could see me, but not Burlin.

When he did, he paused for a minute, then pulled off his red cap and shot out a hand. "Hello. What brings you to these parts?"

Burlin shook his hand and backed again toward the door. "I ran by to bring your wife some flowers from my sisters." He nodded toward the bouquet, then said to me, "I need to get right back, because we're due to leave for Augusta. I hope you feel better soon."

"Thank Georgia and Binky for the flowers."

"I will. Oh, good." He peered at the sky. "The rain's let up some." He hurried out into a light drizzle.

Joe Riddley sank into the chair Burlin had vacated. "Whew. It's been hectic down at the nursery. Everything was flooding." He wrinkled his forehead. "This chair is warm."

"Burlin stayed a few minutes."

"Must have been more than a few minutes, to warm it up like this. You watch him, Little

Bit. He's nice enough, but those politicians like to get their names in the paper, and they don't care whose name appears with them." He looked at the flowers, then back at me. "You get all dressed up after he got here?"

"No, I put this on for a nap. It's a muumuu Walker and Cindy brought from Hawaii. Or maybe it's a caftan. I didn't know he was coming."

"Oh." He sat and twiddled his hat between his hands. So far we hadn't gotten around to putting up a hook by the kitchen door, like he'd had in the old house, and he never knew what to do with the cap when he got home. I kept losing my pocketbook, too. There wasn't a handy regular spot for it on our new kitchen counters. Maybe I'd work on that this week. We'd feel more settled if we knew we had regular places for those two items. They are so much a part of us that our sons keep threatening to bury them with us.

"How's Tad?" I asked.

"He's back at Ridd's, and Ridd called Walker and Cindy and told them to go ahead and stay in New York, since everything's under control."

"But Tad's all right?"

"Hissing and spitting like a feral kitten. Keeps trying to explain what happened and whining that it wasn't really his fault. He nearly bit Cricket's head off for asking if he'd

222

had fun camping without him." Joe Riddley slapped his cap against his thigh. "He doesn't have a clue how to own up to something, say 'I'm sorry,' and get on with his life."

"It's no wonder. Walker and Cindy spend more time explaining behavior and discussing it than correcting it. Which means that their kids don't learn they can be wrong and still loved. We really do need to be more involved in those children's lives, honey."

He stood up and headed for the kitchen. Over his shoulder, he shot back, "That's what I figured you'd say, so I told Ridd to pack up Tad's things and bring him here for the next couple of days. Since you're going to be laid up anyway, he can keep you company."

It took me a minute to get my breath back to respond. "You have wished an angry ten-year-old on me the week I have taxes to do? Come back in here where I can throw something at you."

He peered around the door. "Which is more important, Tad or taxes? I can't talk anymore, I need to feed Bo."

"Title that picture 'Cowardly Rat Feeding Bird.'"

15

"When does our guest arrive?" I demanded when he'd finally stopped making an unnecessary racket in the kitchen. "And who is going to make his bed? Or even find the bed? The guest room is full of boxes."

"He can climb over them." Joe Riddley slammed a cupboard door and opened the refrigerator. "And he can make his own bed. Ridd said he'd bring him after supper. Now stop bothering me, so I can fix ours."

Mama said a wife should always teach her husband to cook so he doesn't have to stop on his way home from your funeral to get himself another wife. Joe Riddley did a real good job with grilled-cheese sandwiches that night. He was trying to avoid talking to me, so he paid close attention to the griddle and didn't burn either side.

Ridd brought Tad by around seven thirty. The boy came in with the enthusiasm of General Lee on his way to Appomattox to surrender. He dragged his heavy athletic shoes so badly that Joe Riddley told him, "Pick up your feet. We don't want a rut in the rug." He put an arm around Tad's shoulders to let him know he was kidding, but Tad pulled away.

Ridd set down a small canvas bag. "We didn't bring all his stuff, just enough for a couple of nights. When he's ready to come on back down to our place, call and we'll come get him."

From the look Tad slid in his direction, we would wait for that moment a long time. Ridd clapped him gently on the arm. "Have fun." Anybody could see that Tad expected to spend the next two days on bread and water.

After Ridd left, Joe Riddley pointed to me on the couch. "Your me-mama is laid up with a sprained ankle, so it's up to us to make your bed. Come on." The two of them headed down the hall. Cricket and his Pop would have laughed and cut up until Cricket collapsed with a fit of the giggles. I didn't hear a sound until Joe Riddley came back, looking disgusted. "He says he'll watch television in his room."

"Tell him I need him to keep me company. Then you go down to the Bi-Lo and get us some lime sherbet. That's his favorite."

He shrugged. "There are better ways to waste money, but I'll go."

Tad sidled in and sat uneasily on the chair that had already held Burlin and Joe Riddley. I could get used to reclining like Cleopatra and letting menfolk pay me court. "Pop's gone to the store a minute. Before he gets back, I want to talk to you, because I need you to do a couple of things for me without telling Pop or Uncle Ridd." I've found that two ways to get somebody out of a shell is to ask them to do you a favor or let them in on a secret.

Tad gave me a listless one-shoulder shrug. "What do you need?"

"You're pretty good with animals, right?"

Interest flickered behind his dark eyes, but his voice was uncertain. "Yes, ma'am. Maybe. A little."

"I want you to teach Bo some new words. He is driving me up a wall. Most of what Hiram Blaine taught him to say is rude, and I'm sick of having him squawk 'sic 'em' or 'back off and give me space' all day. He could use a bigger vocabulary."

A little smile flitted across Tad's face. "He says 'Little Bit!' just like Pop."

I nodded. "Yeah, like he's fussing at me. But I wish he could say something like 'How're you doing, MacLaren?' or 'Here comes Joe Riddley' or even 'Bo wants a cracker.' "

"He doesn't eat crackers."

" 'Bo wants peanuts,' then — I don't care what. The point is, will you try to teach him?"

One slender shoulder rose in a shrug. "Yes, ma'am. I'll try."

"Good, but don't tell Pop. It will be our secret."

He turned his head and looked at me from the corners of his eyes. "What was the other thing?" He obviously thought I had a list of dreadful chores on the tip of my tongue, like Cinderella's wicked stepmother.

"I want you to tell me about the person who was staying in the barn with you."

He pressed back into his chair and didn't say a word. I gave him a sharp look. "Did you promise not to say anybody was there?"

He didn't move a muscle.

"Did you know it was a woman?"

He shifted slightly in his chair. I hated to be the one to tell him, but he'd find out eventually. "You don't have to keep her secret anymore, honey. Lulu and I found her down at the water tank this morning. She's dead."

His face turned so white his eyes looked black. "She can't be dead! She wasn't sick."

I might as well give him the whole story. "Somebody hit her on the head with a pipe."

"No!" He leaped from his chair, fists clenched. "Nobody would do that. She didn't hurt anybody."

"I don't think she hurt anybody, either," I reassured him. "I met her only once, but she seemed friendly and happy. Did she help you hide out?"

He hesitated, then nodded. "Yes, ma'am."

"How did she help?" It was like picking meat out of black walnuts, one chunk at a time.

"She gave me some food. And she shared hay to sleep on. Mr. Spence left just two bales. I needed one for Starfire." He sounded resentful. Hubert had obviously failed to do his duty by the vagrants of the world. "And she kept a lookout while I moved Starfire to the pasture to eat, and she helped me rub him down. She said she used to have a horse." He stopped, then burst out, "She can't be dead. She can't!" He pounded his thigh with one fist.

I spoke as cautiously as I'd approach butterflies on a buddleia. "I'm glad it makes you sad, hon. It makes me sad, too. And mad. I want to try and find out who killed her. Will you help me?"

He kicked the rug. "I can't help. I'm just a kid. Besides, Daddy and Pop don't like you messing with stuff like that. Uncle Ridd, neither."

I gave an impatient huff. "I can't do much messing stuck on this couch. All I can do is think. But to even do that, I need your help. You're a smart kid. And you knew her — maybe better than anybody in town. I want you to tell me what she was like — things she said, anything you can remember about her."

"Did Mr. Spence kill her?"

It chilled me to hear him ask the question that matter-of-factly. Has our world so exposed children to violence that they take it for

228

granted people they know can kill? "Why would you think that?"

"He didn't want her there. She wasn't hurting anything, but he — he —" He lifted his dark eyes to mine and stammered with indignation. "He — he came down yesterday morning and caught her carrying our garbage to the woods to bury it. She buried the *garbage*, Me-mama. She didn't mess his place up! But he yelled at her — real loud. Told her to 'Git!' and 'Git off my propity'" — Tad's accent was a fair imitation of Hubert's — "until she ran away."

I felt real discouraged. If Tad hadn't seen her since Monday morning, we were at a dead end. "So she never came back?" I prompted, when he didn't say anything more.

"Oh, yes, ma'am, she came back. She just went over to the pond and waited for him to leave. She liked the pond. She stayed over there with Starfire a lot. She said it was a real peaceful place." He sat back down and sighed. "Nobody ought to have killed her."

"Did she tell you her name, where she was from?"

"She said to call her Bertie, but the way she said it, I don't think it was her name. And she said she'd call me Son, so if the police came looking for me, she could say she didn't know anybody by that name." He sighed. "She talked funny sometimes and didn't make sense, and she muttered a lot, but she liked whistling at birds and talking to squirrels, and she hummed a lot. She didn't hurt anybody. If I'd had a barn, she could have lived there forever and ever!" Tears filled his eyes and spilled out onto his cheeks. He swiped at them angrily.

"Here." I held out a box of tissues I keep by the couch. He snatched the whole box, then clutched it to him and backed into his chair again like it was the only safe haven in the world.

My own eyes stung. "If I'd had a barn, she could have lived there, too," I said softly. "Bring me a tissue, too, please." We sat and cried together, but I didn't know if I was crying because Bertie had died or because Tad defended her so valiantly.

He sat with his head bowed, tears dripping onto the box, for several minutes. Then he gave a big sniff, blew his nose, wadded his tissue, and left it carelessly on the table beside his chair.

"There's a perfectly good wastebasket at your feet," I pointed out. "When was the last time you saw her?"

He dropped in the tissue and muttered, "After supper last night. She went to Myrtle's and brought us something back. Just cold meatloaf and green beans" — his face twisted in distaste — "but she said beggars can't be choosers. Then she told me she had to go meet somebody, and she'd be back. But she never came." His voice dwindled, and his eyes looked far away. Was he remembering sitting in the dark with his horse, waiting for a companion who never returned?

He scrubbed one cheek with his fist, and his voice was angry. "She should have known better than to go wandering around town alone at night. Did somebody rob her?"

"What could they have robbed her of?"

He shrugged. "Not much. She just had an old knapsack with some stuff in it — a dirty hairbrush, a few clothes, a couple of pictures, stuff like that. And a battered guitar. Didn't you see them?"

"They were there. Do you know who she was going to meet?"

He shook his head. "No, ma'am, but she wrote them a letter."

"How do you know?"

Suddenly he was busy examining the back of one hand.

"I need to know, Tad."

He sighed. "When she got back yesterday morning, she asked if I had any paper. I told her I didn't, but she kept saying, 'A piece of paper. One little piece of paper.' She kept looking all over the barn, too, like she thought Mr. Spence might have kept paper there. Finally, I told her I'd get her some. Seemed like I ought to do something for her, since she'd done stuff for me. She told me to get an envelope while I was at it, so we went down to Uncle Ridd's —"

"Nobody saw you?" I knew the answer, of course, before he replied.

"Aunt Martha's car was gone, so I guess she was working. Everybody else was at school. We didn't take anything except a pen and some paper and an envelope from the desk in the den. And" — he turned pink and looked down at his hands — "and we made us some lunch. She washed everything real good, so nobody would know."

"Ridd and Martha would never begrudge you something to eat," I assured him. "But I wish you'd left a note saying you were okay. We'd have all slept easier."

He scuffed his feet on the rug. "I was in a hurry, in case Aunt Martha had just gone to the store, or something."

"When you got back to the barn, she wrote a letter?"

"Yes, ma'am. Then she said she had to go somewhere and went up the road."

"Do you know whether she mailed it or delivered it?"

"She didn't have a stamp." His tone implied that I ought to have known that, since he'd already told me. Then his voice changed and became thoughtful. "But when she got back with supper and I asked if she'd delivered it, she laughed and said she'd given it to the mailman with the purple truck. I don't know but one purple truck, Me-mama, do

232

you? And it doesn't belong to a mailman. It belongs to that stinking old nut who thinks somebody buried treasure on his farm."

"Hector Blaine's not that old," I corrected him. He was a good bit younger than me. "But you're right that he stinks, and he does think the Confederate treasury is buried on his property. That isn't utterly far-fetched. A lot of folks think it's buried around here somewhere. It got this far at the end of the War, and there's no indication it ever left. Hector's convinced it's buried on his land. However," I remembered to add, "I doubt your mama wants you calling any grown-up a stinking nut."

Tad slewed his eyes my way. "That's what Daddy calls him."

"That's not my fault. I did all I could to raise your daddy right. When you're with me, I'd rather you called Mr. Blaine a confused man."

"Yes, ma'am. Is he nuts — I mean, confused enough to kill somebody?"

I thought that over. "He's devious and mean," I said, feeling my way as I went, "and he's done time for various things. But if Bertie called him a postman, it sounds like she didn't write him the note. I wonder why she gave it to him to deliver?"

"She musta known him. He dropped her off after dark on Sunday."

It wasn't surprising that Bertie would meet

up with Hector. He was one step up from homeless himself, an unsavory old codger who never worked for a meal he could get for free. I filed that information for future reference and asked, "What happened after supper last night?"

"She said she had to go out again and it might be late before she got back, but I didn't need to worry." His eyes went blank. Was he thinking now that indeed, he had needed to worry? He must have worried as he waited in that dark barn alone all night.

"And you have no idea who she wrote?"

"No, ma'am. She went out under a tree to do it. But she put a picture in it," he remembered. "She came back and got it out of her knapsack. When she finished, she licked the envelope and put it in her pocket." Sadness slumped his thin shoulders. "Whoever she wrote is probably who killed her." He was resigned now. His sadness trailed out in two sentences I wished we could put on her tombstone: "She never hurt a single soul. She just liked being free."

"Did she tell you why she dressed like a man?"

"Yes, ma'am. She said it was so people would leave her alone. You know how people are, always saying you have to take care of girls — even if girls sometimes beat up their little brothers or play like they're gonna drown their cousins." He spoke darkly, from personal experience. Then he heaved a sigh from the toes of his heavy shoes. "I guess she didn't want people taking care of her. No-body should have killed her, either. She wasn't hurting anybody."

Seeking to distract him again, I said, "After she left, when you were by yourself at the barn, it must have been pretty lonely."

"That night it was," he admitted, "but today I was mostly hungry. And I wasn't by myself very much. Mr. White showed a lady the house, then you and Aunt Martha came." White's Realty was handling Hubert's prop-erty and the White family lived down the street from Walker and Cindy. "I nearly got caught, but I didn't." I was glad to see color returning to his face. "I had taken Starfire up to the pasture to eat, like I always did in the morning" — to hear him talk you'd think he'd lived in that barn for months — "and I was coming back to clean out his stall when they turned in. I shinnied up a tree so they wouldn't see me, and it sure was good I wasn't in the barn, because she wanted to see it. She said she wants to get a horse." He looked anxious again. "Mr. Spence said Uncle Ridd can keep Starfire in his barn until they get theirs rebuilt, but you reckon he'll be all right without me?"

"He'll adjust," I promised, without a clue about whether horses adjusted or not. "Do you think the woman and Mr. White noticed

235

you all had been there?"

"I don't know. I'd buried our garbage from last night, but I hadn't swept the manure out of Starfire's stall." Sounded like Tad had been learning new habits while he was away.

Lulu raised her head from down near my feet and uttered a sharp bark, then jumped from the couch and ran to welcome Joe Riddley. "Go help Pop carry the groceries in," I told Tad. "I wouldn't be surprised if he doesn't have some lime sherbet in his bag. But don't you tell him what we've been discussing, now."

"I won't." Tad jumped up to obey, looking a lot more his old self. He came back in a minute, carrying a bowl of green sherbet and a box. "This is for you. Pop's getting ours now. But look what he bought me." He held out a paint-by-number kit, showing a brown horse. "If I change the colors to black and gray, it will look just like Starfire." As soon as I took my sherbet, he started tearing off the plastic wrap. "Mama will just love this picture."

He carried the box to the dining room table. "Be sure you put newspaper under that," I reminded him. "It didn't matter down at the other place — that old kitchen table has been beat up and painted on for over a hundred years. But now that we've only got this new one, I want to keep it nice as long as possible."

Tad spread out paper and started painting. His tongue stuck out of one corner of his mouth as he concentrated. His granddaddy leaned over his shoulder and said, "Why, you are a real good artist, son." He set a bowl of sherbet down on the table where Tad could reach it.

"I like to paint." Tad set down his brush and moved the sherbet bowl to the newspaper. "But don't mess up this table, Pop. Me-mama will kill us both."

How frequently do we say that when we don't mean it? But somebody killed the homeless woman named Bertie. Was it Hubert? Hector? Another vagrant who had staked out the water tank as his own private patch?

First thing the next morning, as much as the prospect pained me, I needed to talk to Hector Blaine.

16

Hector Blaine was the last of a notorious family. His granddaddy made enough running a still during Prohibition to buy a little farm, but his daddy, deprived of the still by the federal government, refused to stoop to farming, so his family lived mostly on what his wife made teaching. After she died, nobody knew how they survived. Hector's brother Hiram, a disciple of Amos Pickens, earned a stint in state prison for trying to add vinegar to the town water supply to repel aliens from Venus. Hector had done several stretches for assault and robbery. I didn't want him coming to our house. He hadn't bathed in recent memory, and took far too literally that what was mine was his. Anything he couldn't wheedle out of you, he felt free to come back when you weren't home to "borrow."

But even if Hector wasn't one of my favorite people, I felt sure I could get information from him one way or the other. So I asked Tad at breakfast Wednesday, "How about if you come to the office with me until its time to go to school?" I might need him to prime Hector's memory.

He turned to his granddaddy. "You got games on your computer, Pop?"

"I don't know, but I reckon you'll know how to figure that out," Joe Riddley told him.

"You and who else?" Bo demanded from his place mat.

I gave Tad what I hoped was a significant look. He handed Bo a piece of apple on one finger. "Bo wants some apple," he said softly. "Bo wants some apple. Bo wants some apple."

Bo flapped his wings and squawked. "Back off. Give me space!" Tad laughed and Joe Riddley and I exchanged a happy smile. We hadn't heard that sound for a while.

As soon as Joe Riddley dropped us at the office, Tad slung himself into his granddaddy's chair and started pounding the computer keyboard. I was afraid he was deleting our entire inventory, but in a few minutes he had a game up and running. "I don't have this one," he said with satisfaction.

I called Phyllis to make sure I could get my hair fixed at ten, then sat at my desk wondering how to find Hector when I couldn't drive down to his place. Tad finished his game and turned. "I won. Why aren't you working?"

"I'm trying to figure out how to get Hector Blaine over here."

"Call and tell him to come. I mean, you're

a judge and everything."

I didn't want to lower Tad's opinion of judges. "He doesn't have a phone."

"He must be plumb poor, then." Was that sympathy I heard in his voice? Two nights in a barn with a homeless woman might have been good for the child, but I didn't want him wasting newfound compassion on Hector.

"Plumb no-count," I answered bluntly. "He had a phone, but the company turned it off when they found out Hector had wired three other houses into his line and was charging them so he'd have money to buy liquor. Hector's smart, but dishonest as they come. He's probably hanging out down at Hardee's right now, trying to wheedle breakfast out of some gullible tourist."

"Want me to go look?"

"You are my pride and joy. If he's there, tell him the Judge wants to see him today."

While Tad was gone, I decided to make my maiden voyage to the bathroom in the wheelchair. Thank goodness, Joe Riddley's parents had made all the doors in the place wheelchair accessible years ago. They'd done it from compassion, not compulsion, but it turned out a blessing for themselves after J.R.'s accident.

"You think you're doing this for somebody else," he'd told us the first day he wheeled himself in in his chair. "You never imagine you're doing it for yourself. But accidents happen to anybody."

As I wheeled myself through our office door and back to the ladies' room, I reflected that if builders remembered that, there wouldn't be a narrow door in the world.

Coming back, I smelled Hector before I saw him. The air outside my office reeked of stale clothes, an unwashed body, cheap wine, and chewing tobacco.

He lounged in the wing chair, turning a filthy felt hat around and around in hands so grimy, I declined to shake. Tad perched unhappily on his grandfather's desk chair. When he saw me, he turned so Hector couldn't see him and screwed up his face in a *yuck* position.

"Tad, why don't you swap chairs with Mr. Blaine?" I suggested. "Pop's chair is bigger, and Mr. Blaine would be more comfortable in it." He'd also be less likely to leave permanent stains and odors on leather than on my new slipcover. And being nearer the air-conditioning vent, Tad could resume breathing.

I got myself into my own chair while they were making the change. Tad bent to help lift my cast onto its potting-soil cushion on top of the upturned bucket.

"What happened to you?" Hector wiped a dribble from the corner of his mouth, and I saw a suspect lump in one cheek.

"I sprained my ankle. You'd better not spit on my floor."

"Wouldn't think of it." He pulled a can from his jacket pocket and spat in that. Then he jerked his head toward Tad. "That youngun said you wanted to see me." He sounded surprised. Generally I tried to avoid him.

"I do. Would you like a co-cola?"

He narrowed his eyes and peered at me like he thought somebody had abducted the real Judge Yarbrough and left a nicer changeling in her place. "Reckon I do," he finally allowed, " 'Less'n you got somethin' stronger." He spat again.

"Coke's all I've got. Tad?"

Tad stirred, but before he could start for the cup in Joe Riddley's bottom drawer, I reached for my pocketbook and pulled out a dollar. "Go ask one of the clerks for change, and bring Mr. Blaine a Coke." I didn't want Hector knowing where we keep spare change. Between Joe Riddley going back and forth to the nursery and me popping down to the jail, our office is often empty.

I wanted to be fair to Tad, so I didn't ask any important questions before he got back. Instead I asked, "How are repairs coming along on your house?"

A young lawyer in town, Jed DuBose, was underwriting the process of bringing the old Blaine place up to code in memory of Hector's sister, Helena, who had raised him. The original plan was for Jed and Hector to work together evenings and weekends, but the last I saw Jed, he'd complained, "I'd like to see at least the roof finished in my lifetime, but it never will be at the rate Hector works." I'd suggested that Jed spend what free time he had with his pregnant wife and use the money he made as a lawyer to pay other people to fix up the house. Joe Riddley and I have always believed one of the best things any of us can do with our money is hire other people who also need to earn.

Hector huffed in disgust. "Jed's got builder fellows crawling all over the place. I know he don't have much spare time to put in, but I don't like strangers on my propitty. I spend most of my time nowadays making sure they ain't out back digging for the treasury. Besides, they keep expecting me to move my stuff so they can work. I like my stuff where it is."

I didn't tell Hector it had been my idea to overrun his property with strangers. Instead, I sympathized with him over the problems builders caused just like I'd been harassed by them every day of my life. I also jotted "builder" on a scrap of paper, to remind me to call somebody about building us a new porch. It had occurred to me that instead of regretting our old one, we might as well add one to the new house, off the dining room.

Hector droned on, an endless litany of complaints about life in general and bankers who wouldn't lend him money using the Confederate treasury as collateral, in particular. When Tad returned, Hector took the Coke and drained about half of it in two long gulps. When he swallowed, his Adam's apple jumped like it would leap from his throat.

I asked, "Who was that you carried down to Spence's place in your truck Sunday evening?"

Tad had said "late afternoon," but I knew Hector would consider anything after two "evening." I also knew Hector would take his time answering, but Tad wasn't experienced in dealing with him. "The lady," he said impatiently after Hector had studied the writing on his drink bottle for well over a minute.

Hector threw back his head and let out a guffaw. "That weren't no lady, boy, that were Bertie. She was no more a lady than I am." He laughed again.

Tad was growing pink. Before he could chivalrously rush in to defend his friend, I said, "Did you know it was a woman?"

"Of course. Me 'n' her were like this." He held two fingers up close together.

"Do you know her full name?"

Hector took time to spit again before he shook his head. "It never come up. She was just in town a few days before somebody whacked her upside the head. You know that — you found her." I suppose that was to let me know he was well connected to the Hopemore grapevine.

"Have you told the police what you know about her?" I asked.

At the word "police," he shifted in his seat and slid his eye toward the door to make sure his escape route was clear. "Don't know nuthin'. Never laid eyes on her until Sattidy, when we met down at Myrtle's. Had a bite to eat together, is all."

Tad's eyes widened. "You eat at Myrtle's?" I could tell the child was having trouble picturing Hector and his new friend in one of the booths, but it wasn't the time or place to explain that they'd met around by the back door. Hubert didn't need to frequent Myrtle's back door, of course. Jed had arranged for almost every store in town to open Hector an account and send him the bills each month, but to get in the front door of Myrtle's, Hector would have to wash and change his clothes. To his way of thinking, that would be a stiff price to pay for food he could get free out back.

"You saw her again on Sunday." I'd found that statements sometimes worked better than questions with Hector.

He nodded. "Yeah, ran into her down at the Bi-Lo Dumpster. I told her I'd get us some eggs and bacon if she knew how to cook it. I got credit at Bi-Lo, you know." He beamed at Tad and me as if he were a major stockholder in the grocery chain. "She was a right smart cook, as it turned out, but she

245

warn't too complimentary about my house-keeping. Made us eat out on the porch." He wiped his nose on the back of his hand.

"Did she say where she was from?" I asked. "Or if she had any family?"

"Never mentioned any family, and when I asked where she was from, she just said, 'Here and there.'" He chuckled. "That's exactly what she said, 'Here and there, mostly there.' Said she was just in town for a few days. She had kids, I think, though."

"How do you know?"

"She kept mooning over that baby picture of Jed Helena hung on the wall."

"Did she say why she came to Hopemore?"

"Nope. Just said she was passing through and stopping a few days. I told her she could bunk with me," he added with a nasty leer, "but she said she had other accommodations. Mighty hifalutin word for Spence's barn, if'n you ask me. Old Hubert ought to put him up a sign." He sketched a sign with his hands and peered at me through it. "Spence's Accommodations."

"Did you see her Monday?" I could see Tad was bursting to remind me he'd already told me she saw Hector Monday, but I gave him a warning frown and he subsided.

Hector scratched the whiskers under his chin. "Monday. Lemme think. Yeah, I reckon I did. She give me a letter to deliver."

"To whom?"

He guffawed. "Lordy, Judge, you know I don't read."

I knew. Hector had learned to read like other first and second graders, but he gave it up in third grade and flat-out refused to read after that. He'd been the despair of his poor mother, who had been a Latin teacher before she fell in love with a lovely face and discovered, to her despair, there was no character behind it. The only reason Hector had a driver's license was that Helena went with him when he was sixteen and read him the questions. Hector told the examiner he was having trouble with his eyes jumping that day, and since he'd passed the driving test, she let him get away with it. It would never have worked if the examiner hadn't been very young and as susceptible as Hector's mother to a handsome face and what passed for rustic charm.

"So where did you take the letter?" I asked.

"Over to Annie Dale Wilson's, like Bertie told me to. She said leave it where it could be found, so I propped it on the porch rocker. Annie's done right well for herself," he added in a meditative tone. "She'n me used to go together, you know. And she's alone again now."

The fact that Hector and Annie had gone around together for a little while when she was in ninth grade was one of those memories I hadn't brought out and looked at for years. Hector, of course, had already left school — finding nothing there, so he said, he couldn't live without. He was mighty handsome back then, and Annie Dale was going into her wild phase. Annie Dale's mama took care of that particular problem by baking an apple pie and sending Annie Dale and her daddy over to Hector's to deliver it. Annie Dale told me later, "I didn't know people could live that trashy." Hector's mama was dead by then, and Helena wasn't any fonder of baths and cleaning than her daddy or brothers.

"Of courses, she's got real snooty, now," Hector added, by which I concluded that he must have knocked, but Annie Dale hadn't answered, invited him in, or given him money. Hector was the world's most consistent cadger.

To prove it, he hauled himself up from the chair and said, "Thanks for the co-cola, Judge. I don't reckon you could give me a little something to tide me over until my next check?"

We both knew that the only two things Jed refused him were cash and liquor.

"Sorry, Hubert, I just spent my last dollar bill on your Coke." I didn't mention my twenties or tens. "If you think of anything else about Bertie, will you let me know?"

"I shore will, Judge. Shore will." At the

door he paused. "I already thought of one thing. She could sing real purty. Saw Helena's old guitar on the wall and asked if she could play it. I told her, 'You *may*, but whether you can or not is up to you.'" He snickered at his own wit. "Mama used to say that to us kids. She was a schoolteacher, remember?"

"I remember."

"Well, Bertie could play pretty good. She tuned that thing up and sat there the whole afternoon, plunking out tunes and singing. When we got ready to go, I said, 'Why don't you just take it with you?' I didn't have no use for it, not being able to play," he added, in case I made the mistake of thinking he'd gone softhearted.

He swiped his nose with the back of one hand. "Hubert hadn't oughta hit her with that pipe. She warn't hurtin' nobody, sleepin' in his barn."

17

"Do you know that he did it?" I demanded. "Did you see him? Did anybody you know?"

"No, but who else coulda done it? That Hubert's lost his temper one time too many. Mark my words. They gonna lock him up and throw away the key." He sounded so virtuous, you'd never guess he'd been locked up a few times himself.

He donned his filthy hat. "Nice seein' you, Judge. Be good, youngun."

When he'd gone, Tad fanned the air in front of his face. "Phew! How did you stand it?"

"Didn't you notice how often I blew my nose? I was breathing into my hand."

"You could have handed me a Kleenex," he muttered. "Are you gonna call the police and tell them to arrest Mr. Spence?"

"Not likely."

"But everybody knows he did it."

"Not everybody, honey. Me, for instance, and I know Hubert real well."

Not quite well enough, however. Not well enough to figure out where he was in that half hour he wouldn't discuss.

While Joe Riddley was taking Tad to

school, I called my old friend Isaac James, the assistant police chief. Ike grew up in Hopemore, held a degree in criminology, and would have been chief if our benighted city council hadn't preferred to import a white man instead of promoting a qualified black one. Several of them, I am satisfied to report, had lived to regret that decision.

When we'd exchanged greetings, checked on each other's families, and agreed that Chief Muggins had been a tad quick to haul Tad down to the juvenile detention center, I asked, "Can you tell me exactly what you all have on Hubert Spence besides the matchbook?"

Ike liked Hubert, so he didn't want him arrested any more than I did. "Nothing we can take to a probable-cause hearing yet, fortunately. A search of the barn turned up a few items that indicate the victim was, indeed, camping out in his barn. We have witnesses that Hubert uttered threats against the victim, and other witnesses to a remark he made to you the night of the murder, about taking care of the situation himself. The only tangible evidence we have is a matchbook with his store name on it and a footprint that matches his shoes down at the murder scene. Hubert claims he must have dropped the matchbook and made the footprint when he was down there around five o'clock. Ms. Georgia Tate confirms that she was with him. Her footprint was there, too, and a few threads from a red shirt she was wearing when she went through the hedge. The thing the chief thinks is most significant against Hubert is that he has half an hour unaccounted for after that night's meeting, which he refuses to talk about. Forensics have narrowed the time of death down to some time between eight and ten, which includes the time when Hubert won't say where he was."

I put forth my theories. "Maybe he wet himself and had to change clothes. Old men do that, you know. Or maybe he had to go home and take some medicine he'd forgotten to bring. I don't know if you've ever seen Hubert take his heart medicine in public, but he takes so many pains to hide what he's doing, I've told him somebody's gonna turn him in for taking drugs. Have you checked to see if he dropped by the house before he went out with the fellows?"

"We can check. The biggest thing I see against Hubert is that nobody else in town had a problem with the victim. Folks thought she was a man, of course, but we keep finding folks who thought he was a little spacy, but nice. Myrtle says he never failed to say 'Thank you' for a meal, and she was planning to invite him back after he exceeded the limit of meals your church pays for. Hubert's the only person in town who had a problem with him, so far as we can find."

Who was it who said if you eliminate every

possibility, the impossible must be true?

I refused to believe it yet. As soon as I hung up, I called Pooh's to talk to Otis, Lottie's husband and Pooh's yardman. I liked and trusted Otis.

"Hey, Otis," I greeted him. "Tell Lottie that pie was outstanding Monday night."

"I sure will, Judge. Everybody all right down your way? I heard you got the boy back."

"Got him back and he's doing fine. Listen, I understand the police are real interested in somebody over at your place."

"They sure are, and it's upset everybody. You gonna keep him out of jail?"

"I'm gonna try. Tell me, did Hubert come back there Monday night after the meeting, while we women were in with Gusta? Did he run in for a few minutes and go upstairs?"

"No, ma'am, and I was right here in the kitchen the whole time, watching television. If he'd a come, unless he came in the front door where you all were, I'd have seen him."

"Okay. Thanks."

I was trying to think what else I could ask and who to ask it of when Joe Riddley came in and sat in his desk chair, ready to check the inventory for the week. "I can't for the life of me figure out where Hubert might have gone in that half hour Monday night," I told him.

He didn't turn from the computer screen.

"You've got no reason to figure it out. That's Charlie's business, not yours."

"Yeah, but could Hubert have stopped by the store for anything?"

"He could have stopped by a lot of places, including down by the water tank."

"You know he didn't as well as I do. I can't for the life of me figure out what would be so secret, though."

"Me neither. Only thing I ever knew Hubert to be secretive about was money. He's always been real close about letting folks know what he has."

Joe Riddley went to the nursery and I worked on taxes, but the whole time I was carrying on a private conversation with the Boss upstairs. "You know where Hubert was. Why won't he tell us? If you'll give me a hint, it could save his neck. He's a stubborn old coot, but I don't believe he killed anybody. At least, I hope he didn't. Help!"

That's the first time I ever knew the IRS to be an answer to a prayer. I was typing away on our tax returns when suddenly I put two and two together and got four.

I looked up the number for Wainwright Antiques. "Hey, Maynard," I greeted him, "how's business?"

"Just wonderful, Miss Mac. I got in the whole estate of a family from Macon, and they had some wonderful china you might want to stop by and see."

"Call Georgia Bullock over at Annie Dale's. She collects porcelain. I'm in the giving-away mode right now, not the adding-on mode. But listen, I called about your daddy."

His sigh was so deep it engulfed me. "I'm plumb disgusted with him. If the old cuss would just say where he was for one half hour, he could clear himself. But he clams up and mutters about folks meddling in his 'bidness.' "

"Well, I have an idea. Do you still have a key to the store?"

"Yeah, I had it when he was sick and I was running things, and I never bothered to give it back."

"Good. After he leaves tonight, I want you to go look for a secret stash."

"Drugs?" That was a preposterous idea, and we both knew it.

"No, money. Your daddy made a lot on that garage sale we had together last month, right?"

"More than six thousand dollars. I took anything of historic value, of course, but there wasn't much of that. He and Mama preferred ugly modern stuff. They'd filled the whole place with it, and most of it sold. People thought they were getting treasures."

"He also sold his tractors and mower and your mama's old car, right? For cash?"

Maynard has always been smart. "You think he's hidden all that cash somewhere? Why?"

255

"So he didn't have to deposit it and pay taxes on it."

He thought that over. "He's ornery enough to do that, but he's too smart to keep money lying around where it could burn up in a fire."

"Yeah, but what if he had a good fireproof safe?"

"There's no safe. Daddy took out the one in the store years ago and put up that sign, 'Less than fifty dollars worth of cash on the premises.' He runs back and forth to the bank all day long with little dribbles to deposit. You ought to know that."

"Everybody in town knows it, which is why money would be safe in the store. I have an idea where he keeps it." I told him where to look. "If there's nothing there, you haven't lost anything except a little time. If there is — well, I think he ran by the store that night to make a withdrawal from his private piggy bank before going out on the town."

"That could be it," Maynard admitted. "He never carries much cash for the same reason he won't keep money on the premises — he doesn't want to get robbed. And he claims credit cards are tools of the devil to make a man spend more than he has. But I heard that my old man was standing drinks for the house Monday night like he was buying votes. He's gotten awful interested in politics lately. You don't reckon he's planning on running for office, do you?"

"I sure hope not. We've got enough problems in this state without your daddy helping to run things. Bye, now. Good luck." I hadn't mentioned that Hubert might have been trying to buy the goodwill of a man whose sister he was interested in. That would be between Hubert, Burlin, and Maynard, if it came to that.

Since there wasn't another blessed thing I could do that day, I read the new *Statesman*, which had just been delivered. Gusta would be as happy as I that the *Statesman*'s pictures from her Saturday Do showed her house to advantage, included a lovely shot of her with Burlin and Georgia, and didn't have one single picture of me.

Maynard called as I was winding up for the day. "Daddy shut early to dress for some political rally, so I came on over. You were absolutely right. That old chest freezer at the back is full of money in plastic bags. I didn't touch it, just verified that it's there. But it looks to me like Daddy has enough to take off for a South Seas island. Do you realize if he'd kicked the bucket, I'd have donated that old thing to a thrift store and probably never lifted the lid?"

"You'd have made somebody mighty happy."

"I don't know what to do now, though. I hate to go off and leave it unlocked, but I can't find a key."

"It's been unlocked since the garage sale," I pointed out. "Nobody knows the money is there but Hubert, you, and me, and while I might be tempted to rob the old fool — after all, he couldn't report the theft, could he? — I am in a wheelchair this week. Lock up the store and go on home."

He laughed. "Okay. I guess I lived in New York too long. But I can't wait for Daddy to get home tonight. He and I are going to have a delightful little chat."

I was shutting down my computer when Burlin poked his head in my door. "Hello. About to go home?"

Why couldn't the man leave me alone? I would have snapped off a reply if I hadn't been raised by a mother who sent me daily into the world with that Southern mother's mantra, "Be sweet now." I stifled a sigh. "I'm waiting for Joe Riddley. Did you drown at the barbeque last night?"

"No, but there's always tonight. Looks like there's going to be another shower, and we have a meeting over in Louisville. Before we go, Georgia and Binky asked me to stop by and see how you are feeling."

"I'm feeling better. Still a bit confined, but a sprained ankle isn't life threatening."

"That's good." He looked around to be sure nobody was there, then came to my desk and leaned over to murmur, "I also wanted to say thanks for yesterday afternoon.

I enjoyed it, but I hope I didn't get you into trouble."

He was too close, and I couldn't run away.

I put both hands on his arms to push him away.

A flash went off at my office door.

"Wha — ?" We spoke in unison and saw a camera poised for another shot.

"Stop it!" Burlin commanded. He hurried to the door with his hands in front of his face.

"He's in here," somebody shouted in the parking lot. In another second, the back door to the store opened and pandemonium broke loose. From the noise, there were four or five reporters out there, shouting questions at Burlin and sounding exactly like Joe Riddley's hounds at feeding time. Burlin called over one shoulder, "I'm sorry," as he hurried out.

He had pulled the door closed behind him. Through it, I heard his muffled voice. "Let's go to the parking lot, folks. This is no place for an interview."

Through the window, I saw them press around him asking questions. I saw him grow still, then shake his head. For once, he seemed to have nothing to say. One of the reporters got right in his face to ask something. Burlin shoved him out of the way and headed out of the parking lot, walking fast. They scurried along behind him like a stream of ants heading to the sugar bowl.

How did the reporters know Burlin was at my office? Why were they more interested in him today than yesterday? And would that dreadful picture appear in the paper, as well?

18

I was still shaking and nauseated when Joe Riddley arrived to take me home. "Is something the matter? You look like you've been wrung out and hung to dry."

I took deep breaths to keep from losing my afternoon candy bar. "Burlin Bullock dropped by to see how I was doing, and a bunch of reporters — they —" I couldn't go on.

"They didn't hurt you, did they?" He held out a hand to help me into the wheelchair.

I flung myself at his chest. "No, but they scared the living daylights out of me. They're vampires."

He stroked my hair. "They'll leave as soon as the Bullocks do, and we can all get back to normal."

At the house, he again fixed supper — which, thanks to Clarinda, entailed nothing more than heating up homemade vegetable soup and corn bread and dishing up a congealed salad. During the meal Tad was no longer sullen and defiant, but he was wary — watching each minute to see if he'd done anything else that might make us mad.

I could tell he wished he was at home, where his mama would hug him and tell him it wasn't really his fault the barn got burned — it was an old, dry wood building — and he was a real hero for saving Starfire. Then his daddy — having already pounded things in New York City and gotten over the worst of his anger — would say something like, "I wish you hadn't done it, but I did pretty bad things when I was a kid myself, so just don't do anything like that again." Then Tad could forget the whole thing.

Except he wouldn't forget it. Every time he saw a lighted match, he'd flinch somewhere deep inside, knowing he had burned down his uncle's barn.

Joe Riddley had a meeting that evening, so I let Tad paint his horse for half an hour while I read; then I asked him to fetch us both some lime sherbet and sent up a prayer for help.

He settled into the chair across from me and we ate in silence a few minutes. Finally, I asked, "Do you know the hardest thing to do in the whole world — and the bravest?"

He looked uncertainly at me, waiting for me to give him the answer. I didn't say a word. I wanted him to think about it. He took a bite of sherbet and rolled it around on his tongue. "Climbing a really steep cliff?"

"No."

"Saving somebody's life when it's really dangerous?"

"No."

"I give up. What?"

"Taking all your courage in your hands, going to somebody you have done something wrong to, and saying, 'It was my fault. I did it. There is nothing I can do to take away the fact that I did it, but I am really, really sorry. Will you forgive me? And what do you want me to do about it?' "

He squirmed. "That's not hard." He bent back over his bowl, presenting me with the top of his head.

"Don't you believe it. It's so hard that big, strong men have a hard time doing it. But they need to. You know why?"

He shook his head without looking up.

"Because there's a program written into the universe — sort of a computer game —"

He flicked a glance my way, so I could tell he was interested even though he was pretending his bowl of sherbet was the most fascinating thing in the world.

"What kind of game?" he finally asked, when I hadn't said anything for several bites.

"Well, it works like this. When somebody does something wrong to somebody else, the person who did it starts collecting points for guilt, and the person who was wronged starts collecting points for blame. As the game goes on, each of them gets more and more points, until one person has a whole lot of guilt and the other one a whole lot of blame. As they collect points, they get fatter and fatter."

"Do they get stronger, too?"

"Not at all. Getting bigger is a problem, because at the very end of the game, there's a tiny door they have to go through. Only skinny people can win."

"So does anybody ever win?"

"Yep. There's a built-in eraser, a magic formula that erases points. The person who did the bad thing has to say two secret words: 'I'm sorry.' The other person has to say three secret words back: 'I forgive you.' Then all their points disappear."

"They don't get to fight?" I could tell he was disappointed.

"All brave things don't require fighting, honey. It takes a very brave person to use those magic words, because the other person may turn and walk away. However, if either person says his or her words, their own points get erased, even if the other person doesn't say their secret words back. Those words are the only thing that can make anybody thin enough to get through the door at the end of the game and win."

Parents and grandparents are such fools. We continue to hope that by teaching children the right things, they will immediately jump up like children in soppy stories and say, "Oh, let me do the right thing right now!"

Tad stood up. "I want some more sherbet." As he left the room, I heard him mutter, "It wasn't my fault."

"Horsefeathers," I called after him. "Of course it was your fault. You were smoking in the barn and your match set it on fire." I tried not to sound mad, but I wanted to shake the child until his teeth rattled. "Come here," I told him. Sullenly, he came to stand in the kitchen doorway. "Look, let me spell it out for you. You burned the barn. It was a bad thing to do. But you don't have to live the rest of your life carrying that extra weight around. You need to be brave enough to tell Uncle Ridd and your daddy you're sorry. They may get very angry, fuss for a few days —"

"Especially Daddy," he muttered, scuffing one toe on the threshold.

That's when I got the inspiration I'd been hoping for. "When you tell your daddy, I want you to start by saying, 'Daddy, do you remember when you borrowed Pop's car after he told you not to?' Wait just a minute for him to remember, then say, 'And remember how sorry you were? Well, I'm real sorry that I burned down Uncle Ridd's barn, too, and I'll do whatever you want me to, to show I'm sorry.' "

"He'll put me on restriction for a month. No television, no video games —"

"Don't you deserve that, for burning down the barn?"

"No! I didn't mean to do it, Me-mama. I told you. It was Lulu!" He ran back into the kitchen and I heard him open the freezer door.

265

In a few minutes he carried back another bowl of sherbet and asked, like nothing had happened in between, "What happened with Daddy and the car?"

"Your daddy had just gotten his license and wasn't an expert driver yet. One night when Pop and I went to a meeting in my car, Walker took Pop's car to go see a friend. The friend's road had a deep drainage ditch on each side, and Walker backed into one of the ditches. His back wheels were a good three feet lower than his front ones." I saw a flicker of a smile on Tad's lips. "It's funny now, but it wasn't then. To make things worse, his friend's daddy went and got his truck and a chain to pull him out, but the roads were slippery from a shower, and the truck slid into the ditch on the other side. In the process, it pulled your granddaddy's bumper off. Poor Walker had to call Pop to come with his tractor to pull out both the car and the truck."

"Did Pop kill him?"

"You're here, aren't you? But Pop got real mad at Walker because Walker kept trying to give us all kinds of excuses for what he'd done — he needed to go over to that boy's house, the bank was slippery, the family didn't have enough light to see the ditches. Pop finally told him to hush, that he didn't want to hear another word out of him until he was ready to say 'It's my fault. I did it,

266

and I'm real sorry. What do you want me to do about it?' I thought Walker was going to live in silence forever. He didn't say a word for three days. But one day Pop came into the kitchen just as Walker was coming in from the hall, and Walker started to cry."

"Daddy cried? He never cries."

"He did that day. And he said, 'I can't stand this, Daddy. I'm sorry. I'm real sorry. It was all my fault. What do you want me to do?' Do you know what Pop did?"

"Took him out and beat him with a belt?"

I was horrified. "Does your daddy hit with a belt?" I couldn't believe it, but mothers don't always know their sons.

Tad shook his head. "No, ma'am, but my friend's daddy does."

"What Pop did was hold out his arms and give your daddy a hug. Then they went out to look at the car, and Pop told Walker he had to keep it clean for the next three months. Cars get real dusty going up and down that gravel road."

"That's all Pop did to punish him? Daddy would have grounded me for life." He set his bowl on the table. "Well, I need to go do some homework."

"Carry that bowl to the sink and rinse it out," I told him. "And while you're going, take mine, too." After he'd gone, I lay there and muttered, "Sorry, Boss. I blew that one."

The phone rang in a few minutes, and it

was Walker. "I heard Tad's staying at your place a few days. Can I talk to him?"

I wanted to beg, "Be nice," but I made a rule years ago not to tell my children how to raise their children unless they ask. What makes me think I'm such an expert, anyway?

"Tad," I called. "Your daddy's on the phone."

We didn't have an extension in the guest room, and he must not have known about the one in our bedroom, because he went to the kitchen. I heard him answer tentatively, "Hello, Daddy." Then his voice went real soft. In a few minutes I heard him laugh, then hang up.

He came back to the room. "Daddy laughed when I asked him about getting Pop's car in the ditch. He said that now, every time he asks to borrow Pop's car, Pop laughs and tells him not to drive it in a ditch."

"Yeah. I forgot to tell you about that part of the game. When you use the magic formulas, not only do your points get erased, but your memories do, too. Even if you remember the bad thing that was done, it seems funny or unimportant. Did you tell your daddy about the barn?"

He got real interested in a wart. "I started to, but he said we wouldn't talk about it now, that it was done and there wasn't anything we could do about it." His shoulders bowed under the weight of that.

I wanted to "smack Walker upside the head," as Clarinda or Hector would say. Tad stood. "I guess I better go back to my homework. They give us too much, Mama says."

The phone rang again as he walked toward the door. "Answer that for me," I requested.

He picked up the receiver and his eyes grew wary. "Yessir? Oh. Yessir, I know. That's what Me-mama said." Long pause. I was about to gesture for him to hand me the phone when he took a big breath and words tumbled out. "I am sorry. I'm really, really sorry. I didn't mean to burn down Uncle Ridd's barn or cost you all that money, but I did it." Tears streamed down his face. He grabbed a tissue and swabbed them, but kept talking. "I wish I hadn't. Can you — uh — uh —" He slid his eyes my way, pleading for help.

"Forgive," I said softly.

"Can you forgive me? Please? I'll do anything you tell me — What?" Another long pause. "Yessir, I can do that. Thank you. I love you, too."

He hung up and turned away. "That was Daddy again," he said, wiping his nose. He nearly set the tissue on the table, then remembered and took it to the wastebasket. "He said he remembered that part you told me, about him and Pop." He heaved a big sigh. "He said I need to call Uncle Ridd, too."

269

"Shall I dial his number right now?"

He lifted his chin. "Might as well get it over with."

I called Ridd and told him to come up for a minute. Tad had something to say to him. When he got there, he looked edgy, as anxious as Tad for this to be over.

Tad threw me a pleading look, but I didn't say a word. He took a big breath and said, "Uncle Ridd, I'm — I'm sorry I — I burned down your barn. I want you to forgive me." He had a ways to go — it sounded more like a command than a plea — but at least he went on. "I'll do whatever you want me to. I could wash your truck," he suggested quickly.

Ridd hesitated, then put out his hand. Tad looked at it uncertainly, then put out his own. "I forgive you," Ridd said solemnly. They shook. "How about if instead of washing my truck, you —" He stopped, and I suspected he was thinking furiously, trying to overcome his belief that Tad couldn't do a thing.

"He could help you scrape and paint your house," I suggested. "He's a good painter."

Tad blinked, probably thinking it was a long way from painting by numbers to painting a house. Ridd thought it over, then nodded. "We'll think how many hours would be fair, and you can help me scrape and paint the side the firefighters damaged. Fair enough?"

Tad nodded. "Yessir." His head was high, his eyes shining.

Ridd reached out and rumpled his hair. "I wish you'd come on down to our place again. We sure miss you. Aunt Martha was saying not an hour ago that she wished you were there to help her figure out how to do something on the computer."

He turned to me. "Could I go now, Memama? I mean, if you need me to help you —"

"I'll manage," I told him. "Run and get your things, and you go on down and help Aunt Martha. But anytime you want to come spend the night, give me a call, okay?"

I watched them go out, Ridd's hand resting lightly on Tad's shoulder and Tad's arm around his uncle's waist, and thought that confession is like a waterslide. It looks easy when it's somebody else doing it. But standing at the top of that chute looking down —

"I'll get around to it," I muttered crossly to nobody in particular. "Don't rush me."

19

I lay there thinking that if Tad could do it, I ought to be able to do it, too. But I wanted to wait until Joe Riddley was real mellow. It's one thing to confess when the other person knows they've been wronged. But to inform Joe Riddley I'd been carrying on with Burlin behind his back — well, I couldn't do it while I was stuck in that cast. It complicated my life enough already. I'd figure out the best way to tell him once it was off.

He came in around nine thirty and was delighted when I explained what Tad had done. But he said, "I'll miss having the kid around. That was a great idea you had, inviting him here."

Great idea *I* had?

He slung his cap onto a living room chair. "I'm going out to the garage a little while to set up my shop. Call me for the ten o'clock news."

I got so interested in my book, I almost forgot the news. When I switched it on, the announcer wore a bright red smile to report that the economy was up, although I doubted if that fact would affect her six-figure salary one way or the other. Then her face grew grave. "We now bring you a late-breaking story."

I was so busy wondering if television news reporters practice facial expressions in front of a mirror at announcing school — whether they have a list of looks they have to master, like "caring," "serious," "tragic," "delighted" — that the picture took a second to register on my brain. Then I yelled, "Joe Riddley, come in here! It's our murder."

He arrived in four long strides and sank into the handiest chair. The screen showed the Hopemore water tank in all its faded glory.

A screwdriver fell to the floor unnoticed as Joe Riddley said out loud what I was thinking. "With all the murders going on around the country, why would national news report on a homeless woman killed under a small-town water tank?"

The reporter told us in a bland, modulated voice. "Fingerprints have confirmed that a woman found murdered beneath a water tank in Hopemore, Georgia, yesterday morning is the wife of former congressman Burlin Bullock."

Now I knew why the barracudas had circled Burlin.

Neither Joe Riddley nor I said a word as the water tower gave way to a video clip in which a stocky young woman with shoulder-length blond hair and a friendly square face

273

waved to the camera. She could have been the granddaughter of the woman I'd found. How could one woman age so much in less than forty years?

In the film, she held a small dark-haired boy who clutched her tight around the neck with one arm. It was obvious they enjoyed being so close. Beside them stood a younger Burlin, looking proud, but unfinished, somehow.

The next clip showed the same woman dashing from a courthouse, shielding her face with a clutch bag. I hadn't heard a word the announcer had said for some time. I tuned back in as she was saying, ". . . convicted of killing a five-year-old child in a drunken-driving incident."

I stopped listening again.

The camera returned to the water tank, making its pitiful debut on national news. "I hope everybody in town is watching," I told Joe Riddley, "and that they'll all notice how tacky that thing looks. I just hate for the whole country to see it looking like that."

The clip ended, appropriately, with a shot of a buzzard glaring down from one of the struts.

During the series of commercials that followed, we sat silent.

A light rain fell outside, a steady *drip, drip, drip*. Droplets of sorrow for poor, poor Sperra. I wondered where she had been all those years she was supposed to be dead, who they had buried in her place, how that had happened. Was her "first" death simply a publicity ploy? Had they paid her not to come around again? Or was it an honest mistake?

I tried, but could not imagine the paths you'd need to travel to get from a congressman's house to Hubert's barn. I remembered that Burlin had mentioned she used to be a folk singer and felt I'd drown in sadness as I thought of her perched on Hector's broken-down porch singing and strumming Helena's old guitar. Given the state of the rest of Hector's house, I doubted if the guitar had been in very good shape. The fact that Sperra would play it at all — and accept it as a gift — showed how hungry she must have been to perform. I found myself whispering, "Thank you for giving her that last happy afternoon before she died."

Had it been hard to give up her singing? I hadn't said anything at the time, but it had irked me how casually Burlin had said "she gave it up" in the same sentence with "of course."

I looked across the room at my husband in the shadows. "I need to thank you for something."

"What's that?" Joe Riddley bent to pick up his screwdriver.

"For never thinking I ought to give up who I was because I married you. For letting me be myself, and never expecting me to turn into somebody whose only role in life was to help you become who you could be."

He grunted. "Good thing I didn't. But if I hadn't liked you the way you were, I wouldn't have married you." His dark eyes rested on me briefly. "Let's stay up to see what they say at eleven." He headed back to the garage.

Outside the windows, night closed down around us like mourning. While Joe Riddley puttered in the garage, I lay there thinking how dreadful Sperra's life had been. Bo perched on the back of a dining room chair, preening his breast feathers and muttering soft obscenities. I didn't bother to hush him. For once, he was expressing my feelings exactly.

After a while, Joe Riddley came back in. "I don't see how it can be true," I told him. "Burlin and Georgia both told me Sperra died twenty years ago. Georgia said they had a quiet funeral."

He gave a sour grunt. "Now they'll have to have a public one." He sat back down in his chair and reached for the remote to change channels.

This one, too, showed the famous Hopemore water tank. Then the scene changed to Annie Dale's front porch, where the Bullocks stood in a family tableau. The shot had been taken at dusk, so I presumed they had canceled their evening meeting.

Lance stood in the center wearing his navy blazer with khaki pants. Georgia was to his right, in her navy suit, white blouse, and patriotic scarf. Renée was behind Lance, next to Burlin, and I couldn't see what either of them were wearing, but Binky, to Lance's left, was again in her navy dress and pearls. I wondered if she were one of those women who bought one good traveling outfit and figured she could wear it daily because so few people saw her twice — or noticed her at all.

I also wondered if they had deliberately arranged themselves artistically, the three tall ones in the middle, or if that was just a familiar way to pose. Edward stood by Georgia, holding her arm. All the men looked appropriately somber. Binky dabbed her nose with a handkerchief from time to time, but Georgia was composed and beautiful. Edward had his full attention on Lance, as if transmitting his speech by mental telepathy.

"We are as baffled as anybody," Lance assured the viewers. "We were informed twenty years ago that Mama died in a fire. We've never had any reason to believe otherwise. For her to turn up here, like this —" His voice broke. He ducked his head and turned away.

Burlin reached out to the camera. "Be assured, we will get to the bottom of this.

This is terrible for all of us." He turned to indicate Georgia, Binky, Renée, and Lance, who now held tightly to his wife's hand. They nodded in unison.

I held my breath, afraid I'd see that shot of me with my arms on Burlin's, but it didn't appear. Instead, the camera shifted to Chief Muggins in front of our police station. He stood with his chest thrust forward, his head held high, and every cap on his teeth bared in a smile. "We are on top of this," he promised. "I expect to make an arrest in a very short time."

Now, there was a promise designed to ruin my sleep.

20

Even before I woke Thursday morning, my subconscious started worrying about whether my picture would be in the paper. I came to consciousness ready to do whatever it took to be sure I saw the paper first. It was an hour before I usually got up, so maybe I could camp on the stoop and catch the paper man as he drove past. He might make an exception and bring it to our door.

I hauled myself and that heavy cast out of bed, hopped by the bathroom to brush my hair and teeth, then shoved the walker ahead of me down the hall. Lulu was delighted to see me, and squirmed around my foot. I obviously couldn't take her for a walk, but I hopped over to let her out the back door. "Don't you go out of our yard," I warned softly, although I don't know how I thought she could figure out where the property lines were.

The light rain was still falling. She gave me a reproachful look to say "It's all your fault," and squatted quickly on the soaked grass, then dashed back in and shook herself all over me.

I hopped to the front door and propped on

the walker, glumly regarding the paper. It lay in the grass only twenty-five feet away, but it might as well have been a mile. I couldn't hop down our front steps. Even if I could, I couldn't hop that far across even short grass, and with all the rain we'd been having, ours was a foot high.

"Can you fetch?" I asked Lulu, who had come in with me. "See the paper? Go get it, girl."

She gave me a look that said "If you think I am going back out in that rain, you can think again." Then she did her three-legged hop to her breakfast dish to show me that people who lost the use of a leg didn't *have* to be helpless.

"Ungrateful wretch," I muttered.

I looked up and down the sidewalk. At barely past five, the street was completely deserted.

I considered the problem while I started coffee. I couldn't bear for Joe Riddley to open that paper before me. Could I reach it if I went down to the sidewalk in my wheelchair, then hopped on the grass just a few feet? I hopped through the kitchen and into the garage, got into the wheelchair, pushed the button to raise the door, and headed down the drive.

I knew it was a mistake as soon as I felt the mist on my head and shoulders. To make things worse, the driveway was a slight incline, and slick. Next thing I knew, I was whizzing toward the street, picking up speed as I went.

Maybe some people see their lives flash before them in times of danger. All I could see was myself sprawled in the street in my nightgown. I found the brakes about the time I bumped across the sidewalk. By the time I'd jerked them both up against the wheels, I was rolling smack into the lights of an approaching car.

The wheelchair swerved on a slick spot. The car lights blinded me. I heard the squeal of tires and flung up my arms to cover my head before the crash.

A white Mercedes stopped five feet from my left wheel.

Trembling so hard I could not move, I sat there feeling stupid, helpless, and very wet.

Georgia Bullock jumped out. She wore a pale silver raincoat to match the car. "Mackie?" She clung to the top of her door. "I thought I'd killed you! What on earth were you doing?" Her face was chalky in the dim light.

I spoke through chattering teeth. "Coming to get the paper. I lost control on the hill." I wrapped my arms around my chest to keep myself from shaking apart.

"Hill?"

I followed her gaze up the drive. The grade was very slight from one end to the other. I tried to laugh, but it wasn't one of my better efforts. "It felt like a mountain, coming down. Better than a roller coaster."

"Whew!" She let out her breath, and I saw she was trembling, too. "Abigail wanted to bring you a note, but she's so exhausted, I told her to sleep, I'd bring it. We were both lucky I was driving slow, looking for the number." She shut the car door behind her, took an envelope from her pocket, then stuffed it back again. Her hands were shaking too hard to grip it. "I never imagined I'd find you up this early — much less run you down."

"You're up early, too," I pointed out.

"We never went to bed." As she came closer, I saw dark circles under her eyes. "We've been trying to decide what to do. I don't know if you heard —"

"I saw you on the news. I'm so sorry, honey. If you'll push me up the hill, I've got coffee made, and Joe Riddley won't be stirring for an hour or more."

"Coffee would be heaven." She wheeled me into the garage and would have gone in the side door, but I waved her to stop. "I have to use the walker from here on." I hopped ahead of her into the kitchen. She shed her raincoat as she came in. Under it, she was still wearing the navy pants and white blouse she'd had on the night before, but without the jacket and scarf. Fine lines of weariness fanned out around her eyes. When she reached a dining room chair, she collapsed onto it with a grateful sigh.

The walker had a tray, so I carried in two coffee mugs, spoons, and a pint of half-and-half. We'd moved the coffeemaker to the dining room table since my accident, so I didn't have to get up to refill my cup, and sugar and napkins were also on the table. Thank goodness, because Georgia sat at the table as if she didn't notice a thing I was doing, and my leg would never have survived another trip. I sank into a chair around the corner from her. "Drink up." I wished I could go put on something dry, but hopping even the short distance to our room was impossible.

"Thanks." Georgia filled a mug and held it to her cheek, looking desperate for warmth. "This is so awful! I don't know what we're going to do. All these years, we've thought Sperra was dead. Now, to find her here, living like that —" Was she conscious that she was echoing Lance, or was that part of a prepared speech they had come up with?

I had no idea what it was like to live in a family where every word you uttered could be taken down and published across the country, where every outfit you wore was critiqued by the fashion conscious, where you had to watch yourself every second in case some private emotion made its way onto a television screen. I thought of Renée as I had seen her in a few unguarded moments and knew she had better develop a thicker skin and actor's skills before her husband faced election day.

Georgia dumped three spoonfuls of sugar into her mug, followed it with a hefty dollop of cream, then gulped the coffee as if she needed the sweet warm brew to survive.

"Why wasn't Sperra dead?" I wondered aloud. "I mean, why did you think she was?"

She sighed. "That was my fault — mine and Abigail's." She leaned across the corner of the table, maybe worried that Joe Riddley might show up and hear.

"Sperra never lived with Burlin after the trial. She was sentenced to a rehab prison that kept her only two years. After that, they let her out, saying she was cured. That was a joke. A week later she turned up on Burlin's back porch drunk and unconscious. Lance, who wasn't quite seven, found her and ran screaming into the house that his mommy was dead. It gave him nightmares for weeks."

"Poor baby!"

"You can't imagine. Abigail and I both begged Burlin to divorce Sperra and get a court order forbidding her to come to the house, but he convinced us that a divorce would mean more publicity, and Sperra had a nasty streak when she was drinking. None of us knew what she might do or say in court. So he opened her a bank account and told her he'd put money in it every month, but he'd close it if she ever came back to the house again. She stormed out and showed up a few weeks later out in Spokane, where she had a college roommate. We told people she had moved to Paris — she'd been a French major in college — and Burlin made arrangements with the roommate to pay her bills. For the next seven years, Sperra bounced between sobriety, drinking binges, and rehab centers. In the rare times she was sober, her roommate looked after her. Abigail kept begging Burlin to get a divorce because she was terrified Sperra would come back and kidnap Lance, but Burlin said he had no plans to remarry and he didn't want the publicity. Then the roommate out in Spokane called and said Sperra had disappeared. We had a miserable year wondering every day if she'd show up again on his back porch. Can you imagine how awful that was?"

"No, I can't."

Georgia was talking more to herself than to me by then. I got the feeling she had been needing somebody she could tell this story to for a very long time. "Then Abigail got a call. It was for Burlin, actually, at his office, but he'd taken Lance skiing in Switzerland for his sixteenth birthday. The caller ran a homeless shelter in Atlanta, and said that during a routine drug search of his residents, he'd found a gold locket engraved 'With Love, Burlin,' and some identification cards for Sperra Bullock in a woman's backpack. The woman wouldn't say where she'd gotten them, but he'd recognized the name and thought Burlin ought to know."

She paused to heat her coffee from the pot and take a swallow. I reached for the pot and refilled my own cup. "Abigail and I were both terrified it was Sperra. Abigail was dithering about whether to go see or to call Burlin, but I told her we should just go — although I had no idea what we'd do if it was. When we got there, though, it wasn't her. We explained to the woman that Sperra was our sister-in-law and gave her the story we'd concocted on our way down — that Sperra was living in Paris, had come home for a visit, and been mugged. We said her purse and all her jewelry had been taken. The woman insisted she 'hadn't mugged nobody.' " Georgia's voice took on the cadence of country Georgia. "She said that she'd gotten the things in New Orleans during a fire. She'd been in the bathroom of a homeless shelter in the middle of the night when the alarm went off, and she'd snatched up the backpack and run out the back door. She claimed she was 'real glad to give us the things, but she could use a little something to reward her for finding the locket.' I wouldn't have given her anything, but Abigail gave her twenty dollars."

Georgia bit her lower lip and exhaled years

of frustration and anger. "I got on the phone to the New Orleans police, and asked about the fire. They had to check, but eventually called back to say it had happened over a year before, and they gave me the name of the woman who ran that shelter. She said the fire started in a women's dormitory, and while they were able to save most of the building, all the women sleeping in that one room had died of smoke inhalation and their bodies were long buried. When I asked about Sperra, she confirmed Sperra had slept in that room. She uses the nickname Birdie."

"Birdie," I murmured, "not Bertie." I reckoned it was the man's suit that had made Tad and Hector hear her wrong.

Again, Georgia didn't seem to hear me. "Can you imagine how it felt to know a member of your family had been living in a homeless shelter? We couldn't let the papers get hold of that. And we didn't want to exhume thirty bodies to make sure one was hers. We were certain enough to plan a small memorial service and to put up a memorial stone in the family plot in Oakland City Cemetery. All the way home from her service, I whispered, 'Thank you, God. Oh, thank you, thank you, thank you.' As far as we were concerned, years of fear and worry were over." She set down her empty mug as if it had become too heavy to hold. "They have been, until now."

"But if one woman was in the bathroom, Sperra could have been, too." I was thinking out loud, trying to work it out. "She probably was, in fact, if her backpack was there to snatch. From what I understand, theft is common among homeless people, so they keep their belongings close by, wherever they go."

"You are amazing!" Georgia told me. "Abigail *said* you do a little detecting. Her note asks if you'll help us. I think it's an imposition for us to ask, but if somebody doesn't find out pretty soon who killed Sperra, Lance can kiss this election good-bye."

I was tempted to say I'd help, but I know my limits. Right then they included a cast, Joe Riddley, and a serious lack of knowledge. "You need a professional. I don't know a thing about this. The murders I've helped to solve have all been local, except one, and that one was literally dumped in my lap."*

"Here." She cupped her hands around air and held them out toward me with a trace of the old twinkle in her eyes. Then she said, "No, I'm just kidding."

I sighed. "I'd help if I could, but I didn't know Sperra, and don't have any idea who could have killed her — or how to set about finding out."

She sipped her coffee again and looked out

*When Did We Lose Harriet?

the window into the rain. "We've talked about nothing else all night, as you can well imagine, and I'm inclined to believe it must have been Hubert. Chief Muggins said he'd been threatening her because she'd been living in his barn. Can you imagine that? Living in a barn?" She wrinkled her nose, then went on without giving me a chance to reply. "For the life of me, I can't think of any other reason for Hubert to ask me to walk down by the tracks that night. Frankly, it made me a little nervous, it was so deserted down there. But it was still light, and people were not far away."

"You were scared of Hubert?" I was astonished, and didn't mind if she knew it.

She laughed. "Heavens, no. But I was scared somebody might bother us, and Hubert had told us he'd had a heart attack. He wouldn't be much protection."

She lifted her mug and set it down immediately. I knew the coffee had to be stone cold, so I hopped to the sink, dumped it, then brought the mug back. "I don't believe it was Hubert. I've known him all my life."

She gave me a grateful smile, but her gray eyes grew serious again as she refilled her mug. "Then why did he insist on our going to the water tank? He told me he had climbed up there back in high school to paint somebody's name on it, and he wanted to show me how he'd done it. But what if he wanted to go and leave evidence he'd been there, so if he dropped something later when he went back to kill Sperra, I could testify that he'd been there earlier? Edward said last night that anybody who commits a murder leaves some evidence at the scene. What if Hubert was planning it ahead of time?"

"Hubert's not that devious." But I couldn't help remembering that he'd managed to paint my name on that tank nearly fifty years ago and I'd never known it until this week. "He told me you wanted to go to the tracks," I remembered.

She'd been about to sip her coffee. She set it down, puzzled. "What on earth for? I hate trains. You can ask anybody who knows me. Agnes Scott is near the tracks, and the trains nearly drove me batty. Everybody else got used to them, but I never did. And I can't conceive of any reason why I'd want to see a water tank, can you?" She sighed. "But maybe Hubert did just want to show it to me. I said I wanted a walk — I needed exercise. We've been eating too much and sitting too long on this trip. But we walked too far. I barely had time to shower and change before the meeting." She got up and paced back and forth several times, then went to the front window and stared out through the blinds, like the rain might provide some answers. She asked, without turning around, "If Hubert didn't kill Sperra, who did?"

I'd been doing some thinking while she was talking, and I had a question of my own. "You all didn't stay up all night because you were afraid Hubert did it."

She turned and looked at me for a while, like she was also thinking. At last she said, "You are smart, Mackie. Burlin always said you were. We —" She blinked several times, pressed one hand to her lips, and shook her head, warning me she couldn't speak right then. She came back and sat down, and started drawing a little design on the tabletop with one finger. I couldn't tell what it was, but she traced three of them before she swallowed hard and said, "We're terrified they're going to say Lance did it."

That dammed my creek. I had to take several breaths before I could ask, "Why on earth would anybody think that? He didn't even know who she was, did he?"

She nodded. "He admitted last night that Sperra sent him a note Monday afternoon, asking him to meet her at the water tank between eight thirty and nine that night. We all saw Annie Dale deliver it. We were meeting in a sitting room she's let us work in. Lance read it and stuck it in a pile of papers he was working on. We figured it was from some gushing female — he gets a lot of those. We never imagined it was from her. We thought she was dead!"

"Why was he sure it was from her, then,

291

and not an imposter?"

"He said she drew a little bird at the bottom, like this." She reached for a pencil I keep near the table for doing the crossword and traced a design on her paper napkin: a figure eight lying on its side, with three V's making a beak on the small end, a tail at the other, and two legs. "It was a joke between them when he was little. He could draw it by the time he was three. It stood for Sperra — sparrow." Georgia shoved her manicured fingers through her bangs, leaving them in disarray. "I wish Burlin had never married her. We all begged him not to, the first time he brought her home. She came from a good family — her granddaddy was a senator — but her parents died when she was young, and she had all sorts of weird friends. Burlin met her when she was singing in a nightclub."

"I thought he said it was a folk club."

She gave a slight, one-shoulder shrug. "Same difference. She was earning her keep strumming a guitar. She wore long hippy skirts and hair down to her backside, and she looked and talked like Mother Earth. None of us could see what Burlin saw in her." She frowned at me. "Frankly, I think he was still on the rebound from you."

I refused to take the blame for whomever Burlin had married. "She looked all right in the videos they showed last night. Short hair, nice clothes —"

Georgia's lip curled. "Oh, she cleaned up pretty good. And she'd grown up in political circles, so she knew how to behave — when she wasn't drinking. We figured out later that must have started while Burlin was in the Georgia legislature, a couple of years before Lance was born. It's a miracle he wasn't born with fetal alcohol syndrome — although, to give Sperra credit, she tried to be good while she was pregnant. I always thought the reason she didn't want any more children, though, was that she couldn't bear to give up liquor for nine months again. Oh, why am I going on like this? The poor woman is dead. Whatever she did, it's over. But she put Burlin through years and years of hell, and now Lance — Lance —"

I shoved the coffeepot her way. "Have some more."

She shook her head. "I'm over my limit already. And I really ought to be going, or they'll be sending the police looking for me." She stood up and reached for her raincoat.

"But you haven't finished the story. What happened when Lance met her Monday night?"

"He didn't. Hubert asked them to stay after the meeting, remember? There were a lot of people who wanted to talk, so by the time Lance got home, it was past nine. He says he went to his room and read." She headed for the front door.

"Did anybody see him come back to the inn? Annie Dale, for instance?"

She paused. "He stopped by Abigail's room for a minute, I think. But he can't prove he didn't swing by the tank before he went home. Nobody was with him." She gave a little laugh that wasn't the least bit funny. "For that matter, none of us can prove we hadn't recognized Sperra, or where we were when she died. Renée and I were lost in the wilds of Hopemore. Burlin stopped by the inn to change clothes before he went out with some guys, but nobody saw him, so he can't prove he didn't nip out and kill Sperra while he was there."

"What about Edward and Binky — I mean Abigail?"

She gave me the first real laugh I'd heard from her all morning. "She told me she'd asked you to call her that. That darned kid just won't grow up. She was probably the only child in history to give herself a nickname — that's how she said 'Abigail' when she was two, and Burlin and I started calling her that, to tease her. Pretty soon, she wouldn't answer to anything else. She didn't become Abigail again until she went to work for Burlin, and he and I insisted. He didn't want a secretary named Binky. But I think she secretly calls herself Binky still." Her spirits seemed lighter as she opened the front door, then turned back once more for what

Mama used to call "some tarrying talk."

"I forgot to answer your question. Abigail was working in our sitting room all evening, and Edward drove straight from the meeting to Augusta, to meet with some members of Lance's committee there. They had to finalize details for the rally the next evening. Lance was supposed to go with him. Edward was mad as blazes that he wouldn't, and now we all wish he had. But I doubt if either Edward or Abigail can prove they were where they say they were, any more than the rest of us can." She rubbed one cheek with her hand and heaved a sigh that came from her toes. "Who knew we all ought to document our every move? You don't expect something like this."

I got myself to my feet and reached for my walker to see her out. "But like you said, nobody commits a crime without leaving evidence. The police are probably sifting every square inch of dirt by now. What about Annie Dale? Can she help alibi anybody? Has Chief Muggins even talked to her?" Probably so. Since this was now a story worthy of national attention, Charlie would be interviewing everybody with any connection to the newsworthy Bullocks.

Georgia nodded. "Last night. But she wasn't home Monday night. She'd told us earlier that since we wouldn't need dinner, she was going to spend the evening with somebody with the improbable name of Smoke."

"Not smoke, it's S-m-o-a-k," I told her. "Smoak Wilson is her mother-in-law. She's ninety, but spry as can be. Annie Dale goes over there a couple of evenings a week."

"It's too bad Monday happened to be one of them." Georgia usually had excellent posture, but right then, her body drooped in weariness. "Well, I'd better be going. I didn't think you could help us, but I promised Abigail I'd deliver the letter. Oh — I almost forgot!" She dragged it from her pocket again and handed it to me. It was limp and a little damp, addressed to "MacLaren C. Yarbrough" in a sprawling hand.

I opened it and read two scrawled sentences: "Mackie, we need you to help us, please. Can you come see me this morning?"

I shook my head. I was saying, "I really can't think of a single way I can help you," when Georgia finally lost her excellent control.

Tears filled her big gray eyes, and her shoulders shook with sobs. She leaned her head against the doorjamb and bawled. I hopped to the tissues by the couch and put one in her hand. It left smears of mascara down both cheeks. "I can't bear this, Mackie." Her words came out in gasps. "I can't! To get this close — this close — to the governor's mansion and lose it because of a homeless drunk!" She scrubbed her eyes again, but still they poured tears. "Lance has worked so hard. We all have. But if this thing doesn't get solved soon —" She ran out of words and could only shake her head. She reached out and clasped one of my hands with a valiant attempt to smile, then pulled up her hood and dashed out into the rain.

It was falling harder now, heaven's tears covering the sad streets of Hopemore.

Near the sidewalk, Georgia picked up my paper, then ran back through the rain to thrust it at me. "Here. But I doubt it's worth getting run over for."

As she hurried away, anybody seeing that silver raincoat might think the moon had dropped by our place for a visit. To me, it looked like one big teardrop.

I was relieved I hadn't made the front page. All the Bullocks had, though, standing in the same tableau that had appeared on the eleven o'clock news. I was about to lay the paper down when I thought to turn the page.

There I was, under the headline "Old sweetheart offers condolences." It looked for all the world like Burlin and I were about to embrace.

21

I didn't care if Joe Riddley was grumpy that early. I didn't care if he would be more mellow after he ate. I snatched up the paper and hopped down the hall at record speed. Shoving his legs over, I sat down beside him. "Joe Riddley? Wake up. I have to tell you something."

He muttered from beneath the covers.

"Wake up." I shook his shoulder.

He didn't bother to open his eyes. "Is the house on fire?"

"No."

"Has somebody gone to the hospital?"

"No. But —"

"Is somebody dead?"

"You're gonna be dead if you don't wake up and listen to me. I have to tell you something." I shook him again.

"Will I like it?"

"No, you won't."

"Then wait until I've had my breakfast." With a mighty heave, he turned his back toward me, practically pitching me off the bed straight onto my bum leg.

I scrabbled back up and wiggled to make him give me sitting room. "I can't. I have to tell you *now*." If I didn't, my courage would desert me.

He heaved a sigh and turned back over, again jerking the covers from beneath me and nearly spilling me onto the floor. He put both our pillows behind his head and shoved himself up so he was propped and comfortable. "This had better be good."

"It's not. It's terrible." Tears clogged my throat. "It's — I don't know how to begin."

He glowered. "You wake me up at dawn to tell me something that is so infernally important it can't wait, then you don't know how to begin? How about, 'I'm sorry I woke you up, honey — why don't you go back to sleep'?"

I took a deep breath. "How about, 'I'm sorry I wasn't faithful to you after you left me up at college?' Or 'I did date Burlin Bullock for a while up there. Can you ever forgive me'?"

He punched the pillow behind him to get more comfortable. Then he closed both eyes and didn't say a word for two hundred years.

"I'm sorry," I repeated desperately. "I wish it hadn't happened." I also wished I hadn't said anything. I wouldn't have, dang it, if Burlin hadn't come to town. I'm not one of those fools who think married people ought to tell their partners everything. That may make *them* feel better, but it generally makes the partners miserable.

About as miserable as I felt waiting for him to speak.

But I couldn't have let him find out from somebody else.

I hardly breathed until he finally stretched, yawned, and forced his eyes to open. "Okay. Now I'm awake. But for the life of me, I don't see why you couldn't have waited another hour after waiting all these years." He covered his mouth to yawn again, then gave me an approving nod. "So it was Burlin Bullock. Good taste, Little Bit."

I gaped at him. "What do you mean, '*It was Burlin Bullock*'? Did you think there was somebody?"

He rubbed his chin, and his whiskers made a whispering sound in the room. "I figured there had to be. You went to college that fall kissing like a girl. You came home for Thanksgiving kissing like a woman. You hadn't learned that from me."

If he'd punched me in the stomach, it would have had the same effect. "You never said a word."

"What was there to say? Either you'd come back to me or you wouldn't. Didn't seem to be a thing I could do about it except wait."

I huffed. "You could have come to see me. You could have written or called sometimes to say you loved me."

He nodded. "I could have. Should have. I would now, but I wasn't grown up then.

Mama told me I shouldn't neglect you while I was paying for that ring." He rubbed it gently, his finger warm on mine. "But I didn't want to ask you to marry me carrying a load of debt."

I felt sadder than a hound dog on full moon night. I laid my hand on the one that was stroking my ring. "I never loved him. You need to know that. And if you'd paid me the slightest attention that fall —" I jerked my hand away and swivelled around to face him straight on. "Wait a minute. When you came to my hospital room that night, the way you kissed me took my breath away. You didn't learn that from *me*."

He gave me a smug smile. "What's sauce for the goose —"

I raised my fist. "I'll goose you! Who was she? It wasn't Annie Dale, was it?"

He grabbed my arm and pulled me toward him. "I'll never tell. It never meant a thing. Maybe we both needed a comparison, to be sure we had what we really wanted."

"But —" I felt my lower lip quiver. The idea of Joe Riddley with somebody else shocked me to my very soul.

He wrapped me in both arms and whispered into my hair, "How about if I forgive you and you forgive me? Will that be all right? And we don't need to ever mention it again?"

I nodded. "But we'll probably have to see

Burlin around town until they leave. He's making a perfect nuisance of himself."

He nuzzled my neck. "You think he's a nuisance? I'll show you a nuisance. Take off those wet clothes. I don't know where you have been, but you are soaking my covers."

That's all you need to know about that, except that as I was hopping out of the room later to make more coffee, I saw the paper lying on the floor and remembered why I'd gone in there in the first place. I stopped at the door. "You also need to know there's another picture of me in the paper, but it's not what it looks like. I was pushing Burlin away."

He held out his hand and I gave him the paper. He studied the picture, then roared with laughter. "I'd have guessed that even if you hadn't told me. Burlin Bullock probably gets down on his knees every night to thank the Almighty he didn't get stuck with you." He swung his long legs out of the bed. "Now go get my breakfast. I'm heading to the shower."

22

I'd almost forgotten I had traffic court in the south end of the county that morning. Joe Riddley and I considered the problem and agreed that if the rain was over, I ought to be able to drive. I'd need the wheelchair to get into the courtroom, but I could park in the handicapped place right by the front door and call on my cell phone for somebody to come get the chair out of my trunk.

The rain stopped before we finished breakfast, leaving the sky cloud free and a dazzling blue. The whole town seemed to sparkle. It was marvelous to be driving again, too. I felt like I'd been let out of jail. I'd have enjoyed the drive more, though, if Oglethorpe Street — which is also the federal highway through town — hadn't been jammed because trucks emblazoned with various network symbols were parked every which way up and down the street. I inched along until I came to a cross street to a longer but faster route. As I turned off, I worried that I'd be late. Fortunately, my cast made what Joe Riddley persists in calling my "lead foot" even heavier. Instead of late, I was ten minutes early.

The only thing that keeps presiding over

traffic court from being the most boring part of serving as magistrate is the creative excuses people give for speeding, parking improperly, or running into things. If you sat on my bench, you could think it was the nature of trees to leap in front of moving vehicles and of speed limit signs to randomly disappear. We have a lot of invisible ones in Hope County. Or a lot of drivers who think they can fool the judge.

That morning, I sat there trying to look interested and wondering why I hadn't thought to use traffic court as an illustration when I'd talked to Tad about confession and forgiveness. Most of the defendants could have saved us both a lot of time by admitting they were wrong and accepting their fines. I wonder if the courtyard of heaven will be crowded with people who will choose to spend eternity stuck in a long line, waiting to explain to St. Peter that nothing was really their fault.

As you have guessed, my happy mood dissipated in the courtroom. Maybe that's because some attorneys and a few of the accused thought they could smirk at the judge who'd got her picture in the paper twice that week with Burlin Bullock. They left sorrier than they came in.

Finally, we were done. I didn't want to tackle the Oglethorpe Street gridlock, so I decided to swing around and come up along the railroad tracks, approaching Yarbrough's from the back. Since the water tank was on my way, I might as well see what the police were up to over there.

I might have known I wouldn't find Chief Muggins. All the reporters had abandoned the tank. It had served its purpose: to introduce the story. But squatting like a bloated blue spider above the skyline, it was too faded and ugly to hold media attention long. Two days of rain, particularly yesterday's storm, had also destroyed any evidence the police hadn't found. The only remaining signs of the murder at the weed-grown lot were a bedraggled strip of crime tape wound around the hedge and Burlin Bullock, head thrust back to peer up at the tank. I'd have left him to his ruminations, except he looked so alone.

Hoping I wouldn't shred a tire in a jagged pothole, I headed his way, rolled down my window, and called, "How are you, with all this?"

He turned without even a shadow of his usual smile. "Numb. Disbelieving. Trying to drum up grief and finding none. It's hard to resurrect somebody and bury them again in the same day. My feelings have shut down." He looked younger than he was, in white jeans and an emerald polo shirt, but as he turned and strolled toward my car, I saw webs of weariness around his eyes. "I'm sorry about that picture, by the way." He looked both ways. "We seem blessedly free of cameras at the moment, but don't count on our luck holding."

I squinted, looking straight into the sun. "Notoriety seems to be one of the hazards of being friends with the Bullocks. How did you elude the reporters? They're crawling all over town like maggots."

"Nasty, but apt." He obligingly put himself between me and the glare, then jerked a thumb toward a green roof almost lost in trees a block away. "We're staying just over there. I sneaked out the back way."

"Oh. I never realized that the back of Annie Dale's is so close to the tank. Her granddaddy, who built it, was retired from the railroad and wanted to be close to the trains, but I've always approached the house from the front. She has a lovely big garden."

"That's because the house is built at the back of the lot."

I knew why we were talking about houses and lots. Neither of us wanted to talk about what had happened at the tank. I felt sorry for Burlin this morning. He looked absolutely exhausted. I wished I could offer sympathy, but didn't want it misunderstood. I said, "I didn't know if you all would still be in town. You've canceled the rest of your meetings in the area, I presume."

"By mutual consent." He rested one arm

on my windowsill. "We couldn't get five people to show up to discuss the election, but we could fill a stadium to talk about the murder."

Since he'd brought it up, I asked, "Do you have any theories about who killed her?"

He shook his head, then grinned briefly. "I guess I'd be at the top of your list, huh? But I didn't have any reason to kill her. Heck, I buried her twenty years ago. That's what I told the police chief when he showed up bright and early this morning. 'Charming Charlie,' Georgia calls him. I also told him I'll give ten thousand dollars to anybody who provides information that leads to the apprehension of the killer. Maybe that will bring somebody out of the woodwork."

"That was so dumb!" I pounded my steering wheel with both fists.

Burlin drew back and stared. "What's your problem? You told me the other day to improve the local economy. I thought you'd be proud of me."

"Lance got a note from Sperra Monday, right?" I barely waited for him to nod. "The man who delivered that note has the sharpest nose in town for easy money. I'd be willing to bet that ten minutes after word of the reward hits the street, he'll be in Charlie Muggins's office. Half an hour after that, the chief's new cruiser will be sitting in front of Annie Dale's."

He stared at me like I'd cut his oxygen hose.

"Georgia told me this morning about the note," I added, figuring I might as well spell it out, "and that Lance can't prove where he was after the meeting."

"Lordy, lordy, lordy." Burlin kicked a pebble halfway across the parking lot. "Annie Dale said she found the note on a front porch rocker. We figured Sperra had left it there. We never imagined anybody else knew about it. How did you find out?"

"My grandson camped out with Sperra for a couple of days in Hubert's barn. He told me she'd written a letter and given it to Hector. I spoke with Hector yesterday and he said he didn't look to see who it was addressed to — Hector *can* read, but he doesn't. It's a matter of principle with him. But he said he propped it on Annie Dale's rocker. Once she says she found it there, it's a clear chain of evidence."

He was pale under his tan, his eyes bleak. "They're gonna think my boy killed her, aren't they?" When a daddy says that, it doesn't matter if he's wearing a Rolex or overalls, it tears your heart out.

"It would help if he could prove what he was doing for a couple of hours after the meeting. Was he talking on the phone? Sending a fax? Writing e-mail? Did he speak to anybody on the street? He needs witnesses. From what Georgia says, you all do."

"Help us, Mackie." Tears stood in his eyes. "We don't even know what questions to ask. Georgia and Abigail said they asked you to help, but you wouldn't. I am begging you. Please?"

"I don't have the vaguest idea who might have cause to kill Sperra. The only thing I am pretty sure of is that Hubert wouldn't kill somebody that way. So I've already done what I knew to do — find proof that he didn't do it."

"Do that much for Lance. Clear him. That's all I ask. I know he didn't do it. He couldn't. He's — gentle, he cares for people." He sighed. "Abigail keeps telling me he isn't ruthless enough to be a politician. She may be right. I know he wouldn't kill anybody — especially his mother. But I don't know how we can prove it."

"Call a private detective, or one of your high-powered lawyers. You must know some of them."

"By the time they get here, Lance could be in jail. At least come talk to us, won't you? Everybody's over at the house right now, glum and feeling like prisoners. Come have a cup of coffee and ask us some questions. Maybe just telling you what we know will help us. Please?"

I had never seen Burlin so raw and unsure of himself. I liked him better that way. "What about all the reporters?"

"I'll handle them. I promise."

"A cup of coffee, then," I agreed. "But if Chief Muggins finds me there, he's going to accuse us all of conspiracy."

"He can accuse me of anything he likes, so long as he doesn't arrest my son." He came around and climbed in the passenger seat. "It must feel good to drive again."

"Freedom," I agreed. He had been right earlier: We were often on the same wavelength. I'd never tell him, though.

As I turned out of the lot, I asked, "How many of you knew Sperra was in town?"

"Just Lance, so far as I know. He didn't tell us about the note until last night." He hesitated. "But from something Renée said before the dinner Monday night, she knew he was planning to go somewhere after the meeting. He may have told her where, and who he planned to meet. But he says he didn't meet Sperra. We hadn't counted on the meeting going so late, you see — Hubert sprang the question and answer session on us. Lance says Sperra told him to meet her between eight thirty and nine, and he didn't leave the meeting until after nine. Well, here we are. Park over there. And stay in the car until I open your door."

Two reporters were at the car before I turned off the engine. Burlin got out, held up both hands, and said, "Folks, as you can see, this is Judge Yarbrough. But this mistake about the judge, here, and me has gone on long enough. She is a friend of my sisters. I don't know who started the other rumor, but any more misleading pictures or innuendos, and you are likely to find yourselves hauled into court for libel. Understand? She's come here to see my sisters. Please go away now and come back for a press conference at two. Okay?"

They babbled questions, but he shook his head. "Not now. We have an appointment." He fetched my chair, pushed me through Annie Dale's gate, and clicked it behind us — slick as soap on a shower floor. Out of the corner of my eye, I saw the reporters heading for their cars.

I eyed the six steps leading to Annie Dale's wide front porch and I pointed to the side yard. "See that gazebo over yonder? We'll need to meet there. I'd never make it into the house without crawling up the steps. And don't look at me like that. You aren't going to carry me, if that's what you were thinking. But you'll have to push. Even though it looks like Annie Dale's had her grass cut this morning, I don't think I can get myself over there." He obeyed. As I got out of the chair, I said, "Why don't you ask Annie Dale if she'll serve coffee out here? She does that sometimes. And tell her I'd rather have iced tea, please."

He gave me a mock salute. "Aye, aye, ma'am. But you know something I've just realized? All these years, I've told myself that if I'd married you, I could have been governor. I was wrong. If we'd gotten married? *You* would have been governor."

23

Annie Dale's gazebo had been designed for pleasant relaxation. Six comfortable wicker chairs surrounded a large round table covered in a flowered vinyl cloth. Beyond the waist-high railing, bees and butterflies enjoyed an autumn feast of zinnias, sedum, and nicotiana.

I managed to hop up the single step and took the nearest chair. The Bullock clan came out like Noah's animals, two by two.

Georgia and Edward came first. She wore black pants and a black shell with the same chunky black-and-silver jewelry she'd worn to Gusta's Saturday Do. I didn't know if she was dressed for mourning or just didn't feel patriotic that morning. Above the black, she was so pale, I was afraid she might faint. Edward wore navy slacks and a light blue sports shirt like a man who would rather be in a black suit, and he seemed to have more frowns than suits. Monday night, he'd given Burlin the "Why don't you give in and agree with me?" frown. Today's was a "Why are we wasting our time?" frown.

To confirm that, he greeted me with, "I don't know what Burlin thinks this can accomplish."

I wanted to say "Hello to you, too." Instead I said, "Neither do I. Maybe reciting your alibis to me will be good practice for giving them to Chief Muggins later. My guess is the chief is talking right now to the man who brought Sperra's note here."

That shut him up, at least for the time being. He took the chair directly across from me and pulled it up close to the table, ready for business. Then he sat frowning and drumming his fingers in a series of four beats with the accent on the third. To me, it sounded like "Didn't *do* it. Didn't *do* it." I figured he was waiting to find the best spin to put on their stories. Edward did not look like a man who gave up an election until the polls had closed.

Georgia went behind me and sat down to my left. She adjusted her chair so it faced me slightly, then reached out to take my hand. Hers was cold as death. "You said you wouldn't help us," she said in reproach. I didn't know if her problem was that I'd turned her down earlier or that I had changed my mind.

"I said I didn't think I could. I still don't, but Burlin wanted me to at least come hear your stories about that night."

Her eyes were worried. "He said the police know Sperra wrote Lance. Did you tell them?"

"No, I've been in traffic court all morning

314

— presiding," I added when I saw I'd startled her. "But Sperra gave the letter to somebody else to deliver, and I'm sure he'll go after the reward like bees to honey. He's that kind of person."

She looked as if she'd like to say more, but Lance and Renée were joining us.

Of all of them, Lance looked most normal this morning. He looked sleepy, of course — his eyes were pink, and he stifled a yawn as he came across the grass — but he greeted me with his usual relaxed smile. "Judge Yarbrough, right? Thanks for coming. Daddy says maybe you can help us out of this mess." Renée flinched at his choice of words, but he didn't notice. "After that," he continued, "maybe we can give my poor mother the burial she deserves."

That was the first time anybody had talked about Sperra as a person who deserved something. I liked him for it. He went to the chair beside Edward and sprawled casually, wearing his khaki pants and white polo shirt like a man who had stopped by on his way to a round of golf. He left his chair far back from the table so he could stretch his legs and rested his right arm on the back of Edward's chair. "You doin' all right, Georgia?" he asked her.

She sighed. "As well as can be expected. You okay, Renée?"

Renée took the chair to my right and

turned her back slightly to me, stretching her long legs under Lance's before she shrugged and said, "I'm doing all right." She was wearing green again, that sage that exactly matched her eyes. Today it was a cotton shell with white jeans. Her large feet were encased in pale tan sandals, and she wore a large topaz on her right hand. I tried again to picture Renée as a squalling baby, and couldn't. She must have sprung like Aphrodite, elegant and perfect, from a wave somewhere near Galveston.

Burlin and Annie Dale came last. He was carrying a tray of cups, sugar bowl and creamer, spoons, and tall glasses of ice. She bustled after him with a pot of hot coffee in one hand and a pitcher of iced tea with floating lemon wedges in the other. If she were to bring them together, like cymbals, would heat and cold shatter both and shower glass all over us?

It would be a fitting start to this peculiar meeting.

Annie Dale and I greeted each other like old friends who keep meaning to spend more time together. She looked well, her gray hair cut short and brushed back off her face. But I eyed her full lower lip and silently wondered, *Did you teach my husband how to kiss?*

She gave me the same smile she always did, but now I asked myself, *Was it a little sly? Knowing?*

She beamed around the table. "If you all want anything else, just come ask for it." She walked back to the house with a sway to her hips. Burlin and Edward both watched her to the front steps. Laws, that woman was sexy. Why had I never seen it before? And I knew as well as I knew my name that no matter what she and Joe Riddley had once done, if anything, it would forever remain one of life's little mysteries I would never be allowed to solve.

The only chair left was all the way around the table, between Edward and Georgia. Burlin rested his hand on my shoulder briefly as he passed behind me to reach it. We devoted the next few minutes to pouring what we wanted to drink and taking a few sips to clear our palates. Finally Lance asked, "So, what's this about, again?"

Georgia, Edward, and Burlin spoke at once. Burlin waved the other two to silence and said, "Mackie, here, says Sperra didn't bring you that letter. She sent it by a man who is likely to go straight to the police when he hears about the reward. That means they will know she wrote it and sent it here. He'll say he left it on the porch rocker. Annie Dale will say she found a letter there addressed to you and took it to you Monday afternoon."

Lance absorbed this, then nodded. "So I'm going to be suspect number one pretty soon."

317

Edward grunted. "Suspect number only, unless we come up with another one or you come up with a good story. Now, here's what I think we ought to say." His eyes shifted to me.

"It better be the truth," I warned. "Making up stories gets folks in all kinds of trouble. Ask recent presidents."

He flushed an angry red. "I still don't know what she's doing here," he muttered to Burlin.

Burlin looked around the table. "Abigail looked up Mackie on the Internet, and it turns out she's had some experience in solving murders. I haven't read the stuff, so I don't know what she's done or how, but I thought maybe she could help us out."

"Where is Abigail?" I hadn't noticed until then that she hadn't come with the others.

"She's not feeling well," Burlin said at the same instant Georgia said, "Sulking."

"She hasn't been well since Monday," Renée objected, frowning at Georgia.

Georgia gave me a rueful smile. "Okay, she's not sulking. She doesn't feel well." She managed to convey that in her experience of her baby sister, they were the same thing.

"What do you want to know?" Edward asked. "Where we were Monday night after the meeting?"

I nodded. "And if you can prove it."

"Well, I can." Everybody looked at him in

318

surprise. "I left the meeting at ten 'til nine, because I was dry as a rotten log in drought and I wanted to buy a cold orange juice before I headed to Augusta."

Georgia gave a dainty snort. "You and your orange juice."

"Don't knock it. This one may save my skin. The Bi-Lo here closes at nine, which anybody can verify. I went straight there and arrived as the manager was about to lock the door. He let me in, I made my purchase, and as I was paying, I got a call on my cell phone from one of the Augusta people wanting to know when I thought I could get there. The woman at the register had to wait for me to put him on hold while I paid her, so she ought to remember. He and I talked the whole time I drove up, planning strategy for Tuesday's rally. He can verify that. Except for the time it took to drive from the meeting to the Bi-Lo, I'm covered until nearly midnight." He sat back and seemed to challenge the others to come up with equally good stories.

"Why didn't you say all that last night?" Georgia demanded.

"I needed time to remember it all. How about you, Burlin? You were leaving the meeting as I was."

"Yeah, with Hubert. He dropped me off here and I went upstairs to change my clothes. I turned on the TV —"

"He's a television news junkie," Lance informed me.

"— and I think I might be able to remember the stories if I try. I know there was one about a convenience store holdup in Augusta, because Edward was heading in that direction." He rubbed his hand across his mouth, thinking. "I brushed my teeth, put on some casual clothes, and came down to the porch to wait for Hubert. He came by in about ten minutes."

"It would have been close, but you could have run over to the water tank and killed your wife," I pointed out.

"I could have, but I didn't. I got on my cell phone and placed a call, which my cell phone bill will show. I guess I could have talked while running to the tank, hitting my wife, and running back — you may want to check with the other party whether I was huffing and puffing and whether he heard any dull thuds. We were still talking when Hubert pulled up and he had to wait while I said good-bye. He may remember that."

"That sounds pretty good," I congratulated him. "The way Georgia was talking this morning, I thought nobody could prove where they were."

"Except me and Renée," she reminded me. "We were driving around Hopemore all night, trying to find Gusta's."

"But you came by here to change shoes

first, right?" She nodded. "So what were you doing at that time, Renée?"

She gave me a smile that didn't even pretend to be embarrassed. "Sleeping in the car. I've been dozing off and on all week, every chance I get. I didn't see any need to go in, since Georgia said she'd just be a minute. She even pointed to the clock and said I could time her." She gave Georgia a lopsided smile. "The dashboard clock said 8:30 when she left. She woke me when she came back to point out it was only 8:40 — she'd hurried. I dozed some more while she drove around, until she woke me to say she was lost. I helped her find the right place, and we got there as the clock chimed nine. How she spent twenty minutes lost around here, I will never know."

"More like thirty," I told her. "Gusta's clock runs slow." I hated to ask the next question, but somebody inevitably would. "Would you have noticed if the car had stopped and Georgia had gotten out while you all were driving around?"

Georgia didn't look the least bit worried while Renée took time to consider the question. "I'm sure I would have, because I remember that she had to stop twice at the stoplight."

"One light in town, and it caught me coming and going," Georgia said wryly.

"Did you check any of those times with your own watch?"

She held up her arm and pushed back her sleeve. "I don't wear a watch." I remembered at least two people informing me that Renée had no sense of time. How she managed to be a successful professional without watching clocks, I didn't know. Maybe she could teach me when all this was over.

"The same is true for you as for me," Burlin pointed out. "You have ten minutes when nobody was with you. Instead of sleeping, you could have dashed over to the water tank and clobbered Sperra."

"I never dash," Renée said calmly.

"There is that," he agreed.

"Besides" — she reached to pour herself another glass of tea — "I quite liked the woman."

24

If Renée wanted to cause a sensation, she did.

"What do you mean you liked her?" Georgia demanded.

At the exact same time, Burlin said, "You never met her."

Lance reached over and put a hand on her arm, as if to protect her from them both. "Tell them," he urged.

"Well" — her husky voice drew out the word, like a storyteller beginning a tale — "Monday morning I went for a walk. I needed to get away from people for a while. So I trudged out of town along the highway and turned past the Bi-Lo on the first dirt road I came to."

"It's gravel," I corrected her, having spent a fortune on that gravel over the years.

"Whatever." The distinction obviously escaped her. "There was a funny old house near the corner, with things sticking up all over the roof. Then there were some lovely piney woods on one side with a pasture on the other. I could smell hay and cotton dust, and — it just smelled like September, somehow. I walked what would have been two or three blocks, if there had been blocks, and passed a second house with a barn. Then I saw another pasture with a barbed-wire fence and a hill beyond the fence. I wondered what was over that hill, so I climbed through and went to see. At the bottom on the other side was a cattle pond with a short dock."

"And you met Sperra at the pond," I contributed.

She turned to me in surprise. "You're really good! Did you see us, or are you psychic?"

"Neither. Sperra had been camping in that barn, and my grandson was staying with her a few days. He said Hubert drove Sperra away that morning, and she went to the pond."

"Small-town grapevine detecting," Georgia murmured. "The best kind." A breath of wind lifted her bangs from her forehead, and I saw a faint line near her hairline where a plastic surgeon had taken a tuck and wiped away several years.

Renée was talking again. ". . . man, sitting on the dock throwing bits of bread into the pond. He looked harmless, so I sat down at the other end. After a while I said how nice it was to get away from people a bit, and he told me not to swim in the pond because it wasn't clean. I said, 'I grew up on a ranch in Texas. I know better.' We sat a while longer without talking. Then I asked, 'Aren't you hot in that coat?' He said, 'Yeah,' and took it off. That's when I saw she was a woman. We didn't say anything else for a while. Then she said, 'You're his wife, aren't you?' I said, 'I'm Lance Bullock's wife. Is that who you mean?' She jumped up so fast, I nearly fell in the pond in surprise. Then she started waving her arms and yelling at me. 'Don't let him do it! Don't let them make him do it.'" Renée was so involved in the story, she waved her own arms.

"Did you know what she meant?" I asked.

"No, and I told her so." She reached out and touched Lance, but he was looking down at the table. His hands were clenched so tight before him, the knuckles were white. "Shall I go on?" she asked him privately.

"You might as well. You've gotten this far." He still didn't look up.

"The woman stopped yelling and said, 'I'm sorry, honey. I didn't mean to scare you. I get upset sometimes. But I'm his mother, before God and these witnesses.'" Renée gave us all a crooked smile. "The only witnesses being me, a couple of fish swimming near the top of the water, and a few butterflies. Anyway, she came and took me by both hands, and she had tears in her eyes. 'He doesn't have to run for governor,' she said. 'He doesn't want to do it. I can tell. A mother knows these things. Don't let them make him do it. His heart's not in it.' "

Renée paused to take a big swallow of tea. It slid down a throat as graceful as a swan's. Then she addressed Burlin. "I told her my heart isn't particularly in it, either, and she said, 'Don't let them eat you. They'll eat you alive if you let them.' I said, 'I have no intention of being eaten,' and she said, 'You know, honey, I don't think you will.' Then she spread out her arms and gave me a big, smelly hug. She even laughed and said, 'I know I stink, but my heart's pure.' After that, I came back and found you all had already left for Dublin, so I took another nap." She turned to me. "I knew that Lance's mother was dead, of course, and anybody could tell this woman was a bit peculiar —"

In the South, that's how we describe anybody who's not like the rest of us, from a serial killer to a woman who still irons her underwear.

"— but I liked her, whoever she was. Oh — before I left, she ran after me and grabbed my wrist" — Renée rubbed it at the memory — "and asked where we were staying, so she could write —" She stopped. I saw her pressing her lips together and thought she was done, but she whispered, "I wish I hadn't told her. Oh, I wish I hadn't."

"It's never wise —" Edward began in a lecturing voice, but Lance flapped a hand for him to hush. Then he put an arm around his wife and pulled her to him. Renée laid her head on his shoulder and wept.

"It wasn't your fault, honey," he whispered. "It's not your fault. Hush, now. Hush. It's not your fault." His eyes met mine over her rough-cut brown hair. "She told me what had happened as soon as I got back from Dublin. We drove back to the pond to see if we could find the woman, because I figured that whoever she was, if she was that determined to talk to me, I ought to give her a chance." His voice grew bleak. "I never for a second imagined it was really Mother."

"She was probably wandering around town with her letter by then," I said, "looking for Hector. You never did find her?"

He shook his head. "No, but I got her note a little after three. She signed it with a little bird that she taught me to draw as soon as I could hold a pencil and enclosed this picture." He fished it from his wallet and held it up. "I didn't even tell Daddy, though, because I thought I ought to go see her before I mentioned her to anybody."

"What did you do with the note?" I asked. "Do you still have it?"

"Yeah, I've got it. We were all in the sitting room when it came, in the middle of a meeting, and I needed time to think about it, so I shoved it between the pages of the speech I was working on for Augusta. Tuesday, after I heard what had happened"

— he paused for a deep breath — "I got it and put it in our room."

"You'd better go flush it," Edward commanded.

Lance shook his head. "Not for a million dollars."

"It won't matter whether he has it or not," I told Edward. "Enough people have seen it to verify its existence. Why don't you tell us about your Monday-evening schedule, Lance?"

"I would have skipped the meeting entirely — Hubert wanted Daddy to speak, after all — but Edward, here" — he jerked a finger in that direction — "got the bright idea that Daddy ought to say a few words, then turn it over to me. I was in no shape to write a speech that afternoon. I still don't remember what I said, and it didn't matter anyway — nobody wanted to hear me when they'd been promised Daddy. And then Hubert announced that Q & A session, so I didn't get away until a minute or two past nine. I even had to stay after Daddy, because some people had heard I was planning to change parties —"

"Which wasn't your idea," Renée added. "It was theirs." She glared at Edward and Burlin.

"We have discussed the possibility of Lance running on the other ticket," Edward quickly explained to me, as if it were no more important than his deciding to wear a different tie.

"Mentioned it," Georgia added, to soften the effect.

"You were going to make him betray everything he stands for," Renée snapped.

Burlin gave me a rueful grin. "Bullocks never have easy marriages."

I wasn't going to touch that with a ten-foot pole. "So, Lance, where were you after the meeting? And can you prove it?"

"No, ma'am, I can't." His dark eyes were sober. "I came back here —" He dropped his gaze to the table and started scratching at a speck of something on the cloth.

I didn't raise two boys without recognizing when a man-child isn't being truthful. "But not straight here, right?" He looked up, startled. My eyes held his until he shook his head.

He took a deep breath as if he hoped air would give him strength. "Okay, everybody might as well know the worst. I did go to the tank."

"You never!" Was that Georgia, Burlin, or Edward? They spoke at the same time.

"I did," he admitted.

He'd shocked even Renée. Edward made a motion for Lance to hush. Burlin sat there like he'd seen a Gorgon and turned to stone. Renée reached out and took one of Lance's hands in her own. "But you didn't kill her."

"No." He spoke around what sounded like a sob in his throat. "She was already dead when I got there."

"Tell it in order," I commanded.

He took a long minute to compose himself. "I left the meeting place a little after nine. There were only a couple of folks still there by then. Hubert had run Daddy by here to change and promised he'd come back to lock up. I was later than the note had said, but I hoped if it was Mother, she'd realize I could have been detained. She'd been married to Daddy, after all, and that happens all the time in politics. So in case it was her and she was still waiting, I drove to the water tank." He took a gulp of tea like we were sitting in a desert and he was parched. "The streetlights aren't bright over there, but what I could see of the lot around the tank didn't look safe for my tires, so I parked at the curb and walked. About halfway to the tank I started calling, 'Mother? Mother?' The word felt good in my mouth. I hadn't used it for so long."

He stood abruptly and went to stand at the rail with his back to us. But although Annie Dale's lawn was lovely, I doubted that he saw a single plant. His voice was distant, as if he were narrating a movie while the events of that night reeled by. "When nobody answered, I realized if anybody else heard me, they'd think I was nuts, so I shut up and kept walking. I didn't know if she'd meant to meet in the parking lot or right under the tank — I wasn't even sure you could get under the tank, with all those bushes around it. But I prowled around and found one place that looked like a way in, so I pushed through. It was dark in there, and my night vision isn't real good, so I didn't see anybody. It was when I was walking over to the tank that my foot hit something. I had some matches in my pocket. I lit one and saw — and saw —"

"Did you recognize her?" I interrupted.

He shook his head. "Oh, no. Renée had told me about the man's suit and hat, but I forgot that right then. I thought it was some drunk who had crawled through the bushes to sleep it off — or die. He looked so still, I knew almost immediately he was dead. I wondered if Mother had seen him and run away — or even if he'd tried to bother her and she'd killed him. It sounds dumb now, but you get funny thoughts standing beside a body in the dark. Besides, I was still thinking about how I could find Mother."

"Why didn't you call the police?" I asked.

"I was going to, but I figured I ought to be sure the fellow was dead. I didn't want to be embarrassed by bringing them out for a sleeping drunk. When I reached for his wrist" — he paused for a deep breath — "when I felt for his pulse, my finger rubbed a little double mole. Mother had one exactly like that, in the same place. It crashed over me like an ocean wave that this *was* Mother, and

331

she was dead again." He kicked the banister with one toe. "After all those years, I got there late. If I hadn't —" He paused to swallow convulsively. "She was still warm."

Nobody said anything for several minutes. Finally I felt compelled to point out, "But you didn't call the police."

He shook his head. "I went a little crazy. If the police knew who she was, they'd be sure to think I — or one of us — killed her. Nobody knew she was here except Renée and me, and I hadn't done it. I didn't think Renée had, either — I mean, I was sure she hadn't. Hell, I don't know what I thought. Not much, to tell the truth. I just turned tail and ran. My mother was dead, and I *ran!*"

He bent over the railing while sobs shook him. Renée hurried to stand behind him, and now it was she holding him like a grieving child. "How could I have missed her?" he cried. "How could I have come so close, and missed her?"

He slumped with grief. Renée couldn't support his weight much longer. Burlin left his chair and touched her arm. She stepped back to let him hold his son, but hovered nearby, as if protecting Lance still.

Lance sobbed and sobbed. Burlin stroked his back. "Hush, son. Hush, now." Finally Lance quieted down and stumbled toward his chair. He sprawled with his head on the table, his arms flung out beyond it. Renée took a napkin and gently lifted his head to wipe his flushed face. Then she and Burlin returned to their seats.

I felt like a drill sergeant, expecting him to keep talking after that, but we needed to know. "Did you come straight back here after that?"

He seemed to appreciate my matter-of-fact tone. "No, ma'am. I drove to Main Street —"

"Oglethorpe," I corrected him. He didn't notice.

"— and when I saw a sign to Waynesboro, I decided to go to Waynesboro. Don't know a soul there, but it seemed as good a place to go as any. Then, just out of town here, I saw a filling station and noticed I was low on gas. So I stopped to fill up my tank and get something to drink. The man who took my money said, 'You're shaking like a leaf, buddy. What's the matter?' I came within a hair of telling him, but by then I had some sense, so I told him I was low on sugar and needed a Coke real fast. He's bound to remember me. He had to pop the top on my can."

"Since you don't really have a sugar imbalance, that could cause some problems in court."

He looked at me, surprised. "But I do. I've had diabetes since I was fourteen."

Edward figured it out as he went. "If you had driven straight out there after the

333

meeting, it wouldn't have taken you much less time than stopping by the water tank, right?"

Lance shook his head. "Five minutes, maybe, or even less."

"And you came right back?"

"Yeah. I looked in on Abigail, who was working, and told her I was home."

Edward sat back in his chair and lifted his hands. "So what are we worried about? Everybody has an alibi. Lance won't mention the tank detour, and the police will eventually find the killer — or not." He gave a scornful laugh. "It was probably some tramp who'd staked out the tank as his private estate."

"Maybe so," Burlin agreed, "but I think we all owe Mackie a round of thanks for helping us get the stories clear in our minds." He gave me his famous lazy grin. "You're as good as Abigail said you were. Thanks."

Georgia patted my hand. "I didn't know you had this gift."

Edward stood and stretched. "Well, I haven't had much sleep, and we've promised to hold a press conference at two." He checked his watch. "Until then, I'm heading to my bed and recommend the rest of you do the same. We need to look our best."

In an instant, tensions around the table dissolved. Burlin reached for Georgia's hand and gave it a squeeze. Renée patted Lance's shoulder. "You're going to be fine," she murmured. "Let's get some rest."

I'd seen that phenomenon before — the relief when a group of people was finally persuaded none of them had committed some dreadful crime. They took deep breaths of Annie Dale's new-mown grass and relaxed. I hated to spoil their new mood, but I held up one hand.

"We haven't heard from Binky yet. I think we'd better find out what she has to say."

Georgia frowned. "I hate to bother her right now. She's sleeping."

"And nobody would suspect Abigail," Edward agreed. "She's too — too *honest* to kill somebody in that secret way."

Burlin shoved back his chair. "I agree, but like you're always telling me, it's good to anchor loose cannons. Until we hear what Binky has to say, she's a loose cannon, as far as I'm concerned. I'll get her."

Georgia got to her feet first. "No, I'll get her. You know she doesn't like men in her bedroom. Better still, I'll send Annie Dale and ask her to bring us some more tea, too. My ice melted ages ago."

She swung up the walk like a woman whose future was brighter than the immediate past.

We sat there enjoying the buzz of bees and the graceful ballet of butterflies on the goldenrod and buddleia. Then we heard a series of thuds, like somebody falling down the stairs. Burlin half rose in his chair, and poised, listening. We heard Annie Dale call out, and feet running quickly up the stairs.

In another minute, Georgia ran onto the porch, clutching her chest with one hand. In the other, she waved a piece of white paper. Even at that distance, we could see that her eyes were huge. She stumbled across the grass and held on to the rail of the gazebo, gasping. "Abigail's killed herself." Her voice changed to a wail. "Oh, Burlin, Binky's dead!"

25

I reached for my cell phone, but Georgia put out a hand to stop me. "Annie Dale's calling the police. I told her I'd come tell everybody." She pulled herself up the single step, stumbled toward her chair, and drained the inch of pale liquid in her glass. I had the feeling she wished it were something stronger. She crumpled the note she carried in one fist.

"What happened?" Burlin demanded. "Should I go up?" He shoved back his chair.

Georgia touched his arm. "Not until the police get here. She must have taken pills. You know, the ones she took sometimes to help her sleep? She's cold. I shook her, and she's cold! She must have done it before she went to bed this morning. She left — this." She handed him the page.

He smoothed it and laid it on the table. Reading upside down, I made out the scrawled words, "I cannot stand this any longer." That was all. No signature, no explanation.

"You're sure that's her handwriting?" When I spoke, everybody looked at me like they wondered what I was doing there. I was wondering the same thing — particularly since any minute, Chief Muggins would be arriving. He was bound to come himself. The Bullocks were important. If he found me there, he'd be sure to imply I'd had something to do with Binky's death. He'd also be sure of what I saw in everybody else's eyes: that Binky killed Sperra and had been unable to face the consequences of what she had done.

That horror was clearly mixed with their grief. Lance had turned pale and was staring into space like he was trying to fit the word "murderer" to the aunt who'd replaced his mother. Burlin's eyes were dripping tears he kept swiping away with the back of one hand, but the other was clasped over his mouth. Renée had turned her back and was gazing out toward the garden. Georgia wasn't crying, but she trembled all over and, for once, looked her age.

Even Edward, while obviously calculating the damage done to the upcoming election by this latest development, had an unexpected glimmer of grief in his eyes.

I pushed back my chair. "You don't need an outsider around right now. If somebody could push me across the grass and help me get the chair in my trunk, I'd be grateful."

Edward stood. "I'll do it." I didn't flatter myself that he wanted to. His tone made it clear he was willing to do the dirty work to spare the others.

Burlin waved him back to his chair. "I brought her. I'll see her on her way." He offered me a tear-damp hand to help me down the step. As he pushed me toward Annie Dale's gate, he murmured over my shoulder, "I feel like I've just been poleaxed."

"I could not be sorrier for you," I told him. "I liked Binky a lot. But you'd better be ready to face the police. That's Chief Muggins's car parking beside mine right this minute."

Chief Muggins stepped back to let us out the gate, wearing a smile that strengthened my conviction that some of his ancestors were chimpanzees. "Joe Riddley better put a leash on you."

"She is, unfortunately, devoted to the old geezer," Burlin told him, wheeling me toward my car. "I can't make a dent in her affections, no matter how hard I try. She just dropped by to visit the family and offer her condolences. I'm seeing her off."

I gave him a startled smile of thanks as he held my door.

As he pushed my chair to the trunk, he told Chief Muggins in a low voice, "I appreciate your coming so quick. Or haven't you heard that we've had another tragedy?"

Chief Muggins grunted. "I heard on my way over here. That sort of thing tends to happen when the judge is around." It took every charitable cell in my body not to drive over him on my way out.

I pulled into my parking space at the store and used my cell phone to ask for an employee to fetch the chair and wheel me in. Joe Riddley came himself. "You're gonna be thinking you're the Queen of Sheba by the time you get that cast off," he warned as I opened my door, "but don't expect this royal treatment to continue." Then he saw my face and squatted down so his head was level with mine. "What's the matter?"

"Binky Bullock. She — she died." I laid my face against his broad chest and sobbed.

He held me until I felt able to face the world again. Then his hand touched the top of my head like a benediction. "We're unloading cattle feed in the back. I'll take you to the office, but I'll come back in a little while to take you home for dinner."

I couldn't concentrate on taxes. I kept getting swamped by wave after wave of sadness. For Sperra, I had grieved only for a stranger who died too soon. Now I grieved for a fierce, earnest little girl whose dreams got overshadowed by life and for the woman who, in my office four days before, had been so alive and happy, Hubert's name warm on her tongue.

I could shake Hubert for hurting her. Once he and Georgia went for a walk, he never looked back. How dreadful was that for Binky? As hard as it was for me to cast

Hubert as the male lead in a romantic tragedy, she may have viewed him as her last hope. She could even have come to care desperately for him in their two days together.

Hubert? demanded that voice that lurks somewhere in my head. *Rubbish. It's a lot more likely that Binky left Annie Dale's Monday night and killed Sperra, and that she was filled with remorse.*

Nonsense, I disagreed. *Binky would never have crept up behind somebody with a rusty pipe. She'd have shot them down in the street. Besides, she wrote me a note asking me to help find the killer. She didn't kill Sperra, even if she did kill herself.*

Then who did it? You don't think it was Lance.

"That's Charlie's problem," I muttered, startling a poor deputy as he walked in.

"Beg your pardon?" he asked. "I have this search warrant —"

He and I both knew a search warrant wasn't Chief Muggins's problem. "I was talking to myself," I said crossly. "A person has to have an intelligent conversation sometimes."

"Yes, ma'am." He shuffled his feet and didn't quite meet my eye.

"Let me see what you've got." I held out my hand.

What he had was a warrant to search the home of a young man, just eighteen, suspected of possessing the computer, television, and brand-new stereo system removed from his classmate's home the previous weekend. "I figure he wanted the stuff for himself, rather than to sell," the deputy said as I scrawled my signature. "I think we're gonna find every bit of it in his room."

I wished Sperra's murder were that easy to solve.

Chief Muggins thinks he's got it all wrapped up, the voice reminded me. *He thinks Lance did it. He isn't going to be out looking for other suspects.*

I sighed. *Even Charlie isn't dumb enough to think he can arrest Lance on Hector Blaine's word. Anybody knows Hector would lie like a rug to get his hands on a reward.*

He'll verify Hector's testimony by talking to Annie Dale, to confirm she found the letter where Hector said he left it and that it was addressed to Lance. You said yourself that it's a direct chain of evidence.

He'll still need evidence that Lance was at the water tank the night of the murder.

There's bound to be some. After all, he was there.

I hate that voice. I never know if it's my conscience or what Martha, with all her psychology training, calls my shadow. It certainly seems to shadow me at inconvenient times.

My head was beginning to ache with all its chatter, and I'd had enough coffee and iced tea that morning to need a visit to the ladies' room.

As I maneuvered myself into my wheelchair, the voice had one more question. *So if Lance is innocent but Charlie's convinced he did it, who's gonna look for the real killer?*

"I need a mental-health break," I told Joe Riddley as he drove me home.

"You stayed home the whole afternoon you sprained your ankle," he pointed out.

"That doesn't count. I want to pile up on the couch and read that mystery I bought a couple of weeks ago. I haven't even started it yet."

Clarinda, of course, had other ideas. "You can finally get to those boxes in the guest room." Before I knew it, she'd settled me in a chair with five boxes in easy reach and a sharp knife for cutting tape, then returned to the kitchen. I tediously sorted through junk I'd thought I couldn't live without a month before. Now I wondered whether anybody but me would ever want Ridd's first bib, yellow with drool, or the fuzzy wool letter from Joe Riddley's high-school baseball sweater, and where could I put them in the meantime?

Clarinda looked in from time to time, hands on her hips, to make disgusted noises. "This room looks worse than when you started."

"I'm getting there," I insisted. "You have to make a mess to create order."

"Well, I'm not goin' home until we get this mess cleaned up, so you keep working."

Figuring out who killed Sperra Bullock turned out to be a whole lot easier.

As I disengaged my brain and filled my hands with busywork, pieces of the puzzle began to fall into place. By the time I'd unpacked the last box and decided where to put the various pieces it had held, I knew who the murderer was. I just didn't know what I could do about it. I looked at the clock beside the bed. Two thirty. I hopped to our bedroom and the bedside phone.

"Isaac," I said when the assistant police chief came on the phone, "let me tell you a story. See what you think."

"What I think," he said when I finished, "is that you better sit tight and not let anybody in until I've had time to sort this out. And keep Clarinda there until Joe Riddley comes home."

I wasn't sure what he thought Clarinda could do to protect me, but I promised him on both counts. I even had to admit I felt safer with Clarinda around.

I hopped toward the couch with my mystery. "I'm finished," I called. "I've made a list of where everything goes. Now I'm going to sit down with a good book, and I don't want to be interrupted. But can you stay until Joe Riddley gets home? I'm feeling a little jumpy today."

"I'll be here," Clarinda rumbled. "I'll be lucky to get home by midnight, with all this to clear up. You made a bigger mess than the one you started with. Who ever taught you to unpack, I don't know . . ."

Her mutters were a familiar background as I settled comfortably against one end of the couch with my feet propped on a pillow and turned to chapter one. Clarinda moved around in the back of the house, putting away things on various closet shelves.

I was in the middle of chapter two when the doorbell rang. By the time I'd realized I hadn't warned Clarinda not to let anybody in, she was already opening the door.

"The judge is a bit incapacitated," she greeted the visitor, "but come on in. I know she'll be glad of company."

Renée came in with that combination of big-boned awkwardness and grace that made you want to keep looking at her. She was spectacular in gold linen pants and a white silk shell with a gold disk hanging from a chain around her neck. "I'm sorry to bother you, but Lance wanted me to bring you something."

Reluctantly, I closed my book and set it on the coffee table. Renée started fumbling in her huge purse. Clarinda paused on her way back to the guest room. "You all want some tea and cookies?"

"Oh, no," Renée assured her. "I'm fine." She waited until Clarinda trudged away, then repeated, "Lance wanted me to give you these." She held out two old photographs. "Abigail had them in her briefcase. She showed this one to Lance earlier this week and told him she'd looked for it as soon as she knew we were coming to Hopemore, in case you still lived here. Lance didn't think you'd want the police to find it, so he went to get it while Burlin was talking to the chief." She handed me one of the pictures.

I couldn't help smiling as I saw what it was. It had been taken at the Bullocks' lake house that fall weekend years ago. Binky was on Burlin's back with her chin propped on one of his shoulders. I stood behind him on a rock with my chin propped on his other shoulder, creating a three-headed monster. We were all making ferocious faces.

My eyes stung. Had any of us ever been that young?

"Abigail told Lance she was just a child when you met," Renée broke into my thoughts, "but you talked to her like she was a real person. She never forgot that."

I wanted to go somewhere and cry a river. "Poor Binky. She probably didn't get talked to much at all. Her family was so — I don't know, *involved* in things. Politics, society, sports. That whole weekend, I kept wishing I could bring that little girl home with me to our farm for a week or two, so she could just be herself."

"She never was." Renée's smile looked as sad as mine felt. "She gave her whole life to Lance after his mother left, and everybody took that for granted — including Lance. When I came into the family, I expected her to resent me, but instead, she saw me as a sort of ally: Abigail and Renée against Burlin, Georgia, and Edward — all of whom are determined to make Lance into something he's not."

"Governor?"

"Anything political. The only good thing this mess has accomplished is that maybe he can go back to his drawing board and I can go back to my clients. But I'm going to miss Abigail."

"Me, too, and I hardly knew her."

"Lance also found this with the other picture, and we don't know where she got it. We're terribly afraid —" She handed it to me, her eyes anxious.

I held it carefully by the edges. "Lance will want to have it eventually."

She nodded. "He doesn't have many pictures of himself with his mother, and this one is particularly nice. But it didn't come from any of their family albums."

"My grandson, the one who stayed with Sperra a few days, said she had some pictures. I'd guess this was one of them. He may recognize it."

"But how did Abigail get it, unless —" She broke off, turned away, and said thickly, "Lance said would you keep it for him, please? Just for now?"

I shook my head. "I can't do that. This is evidence in a murder case. You both know that — which is why I guess Lance made sure it had your prints and his all over it, and wanted me to put mine on it, as well. Clarinda?"

When she poked her head around the doorframe, I said, "Bring me a sandwich bag, please." I had her hold it open while I dropped the picture inside, then I sealed it and handed it back to Renée. "Take that to the police, or you could face a charge of obstructing justice."

She slid it into her purse with a glum look on her face, then held out one long slim hand. "I don't know if we'll ever meet again, but I want to thank you for being a sane island in the middle of this crazy mess." She spoke quickly and almost ran out the door.

I heard Clarinda rumbling in the kitchen. "What are you doing now?" I called.

"Fixing to finish up in that guest room. That'll take most of the afternoon. Then I aim to switch a few things around in here again. There's stuff still not sitting right on the shelves. It's too crowded, like." She hummed as she pulled down who knew what and thumped it on the countertop. In a

348

minute or two, I heard a crash.

"Ah! Now I see the method in your madness. If you keep rearranging things, you'll break enough so the rest will fit."

She didn't reply, but in a minute I heard co-cola fizzing over ice. She brought me a glass and glared at me as she set it down. "You are too mean for anybody else to work for. You know that, don't you? I just stay because I feel sorry for Joe Riddley."

"And because nobody else will hire you."

"You wish." She stomped back down the hall.

I settled back with my book, wishing I'd bought a paperback. I didn't mind the price — I figured I was contributing to the college fund for the writer's children — but hardback books are so heavy to hold.

I forgot that by chapter four, when it got really exciting. But as I looked nervously about to make sure no villains were lurking in the living room, I remembered something I ought to have thought of sooner: Renée had left the front door unlocked.

26

I was opening my mouth to call Clarinda when the knob turned.

"Hello, Mackie. Sorry to just barge in, but I feel like family by now."

Georgia was still dressed in black. I supposed she had put on her silver slippers for Chief Muggins, and was carrying the matching black-and-silver bag for the sake of her public, but nobody who saw her right then would have thought "fashionable." Words that came to mind were "grief stricken" and "haggard." Her eyes were great gray holes in her face. Her shoulders sagged.

"Are you all right?" I greeted her with concern. "I nearly lost my brother a year ago, so I know a bit how you feel."

She sank into the chair across from me and sighed. "I hate to keep coming to cry on your shoulder, but I can't stand it over at Annie Dale's anymore."

"You've been through an awful lot in one week. How did the press conference go?"

"We couldn't face it. Edward just read a statement to the reporters." She sniffed and held her fingers delicately to her nose. "All I can think about is Abigail, wondering if there was anything I could have done. If I'd gone in to talk to her this morning instead of coming over here, or if I hadn't gone walking with Hubert — she liked him, you know. But that walk didn't mean anything. She was washing her hair and he asked me . . ."

"I miss Binky," I told her. "She was a special child, and a special woman."

Georgia nodded, and a tear fell onto her clasped hands. "She was my baby sister." Her voice was a whisper. "I can't believe she's dead." She reached for a tissue from the box on the coffee table and buried her face in it.

When she opened her pocketbook, I thought she was tidying away the tissue. Silly me. I never expected a gun that small.

From where I sat, all I could see was a little silver ring with a black hole in the middle. It wasn't the ring I had to worry about, though. It was that hole. Not that a bullet that small would be likely to kill me. She'd have to use two or more, and I'd probably bleed to death in the end. Still, I'm as opposed to a slow lingering death as to a quick one, and I have little tolerance for pain.

Deep in my head, a chant began: *"Please, God, please, God."* It's the prayer I do best.

Georgia spoke so low, I almost couldn't hear. "Abigail said you could solve the murder. I didn't believe her, fool that I am. You never *seemed* that clever. But the way you looked at me this morning — you already knew, didn't you?"

"No," I protested — which was true. I hadn't known until later.

She leveled the gun at me. "Don't try to lie. I saw your face when I walked in that door just now. It's a good thing you didn't marry Burlin. A politician's wife has to control her face, and yours is like a book. Anybody can read it."

If so, right that minute she was reading that I'd rather be anywhere else in the world than in that particular room with her and her violent little toy. I wanted to promise her that I'd never tell anybody, that she could go back to Atlanta and live a long and happy life. I wanted to scream the house down so Clarinda would come —

It was thinking about Clarinda that calmed me down. Whatever happened to me, I wanted to try and make sure she got away. "You're talking nonsense, Georgia. Go back to Annie Dale's."

"Are you crazy?" she demanded. "You know what I did." She got up and went to the front window, peered out through the blinds. "But I want to know what I did wrong. How did you figure it out?"

I wished I'd had SWAT-team training in talking my way out of situations. I've never understood that concept, personally. Why would anybody with a gun stand around talking when they could be shooting? Still, Georgia hadn't pulled the trigger, and Joe Riddley has been heard to say I can talk the comb off a rooster. This was as good a time as any to try.

"Well, for one thing, you told me Hubert took you down to the water tank, and you suggested he was making sure if they found evidence at the scene to incriminate him, he could claim it was from that earlier visit. What you didn't realize is that I've known Hubert all his life. He's not that clever. But you are. You were the one making sure any evidence they found could have been left on that previous visit."

She turned. "If you're so smart, how did I know Sperra was in town?"

"You read Lance's note. You were the only one who could have. He said he put it among his papers during the meeting. Burlin told us during his speech that he, Edward, and Lance were golfing that afternoon, Binky went bike riding, and you and Renée were napping. But you informed us all you were writing thank-you notes, remember? Burlin told me earlier that you all used the sitting room for meetings and writing thank-you notes."

Georgia looked like she had forgotten how to breathe.

"So you were alone in that room, knowing Lance had hidden a note in his speech. Of course you looked to see what was so secret. After you read it, you knew Sperra was alive, in town, and hoping to meet Lance at the water tank that night. What you didn't know was how Lance would respond to the resurrection of his mother."

"A drunk!" She spat the words over her shoulder.

"A homeless drunk. That's what you called her this morning. You said, 'To get this close — this close to the governor's mansion and lose it because of a homeless drunk.' That's all Sperra was to you, wasn't she? A homeless drunk. Not a musician. Not a woman. Not a mother or a wife or even a human being. A homeless drunk who stood in the path of the Bullocks' march to the governor's mansion and eventually to the White House. Your daddy told me years ago that it was just a matter of time before a Bullock occupied the oval office. I thought he was joking, but he wasn't, was he? It's been the family game plan for generations. Binky wasn't the loose cannon aimed at the plan. It was Lance."

She shrugged. "He isn't as focused as the rest of us —"

"And he's kind. From what I've seen of him, he would take a drunk homeless mother home and install her in his guest room. That's hard to do in the governor's mansion."

She didn't reply.

I said thoughtfully, "I can understand your

354

wanting Lance to be governor, but it's hard to forgive your using Hubert. It was tacky to persuade him to take you on that walk by pretending you needed to stretch your legs after sitting so long and to gently steer him toward the water tank where you could leave a clear footprint."

Georgia's voice was icy and she still didn't turn. "Have you forgotten I was with Renée the whole time after the meeting, until I joined you all at Gusta's?"

"Not quite the whole time. You went up to change your shoes — muddy shoes, the ones you have on now, the ones you showed us after the meeting. You did change them, but only after you killed Sperra. That way, if forensics tested them and discovered mud on them from under the water tank —"

"I was gone ten minutes!" she blazed "Ten *minutes*. Think about it. I had to go up the stairs and stop by the bathroom for a tinkle — you know how unreliable bladders are at our age. I had to find my other shoes, put them on, and get back downstairs. If you can do all that in ten minutes plus run from Annie Dale's to the water tank and back — not to mention killing somebody while you are there — more power to you. I'm fit, but I'm not in that good a shape."

"Me, neither," I agreed. "But both you and Burlin mentioned that Renée has no sense of time. Besides, she was jet-lagged, dozing any-

355

time she could. I think what really happened was this: You went in the front door of Annie Dale's and straight out the back. You knew Annie Dale was at her mother-in-law's, the men were still at the meeting, and Binky was up in the sitting room, working. You ran the short block to the water tank, surprised Sperra, and killed her. I doubt if you even spoke to her, so it wouldn't have taken long. You ran back to the house, up the stairs, and changed your shoes. Maybe you even stopped for that tinkle, and fixed your face. I noticed your lipstick was fresh but you were breathless when you got to Gusta's."

"Fixing my face takes time," she reminded me.

"Not much time for a person in the public eye. You're used to doing it on the run. That night, I think you ran down to the car, changed the dashboard clock, and woke Renée to verify the time. You'd told her you wouldn't be a minute. Now, you impressed on her that it hadn't been but ten. She sleepily agreed, and dozed again. You drove around a few minutes, changed the clock back to the right time, woke her, told her you'd been lost twenty minutes, and let her help you find Gusta's. It a stroke of luck for you that Gusta's clock is ten minutes slow. That made it very believable that it had only been half an hour since we left you at the community center. But you made two mistakes. It was still light enough then to see, so you went through Sperra's knapsack to make sure there was nothing to identify who she was. You found a picture of her with Lance and brought it back. Binky saw you with that picture, didn't she? Hearing you in the hall, did she come to the door? And when did she take the picture — after she heard that the murdered woman was Sperra?"

"How do you know about the picture?"

"It turned up in her briefcase this morning."

"So maybe Binky murdered Sperra. Had you thought of that?"

I thought about pretending to believe it, but I knew Georgia was right about my face. I've always been a lousy actor. So I might as well let her have the whole story. "Even if you kill me, you aren't going to get away. The police have some evidence you forgot about."

"What?"

"What were you wearing that night?"

"A red pantsuit. You saw me."

"But earlier that day, you were wearing navy. I saw you in the morning, too, dressed for Dublin and you said earlier you went home from the walk to shower and change for the meeting. Even if you kill me, Hubert will probably remember what you were wearing on the walk. He's always had an eye for women's clothes. And the others will remember you changing. What if I told you that one piece of evidence they found on the bushes was bits of red thread? Before you went walking with Hubert, you remembered to put on the shoes you planned to wear that night, but you didn't know about the bushes."

"Those damned bushes!" She seemed to crumple.

Odd as it sounds, I pitied her for a moment. I felt like I was watching something fragile and lovely collapse in on itself. "They scratched me up, too," I said. "I plan to ask the city to cut them back and shape them up in the next week or two."

"I'm afraid you won't be able to do that." She leveled the gun at me again.

PleaseGodpleaseGodpleaseGod!

No angel swooped down to take away the gun, so I kept talking. "Did you kill Binky, too? Did she see you coming back Monday night, and once she learned the dead woman was Sperra, ask where you had been?" Georgia's hand wavered. I plowed on. "Did you kill her to keep her quiet, or did she prefer to kill herself rather than give evidence against you? It's even possible that she couldn't stand to live with you taking every man who ever looked her way. I figure that was what the note was about. It certainly wasn't a suicide note from a woman who made her living writing letters. But it doesn't really matter whether Binky killed herself or you killed her. You can't be executed twice."

"Or three times," she reminded me grimly.

In the kitchen, Clarinda slammed a cabinet door. We both jumped, and Georgia gave her watch a puzzled look. "Who's that? Burlin said your maid leaves at two."

"We've been unpacking boxes, and she decided to stay late."

She walked closer and whispered, "Send her home. We don't need her here."

"Clarinda?" My voice shook a bit, but it's hard to control body parts when they've got a gun pointed at them. Especially when the woman holding it is shaking from head to painted toenails. "It's past time for you to leave. Go on, now."

Clarinda stomped in, wiping her hands on a dish towel. "I told you, I'll go when I get done. You all need something to drink?" She'd heard the visitor. She hadn't seen the gun.

I tried to silently beg Georgia to let her go, but Georgia had already motioned with her head, keeping the gun out of sight. "Sit on the couch, next to Judge Yarbrough."

Clarinda raised one eyebrow. "Folks in this house want something from me, they say please."

She was still in the kitchen doorway. "Run," I urged her in a hoarse voice. "Please."

Now I got her full glare. "What you mean, run? I'm too fat to run."

"Sit over there!" Georgia snapped. She gestured with the barrel of the gun.

Clarinda's eyes got round as Mama's old gravy boat. She stepped back toward the kitchen. "What you doin' with that gun in this house? Mr. Joe Riddley don't allow guns anyplace except locked in his cabinet."

"Clarinda!" Every cell in my body was shrieking. "Don't be a hero! This woman is serious. Run!"

Georgia took dead aim at the dearest friend I had in the world.

I hurled my book with a one-word prayer: *"Help!"* I'm not the best pitcher in the world, but she was only a few feet away and the book was thick and hard.

Thank God for hardback books. That one hit her arm as she fired, and I watched in relief as a small hole appeared in my living room ceiling.

Before Georgia recovered for a second try, Clarinda seized one of our dining room chairs, ran across the room faster than I knew that woman could run, and brought the chair down on Georgia's arm. The gun fell to the floor and skidded on the rug. Clarinda put one heavy foot on it.

Still breathing hard, she said grimly, "You sit down in that chair and be quiet."

She retrieved the gun and looked at it in

contempt. "Little bitty thing like this can't kill nobody les'n you're close enough to shoot 'em in the head." She handed it to me. "Still, it could hurt somebody right smart, so you keep it aimed in her direction while I call 911."

I'm used to obeying Clarinda, so I did as I was told. However, my hands were shaking so bad, I was almost as much of a threat to myself as to Georgia.

Since we weren't the Bullocks, Chief Muggins let Isaac James and a deputy take the call. As Clarinda let them in, I permitted myself the luxury of one long, shaky breath. "You took long enough."

He glared. "I told you to keep that door locked."

He turned. "Georgia Tate, I am arresting you for the attempted murder of Clarinda Williams. Anything you say may be used against you . . ." The preacher at my own wedding never sounded as sweet as Isaac rolling out that Miranda warning.

27

The Bullocks flowed out of town like melted butter, sending back some of Burlin's high-powered lawyer friends to defend Georgia and another to settle with the owner of the Toyota the buffalo restructured.

I couldn't accept the reward Burlin had offered, of course, but was delighted when it went to Clarinda — except for a hundred dollars, which was peeled off for Hector and promptly got poured down his cast-iron throat. Clarinda used part of the money to buy a new black suit in which to testify in court.

I suppose Lance returned to his drawing board and Renée to her clients. I never read any more about him except for one brief article entitled BULLOCK PULLS OUT OF RACE AFTER TRAGIC FAMILY WEEK.

In the perverse nature of our current society, Burlin became more of a celebrity than he had been before. We couldn't turn on the television or pick up a magazine for weeks without seeing his solemn handsome face. He'd become an advocate for the plight of the homeless and the country's crying need for long-term shelters and better mental-health care.

I was glad he'd found something to occupy

his time and considerable energy, and I didn't doubt his genuine concern for mental-health care. Georgia had pleaded insanity for killing both Sperra and "the dearest baby sister a woman ever had," and would spend the rest of her natural life in an institution for the criminally insane.

I wasn't quite sure whether Burlin cared about the homeless or merely cared to make people think he cared about the homeless. I still blame politicians for a lot of homelessness in the first place, since if they hadn't refused to raise the minimum wage for over a decade after 1980, a lot of people wouldn't have been forced to choose between buying food and paying rent. Knowing how comfortably Burlin lived in three houses, I wondered if he really cared that some people don't have one.

Then, one day in December just before Christmas, I got a letter.

Dear Mackie,

Enclosed is a check for a memorial to Sperra and Binky in Hopemore. It has occurred to me that if Hopemore had had some kind of shelter for homeless people, my wife and your grandchild wouldn't have had to sleep in a barn. Christmas seems a fitting time to get people out of barns, doesn't it? I called the Realtor in town, and he tells me Hubert Spence's house and barn are still for sale. If you'd use this to purchase them and endow a shelter in Sperra's name, I'd be real glad.

My guess is that you don't have enough homeless people in town to fill it, but the world being what it is, I'd guess there are some battered women and children who can use the other rooms. Spend some of the money to buy bicycles for the kids. That ought to make Binky happy, up in heaven.

Don't expect us to come for the dedication — we don't look back fondly on our week in Hopemore. But I learned something there. I learned that my plans for other people's lives are not necessarily the best plans — not for you and not for Lance. He's real happy now, piddling around with his old buildings. Renée still travels all over the world, but it turned out that she was so tired all the time in Hopemore because she is pregnant. Can you imagine me as a granddaddy? I wonder if I'll still be around by the time the kid is ready for the White House.

That was a joke. Laugh, dang it!

Georgia is as well as can be expected. I reckon in a few years, she'll be running the place. Like I once said, she's the organized one in our family.

As much as I hate to admit it, you made the right choice in that tall drink of water you married. Merry Christmas. May we all have a happier New Year.

Love,
Burlin

P.S.
I've made the check out to your church. I needed the tax write-off, and besides, I don't want you taking an extended second honeymoon at my expense. Stay happy, dear Mackie, even if you can't stay out of trouble. B.

I'd never seen such a big check before. I sure didn't want it lying around on my desk all day. Our church treasurer was the manager of the bank across the street, so I headed over so she could deposit it immediately.

As I waited for our one red light to turn green, I remembered to be grateful that I walk without crutches. I never appreciated my own two legs until I lost the use of them.

On the sidewalk outside the bank, I saw Gusta climbing out of Pooh's old navy Cadillac and heading toward the bank with the aid of her silver-topped cane.

I couldn't resist showing her the check and telling her what it was for. She paused at the door and gripped my elbow. "Tell me, MacLaren, exactly when were you and Burlin Bullock sweethearts?" Her steely eyes bored into me like they would pierce my very soul.

I had been waiting for that moment, lying in bed rehearsing what I'd say. I let my eyes widen like Georgia's. "Why, Gusta! You know I've loved Joe Riddley practically since I was born. And we both know what deceivers those Bullocks were. Who'd ever believe a word they said? Some people will do anything to get their picture in the paper."

I gave her a smile I hoped was as enigmatic as Renée's and walked slowly toward the bank manager's office, letting my hips sway.

Not one conversation slowed down as I passed. But I had, for once, cut off Gusta's water.

I expected that the deposit of Burlin's check would end my connection with the Bullocks. Who would have imagined that Burlin was a prophet, that in a very few months I'd be off on a second honeymoon and up to my neck in trouble?

But that is another story.

About the Author

PATRICIA SPRINKLE grew up in North Carolina and northern Florida, graduated from Vassar College, and spent a winter writing in the Scottish Highlands before settling in Atlanta. Although as an adult she has also lived in Chicago and Miami, her mysteries and novels reflect her love for and the strength of her Southern roots. Sprinkle is a member of Sisters in crime and Mystery Writers of America. Contact her at patriciasprinkle@hotmail.com or check out her Web site, www.patriciasprinkle.com.

We hope you have enjoyed this Large Print book. Other Thorndike, Wheeler or Chivers Press Large Print books are available at your library or directly from the publishers.

For more information about current and up-coming titles, please call or write, without obligation, to:

Publisher
Thorndike Press
295 Kennedy Memorial Drive
Waterville, ME   04901
Tel. (800) 223-1244

Or visit our Web site at:
www.gale.com/thorndike
www.gale.com/wheeler

OR

Chivers Large Print
published by BBC Audiobooks Ltd
St James House, The Square
Lower Bristol Road
Bath BA2 3SB
England
Tel. +44(0) 800 136919
email: bbcaudiobooks@bbc.co.uk
www.bbcaudiobooks.co.uk

All our Large Print titles are designed for easy reading, and all our books are made to last.